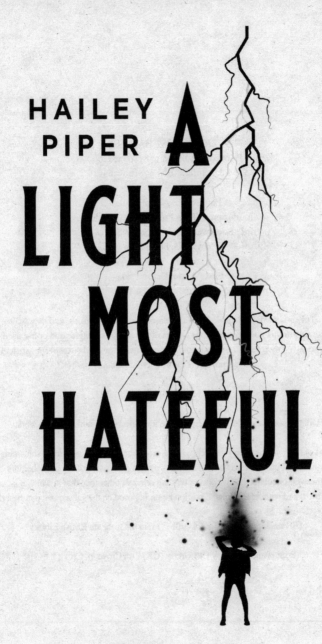

HAILEY PIPER

A LIGHT MOST HATEFUL

TITAN BOOKS

A LIGHT MOST HATEFUL
Print edition ISBN: 9781803364209
E-book edition ISBN: 9781803364216

Published By Titan Books
A division of Titan Publishing Group Ltd.
144 Southwark Street, London SE1 0UP
www.titanbooks.com

First edition: October 2023
10 9 8 7 6 5 4 3 2 1

A CIP catalogue record for this title is available from the British Library.

Printed and bound by CPI Group (UK) Ltd, Croydon, CR0 4YY

To anyone who's ever needed to run,
this book is for you

Why are you like this?

You hate me so much, but I hate you too.

I've always hated you.

Hate. You.

1. WHAT MOVIE IS THIS?

The hill screamed at nightfall, the high-pitched panic of a child caught in a bad dream. Its power rattled Olivia Abram's car windows, her teeth and bones.

She pumped the brakes in the middle of the street, and her uneasy sedan paused only a few yards from the curb where the Mason House stood. No sign of anyone shrieking in its windows, on its lawn, around its neighbors.

Olivia looked out her driver's window at the curb, to the nearest standing streetlight, and then eyed her rearview mirror. Behind her, tongues of pavement formed turn-offs and intersections. Every route in Chapel Hill spread from Main Street, either heading south past the Mason House toward the interstate, or north toward the Starry Wood, the business district, sterile suburbs, and Sunset Pass. An older woman in tank top and shorts walked a yellow Labrador, and both she and her dog looked toward Olivia's maroon Chevy, as though she'd been the one to make the sound.

Which at least meant she hadn't imagined it. She listened for it again, some way to give it a sensible origin, but only crickets sang in the trees ahead.

Had it really been a scream? She had heard a noise, glass shattering across Chapel Hill's sky, no doubting that, but had it been human for certain? Too far away to be the squeal of drive-in speakers gearing up for tonight's show. Maybe some commotion on Main Street? Or maybe Olivia's tire had run over twisted metal in the road, but she couldn't guess why it would make that anguished screech. Another listen would help her figure it out, but the sound didn't come again.

Hills didn't scream, no matter how lonesome.

Olivia couldn't idle here much longer. She pulled forward on the narrow road and beeped her horn twice, interrupting the night with a noise of her own. It came in two flat squawks.

Homes on this side of town stood ancient, almost too old for Chapel Hill, for America, as though they had watched continents divide and stars die. The Mason House was a two-floor house with a split-level breaking the black rooftop between the main area and the risen second floor, where two bedrooms haunted the upstairs. Dark wood formed its skin and organs. Olivia had stepped inside plenty of times, but the house never seemed to welcome her any more than the woman who owned it. Only her daughter offered a kind word.

There was no sign of Sunflower. The front door stood unmoving above the stiff porch of grim planks, empty of a petite silhouette or blond locks. As if no one lived here.

Olivia craned her head out the driver's side window. "Sunflower, where did you get?"

She only then noticed the driveway, where an aging Volkswagen should have sat beside the white Honda. No Volkswagen meant no

Sunflower. And despite the number of bedrooms, only two people lived here.

The door at last cracked open, where a bony frame in a white dress emerged. She shut the door hard, her back to the street. Her face was hidden behind gray-streaked dark locks, as if her head were only made of hair across an endless faceless scalp.

Olivia tensed to drive off. She wanted to escape before Hazibel Mason could descend the creaking porch steps and snag her in unpleasant conversation. This was supposed to be a pick-up-and-drive kind of visit. Nothing to make Olivia late for the Friday night shift.

"She isn't here," Hazibel said, still not turning around, her tone flat and unfriendly. Keys jangled in her hands. "Isn't she with you?"

"Yes," Olivia said without a moment's hesitation.

She hit the gas and drove on before Hazibel could ask another question. Better to spread confusion now and concoct the right lies later. Anything to appease Hazibel's blue-dagger stare.

The sedan slid toward Main Street, where the bars, shops, and restaurants thrummed with life, and the sidewalks and streets brimmed with cars and people. If Olivia didn't know better, she would have assumed Chapel Hill to be fighting its small-town status with small-city aspirations.

No such thing. This was a go-nowhere, be-nobody town. Always would be, as long as it stood. So where the hell could Sunflower be? Her boyfriend Roy Addler's house? The craft shop?

Maybe the drive-in, with any luck.

Olivia drove a block along Main Street before chasing north and turning onto Ridgemont Road. Her home on Cooper Street beckoned from the west side of Chapel Hill, if only she could waste the evening cozy there instead.

But she headed east, passing sterile suburban neighborhoods where slanted rooftops capped timber houses, each looming over nearby lawns and streetlights before disappearing in her rearview. Van Buren Avenue, then Riggs, then Newport all on the right, trees on the left, until Ridgemont Road curved north and sent her driving straight into the Starry Wood.

Night painted the trunks, limbs, and needles in a blue-black hue where the town's light couldn't reach. Their darkness coated Chapel Hill's northern edge, guarding town from a steep descent. You could even stare down that gaping drop from Lookout, but that was east of the drive-in, meant for making out, feeling up, and other activities you needed two or more to do, and Olivia drove alone.

Starry Wood Lane had no streetlights, hiding the forest beyond beneath a black curtain. Switching off the headlights might have given Olivia a meager glimpse of starlight above, but the outstretched tree limbs obscured much of the sky, forming shadow hands that grabbed at her car in passing.

According to one of the astrology books Shelly and Dane kept in the craft shop beneath their apartment where Olivia lived, this August's new moon and the positions of the northern stars promised her that tonight would be okay. But books and stars could be liars, and maybe the not-scream noise meant to remind her of that. There was no such thing as an okay Friday night shift at the Starry Wood Drive-In.

Crossing tree limbs and branches soon thinned from the winding road against the subtle lights ahead. Rows of gravel formed a tight square spreading beneath the enormous drive-in screen, its black speakers rising as sentinels to either side for anyone whose radio might be busted.

Booth Bill sat in a lawn chair where Starry Wood Lane deposited cars into the driveway, a gentle giant of a man. He and Olivia waved as she drove past. He would sell tickets until showtime, and then he would man the projector himself, while Olivia juggled the work of two or three people at the concessions counter. The owner would be sorry if either of them quit, but he knew the same as Olivia. No one in this town ever went anywhere, got anywhere, and no one was coming to make this night any easier for either of them.

Not even Sunflower, it seemed. She was supposed to hop into Olivia's car on the way in, that had been the plan—keep Olivia company through the first film of tonight's double feature. Not to help, but for Olivia to have her best friend against the August heat and nighttime stillness. That would have been enough.

Only a couple of cars were parked in the drive-in's gravely rows, neither of them Sunflower's Volkswagen. Other cars would come, and there was a chance none of them would bring Sunflower. She might have found better things to do than hang around here.

Olivia needed to get her head on straight. She hurried into her red uniform shirt and pulled her dark brown hair into a gentle ponytail. A mounting ache throbbed behind her forehead. She'd have to muscle through it. Pain wouldn't make the double feature any easier, but regardless of lying books, she wanted to pretend the stars had something nice to say.

Tonight's crowd came rowdy. Too many high school graduates and seniors-to-be soon stuffed the drive-in's rows, with little intention of watching the movies. August's retro night—the owner's idea—gave Chapel Hill's teenage populace a substitute location for necking rather than piling their cars at the cliffs of Lookout in a mock orgy of flesh and steel.

The concessions stand was a sticky countertop, a glass window guarding the candy, not the staff, and a sloping roof jutting from a squat white slab of brick at the drive-in's edge. Most of the building's insides offered supply storage, a pantry, and a walk-in fridge. Public restrooms haunted the building's far end, while the locked door to the employee restroom stood a few feet down from the soda-stained tiles where Olivia juggled her responsibilities at the register, popcorn machine, soda fountain, and everything else the owner stuffed back here to accommodate guests.

Rows of cars spit endless customers, approaching with endless requests. Every request for buttered, unbuttered, root beer, clear soda, candy—it all piled on Olivia's shoulders, everyone scrambling to get their share before the screen lit with tonight's spectacle.

She only caught a break when the first movie rolled. Couples retreated to their cars, and most wouldn't return from swallowing soda, snacks, and each other's tongues until the between-movie rush. Only the occasional straggler popped in mid-show. The runtime gave her room to catch her breath, recount the cash in the register, even grab a drink for herself.

And to scan the area again for Sunflower Mason.

She might have gone wandering anywhere amid the rows of parked cars, now ashine with flickering light. Concessions stood to one side of the drive-in, and the windshields offered clearer pictures of the movie than the screen itself at this angle. Had she known the movie, Olivia could have followed the reflected technicolor blur, but retro night meant cinematic mystery meat. She had been too focused on starlight and the half-heard scream to note the title placard outside the drive-in, and now the reflected screen filled with suggestions of spaceships and robots.

No Sunflower amid the cars. No Volkswagen, not even Roy's

Ford rust-mobile. The world stretched empty beneath the encircling trees, busy screen, and starlit sky.

A figure broke from the gloom, the glint of a pinkish face under the movie's glow.

Olivia stood straight and dusted her shirt. This might be another drive-in patron, but it could be Sunflower at last. Olivia needed to get herself together. Be nonchalant, and also excited, and maybe annoyed too. She could say something like, *Look who finally showed up*, or maybe, *I thought you died*.

The eagerness sank into her stomach as the figure grew definition. Hair too dark, shoulders too broad, legs too long. Only the darkness and Olivia's delirious optimism could have convinced her this guy was Sunflower.

He was Roy's friend, Taggart Dempsey. He appeared in his corduroy jacket and ripped-up blue jeans, cocking his shaggy head.

Olivia wanted to shrink away, pretend she wasn't here, ignore him, but then he waved a dollar bill, transforming him from annoying acquaintance into customer. No choice but to attend him.

"What can I get you?" Olivia asked. "Please don't say anything that will make me point to the sign."

Taggart glanced overhead, where a white placard behind Olivia read, WE RESERVE THE RIGHT TO REFUSE SERVICE TO ANYONE. He swallowed whatever he'd been about to say and slid the dollar across a butter stain.

"Twizzlers," he said with a charmless grin. "Cherry."

Olivia passed him two dimes of change and a pack of crimson Yum-Yum Whips. His teeth tore open the plastic and drew out a whip as if snapping a cigarette from its pack. Olivia had seen Hazibel Mason do that a thousand times, as if she sustained herself on nothing but nicotine.

"Think they'll ever get real Twizzlers?" Taggart asked. "The knock-off's never as good."

"I couldn't predict," Olivia said. "You're free to drive to the theater in Langston, ask their concessions."

"How about Roy? Got him back there?"

"No Roy. You couldn't afford him." Olivia bit her lip. Any more words than needed and Taggart would feel encouraged. He dreamed of Roy and himself dating Sunflower and Olivia, but his idea of small-town coupling entitled him to nothing.

His teeth flashed red with licorice. "Haven't seen him? Or Sunflower?" Neither had graced their loser friends with their attention. "I could keep you company. Like a date."

Olivia usually cleaned or knitted under the counter at spare moments, but she had forgotten her scarf project in her bedroom. Just as well; she didn't really need Taggart asking, *Is that a knitting needle, or you're just happy to see me?* for the fiftieth time.

"Devin Shipley's here," she said, chinning at a black Ford down the rows. "He asked me out first, and I can't say yes to you until I've said yes to him. No line cutting."

Taggart chewed half a whip. "Shipley hasn't said two words to you since graduation. He's with Stacy Keppler tonight."

Didn't people in this town have anything better to discuss than each other's personal lives? Olivia had always assumed graduation would flip life's light switch from nonsense to progress. She had forced sudden change when she was fifteen, a runaway hitchhiker from Hartford, Connecticut who landed in Chapel Hill, Pennsylvania. It could happen again, but nothing had changed between graduation and tonight. High school only bled into the wider world. Olivia still worked the drive-in. Devin and his football buddies still shared blue-and-gold letter jackets with high school sweethearts, or new girlfriends if the old ones thought they could escape Chapel Hill for college. Most would thicken their roots on this hill and sprout lifelong jobs and families.

Would Olivia? She had always meant to head for Hartford again and find some resolution with Mom and Dad. She imagined them both still coming home from the family's pet store smelling of fish and dogs and everything they ate, but perhaps their lives had grown while Olivia stagnated in this overlong rest stop.

She pulled a white rag, blotchy with saffron stains, from beneath the counter and wiped at its surface. "Anything else? I'm on the clock."

Taggart tightened his fingers around the licorice bag. "Fine, not now, but I'll keep you company after shift. Not like anyone's waiting up at your house checking a curfew."

Olivia's muscles tensed. Enough scrubbing, and she might wipe Taggart out of the picture, too. "Because Shelly and Dane aren't smothering me."

"Because the Kincaids aren't your parents," Taggart said. "They're only going to care so much."

Olivia glared at him. "That's your game plan? Pissing me off?"

His smirk returned. "It working?"

A lithe figure slid from the drive-in's dimness. "Goodbye, Taggart," her familiar voice sang. Olivia grinned at the sound.

Taggart spun around, licorice swinging. "I'm allowed to—"

"Good. Bye. Taggart." A white hand pressed him out of the way, his body an organic sliding door. He stumbled to one side, eyes fixed intently on his licorice bag, and then moseyed off to find someone else to bother.

Sunflower Mason's corn-yellow hair glowed beneath the concession stand lights. A gentle smirk graced her perfect, petite face, and then she grabbed the counter, hoisting herself overtop, jeans narrowly missing a dried splotch of butter. Roy's red-and-black jacket billowed around her shoulders, two sizes too big. Her sneakers slapped the brown tiles.

Olivia dodged out of the way. She said nothing, only stared in disbelief.

"What?" Sunflower asked. "Why scrub the counter if not for little old me?" A smile pressed at her porcelain cheeks, and mascara-clad lashes fluttered over pale blue eyes.

Olivia could fall into those twin skies. "You know it."

Gravel crunched under sneakers closer to the rows of parked vehicles, where Taggart probably hunted for Roy. Olivia had every right to ask why Sunflower hadn't waited at her house, why Olivia had been forced to cross paths with Hazibel, but after shooing Taggart away, to question might sound ungrateful.

Sunflower scoffed in his direction, a bad taste on her tongue. "Got enough headache without buddy boy there," she said. "Any Motrin?"

"Your head, too?" Olivia asked.

She made for the personal effects cabinet, where her purse nestled inside, alone. Her fingers prodded the jumble of lipsticks, tampons, candies, and a thousand other things for the Motrin bottle. She should have popped one when she arrived. Even with her headache having mostly subsided, invisible hands squeezed her head, stormy tension filling the air with a threat of thunder. She glanced above the screen-lit parked cars, where the night remained starlit, not a cloud in the sky. No reason she could see out there for the pain. Maybe her period was coming early this month.

Her nail scratched a plastic cylinder, and she snatched the Motrin bottle before her purse could swallow it again.

"Thanks for clearing Taggart," she said, batting a couple pills into Sunflower's palm. "But he won't leave once Roy shows up."

"Roy's not coming," Sunflower said, helping herself to the soda fountain and chasing the Motrin with Mountain Dew.

Maybe the stars were right and tonight wouldn't be an absolute disaster. "Hang here," Olivia said, beaming. "We'll half-watch the movie, and you'll play Taggart repellent."

"He's not coming, and I'm not staying." Sunflower cupped a hand beneath the fountain drink's ice dispenser and then crushed the gathered chips against her forehead. "Heading to Lookout."

Olivia scrunched up her face. "Roy and Taggart?"

Sunflower batted those lashes again. "Me and Roy."

A long stare stretched between them. Hazibel Mason went out each Friday night, usually with friends, sometimes on a date. She wouldn't be home to expect Sunflower's return. Any other night, Roy and Sunflower meeting at Lookout wouldn't have meant more than groping and necking. They would drink, stargaze, and maybe watch the lights of distant towns beside other couples. But Lookout was empty tonight, every other rambunctious duo having gathered at the drive-in to make-out beneath the shimmer of retro film. Sunflower and Roy could do the same, but they weren't.

Which meant they had other plans. Had been making them. Reason enough for Sunflower's absence earlier and a much longer absence when she laid on a leather back seat at Lookout.

"Oh." Olivia almost laughed. "And you decided this, when?"

"Morning impulse." Sunflower scratched the back of her neck. "Positive by noon. Don't make that look, I'm already nervous."

Olivia patted her face for some alien expression and found herself gaping. She forced a smile, took Sunflower's arms, and pressed forehead to forehead.

"Easy, easy," Olivia said, her voice softening. "No need for nerves, Sunshine. You're the most amazing person in the world."

Sunflower exhaled hard. Her forehead nuzzled Olivia's, and then her smile flared with certainty as she dipped back.

"Am I good?" Sunflower asked. "Looking sleek, Liv? Check me out."

Olivia guided Sunflower in a slow spin, examining every inch from her raggedy jeans to her manicured nails and tussled curtains of hair. Her locks had mussed in the back where Sunflower scratched her neck, and Olivia smoothed them together again. Her fingers traced skin, where a faint, risen blemish formed a crescent moon—Sunflower's birthmark. Olivia had always found the mark funny. Sunflower—partly named for one celestial body, skin bearing the resemblance of another.

Hurricane wind swept beneath the birthmark, and Olivia realized she'd let her touch linger.

Sunflower tilted an impatient head. "Good?"

Olivia spun Sunflower to face front. Good didn't cover it. "You're gorgeous."

"Gorgeous?" Sunflower snapped into a shrill giggle. "I'm so nervous, I need to pee."

The concession stand clutched at Olivia like a child needing a mindful mother. "I can't go with you right now, but—" She pointed to where the public restrooms jutted down the building.

Sunflower wrinkled her perfect nose. "You'd make your best friend slum the public cesspool?" Every word dripped audacity.

"I clean those up every shift," Olivia said, but Sunflower's face was too bright-eyed, too sweet. Deflated, Olivia plucked the staff restroom key off her hip ring. "No one else."

Sunflower snatched the key, pecked Olivia's cheek, and darted past the popcorn machine to the black door marked EMPLOYEES ONLY. Olivia would have watched the door shut, but a figure approached the counter out the corner of her eye. Not Taggart; a real customer, though Olivia couldn't remember their name.

Besides Shelly and Dane, with their devil-may-care approach to taking in the hitchhiking stray, no one had opened up to Olivia like Sunflower. Small town law dictated that once an outsider, always an outsider, with Olivia rendered more a mild curiosity than someone to get to know. Certainly not a friend. Sophomore year, Olivia's first day at Chapel Hill High, nearly everyone had treated her like a rusty nail jutting from the floor. Step too close, she'd run their feet through.

Not Sunflower. *Olivia*, she had said, appearing in the courtyard that September lunch period, a golden halo circling her head. *That's a pretty name. I've always liked that name.*

She couldn't have seen anything but a gawky short girl with big features on her small face and bright brown eyes that no one ever called beautiful. Where Sunflower had grown lean, Olivia was more a marshmallow. While Sunflower's smile gleamed perfect, Olivia's lips peeled from her gums when she grinned or laughed. Attractive, Olivia felt—hoped—but uninteresting, as much an ordinary part of the scenery as Chapel Hill's bricks and parking lots.

And yet, she and Sunflower had become glued to each other that day. Nothing had changed since except the swelling in Olivia's heart.

The customer departed, cradling a box of Rocket Raisin-Nauts and a Diet Coke, as the staff restroom door whined open. Sunflower danced out on sneakered tiptoes.

"I still have a headache," she said in singsong.

"Maybe tonight's not the night?" Olivia asked.

"Tonight's perfect." Sunflower glanced at the moonless, cloudless sky, as if the stars had aligned solely for her to stretch across Roy's back seat.

Olivia's cheeks burned. "Break a leg, Sunshine. And if you need me—"

Sunflower squeezed Olivia. "Butterflies, nothing worse."

Olivia only meant to say that she was here, would always be here. She kissed Sunflower's cheek. "Love you."

"Love you back." Sunflower broke away.

Her soft hands trailed Olivia's uniform sleeves, her hands, and then she hopped the countertop, back to the rest of the world. A few boys from the letter jacket crew milled between rows of cars, cigarette smoke rising between them. Half a dozen blue-and-gold sleeves raised Sunflower's way, and she waved back at them.

And then the night sucked her in.

Olivia slumped beside the register, chin in palm, and stared at the drive-in's black tree line. A strange cry swelled from the speakers, the film throwing out something between an animal roar and a synthesizer shriek. Had an amplifier test caused the scream Olivia heard outside the Mason House? She'd been idling on the far side of town though, and after the drive here, attending customers, hearing Sunflower's news, she couldn't be certain she even remembered the scream accurately. It might have been a tire screech. A dying raccoon.

Her imagination playing with her, some extrasensory bullshit warning she might be losing her best friend.

Olivia pried her face from her palm. No, that wasn't true, she wasn't losing anyone she hadn't lost already. Sunflower was a sweet, carefree creature. Small towns made few like her. Her plans with Roy tonight wouldn't change anything the last couple years hadn't made clear between her and Olivia. A cheek kiss, holding hands via commiseration, nights gossiping and giggling—these would stay. They were friends, and nothing would change.

Wasn't that Chapel Hill's way? It wouldn't offer Olivia any deeper of a future than Hartford ever had. She had escaped that emptiness once, but back in Connecticut, she'd had no one. Parents who couldn't understand. A world that would only take. Chapel Hill clutched tight, but it wouldn't steal anything that didn't belong to it. Olivia could find passive, unchanging stillness here and maybe settle with that. She wouldn't run. Wouldn't leave Sunflower.

The staff restroom door whined open, snapping Olivia from a trance. How long had she been staring into space? She didn't know the movie and couldn't make out the screen clearly, so glancing at windshield reflections of the current scene couldn't tell her how much of its time had passed, let alone her own.

Sunflower couldn't emerge from the restroom again without heading back inside. Someone else must have sneaked in while Olivia was staring into space, thinking of screams and Sunflower and disappointing futures. She couldn't see who hovered in the doorway. Only a hint of scalp lightly coated in spines of dark red hair cut past the doorframe. No one Olivia knew.

"That bathroom's employees only," she said. "I'll have to ask you to leave."

"That what you call that stint between you and Blondie?" the stranger asked, their voice sun-dried and crackly. "Employees only benefit?"

"No customer entry. Please leave."

The stranger's head bobbed as if shrugging. "Didn't buy anything. Guess Blondie didn't either."

They emerged before Olivia could again ask them to leave.

She had hoped for some lost high schooler, the kind she could handwave from the employee side of the concessions counter. Someone full of attitude, maybe, but who would buckle when pressed and return to the vehicle rows.

The lithe figure unfolding from the doorway melted her expectations. Most people overshot Olivia by a few inches, but the stranger towered, their face looking twenty, maybe twenty-one, limbs of wiry muscle, their cropped hair shifting from dark crimson to blood-red in the light.

"I don't know you," Olivia said, fighting a tremble in her voice. "You can't be here."

"Call me Christmas," the stranger said. "I bring joy wherever I go."

Their encroaching shadow covered Olivia. Limbs and spine folded again in an awkward squeeze as Christmas half-stepped, half-slid over the concessions counter, black jacket crinkling at their elbows, jeans straining not to split at the knees.

Olivia didn't realize she'd been shaking until the useless countertop divided her from the lanky newcomer.

"There," Christmas said. "That make it easier to talk to me?"

Olivia studied the register as if it were her boss. "I'm on shift. Attending customers."

"What if I decide to buy something?" Christmas folded their arms beneath their chest and leaned in. "You got to talk to me then, yeah?"

Would this shift never end?

Olivia threw on a generic customer service smile. "What can I get you?" she asked.

"Clarity," Christmas said. "One minute, I'm at Steve's. You know the bar? Next, I'm here. Now, being no shot glass of a girl like you, I can hold a drink, so there's no way I got that black-out drunk since dusk. I wonder, is this some oasis? A mirage?" They reached a long-fingered hand over Olivia's forearm.

Her skin buzzed from wrist to spine, and she drew back her hand.

Christmas smirked. "Too solid for my imagination." They lifted their outstretched arm and flexed the fingers. "Or am I the illusion? I want to hear Olivia's thoughts."

Olivia blanched. How could this stranger know her? Had they been asking around? No, she realized, her dull red uniform bore a name badge over her left breast. Her eyes cut to Christmas's chest, as if she expected everybody to wear one.

"Missing Blondie?" Christmas asked. "No, you want out of this conversation, but you're stuck in the retail cage."

Olivia's tongue stiffened. "If there's nothing I can get—"

"Get me?" Christmas's dry voice flattened to a growling hum. "Yes, you can get me."

Olivia gestured to the backlit menu board, her hand a quivering baby bird cast from its nest too soon. "You can customize your popcorn," she said, reciting script. "Butter, extra salt. Coke, Pepsi, a variety of—"

"I want your heart," Christmas said.

2. DEVILS

Olivia didn't believe in any hells of the Christian sense, but caught in the clover-green gaze of Christmas's eyes, for a split-second, she believed in the Devil.

"My heart?" she whispered.

"Ever hear the two rivers theory?" Christmas asked. "Each of us flows through the world like a river, trying our best to steer clear of each other. Sometimes, two rivers run parallel. And sometimes, it rains."

Olivia listened, almost expecting raindrops to patter across the roof. The stars still shined too bright for storms, and yet she kept looking skyward. The night looked too clear, its lack of hiding places suggesting it must be hiding something.

"Flood those rivers, and they'll make inroads toward each other," Christmas went on. "Exchange fish, frogs, what have you. The rivers swap spit, stop being two rivers. End up a mess."

They now leaned entirely over the counter, their face and teeth consuming Olivia's sight. *All the better to eat you*, said that wolfen grin, ready to skin Olivia alive.

"You kissing her, or what?"

Taggart appeared at Christmas's side, the Yum-Yum Whips bag crumpled in his fist. He'd either eaten every whip or handed them out to non-friends across the drive-in. His voice yanked Christmas back, a snake recoiling from the concession stand to the real world. Air flooded Olivia's lungs. She hadn't meant to hold her breath, and now she wheezed.

"This guy bothering you, Liv?" Taggart asked.

Freed from the concession window, Christmas unfurled to full height and crested Taggart with ease.

His lips formed a quavering O. "Or—"

"Or what?" Christmas asked.

Taggart should have risen up, forced some empty bravado to compensate for his size and hesitation, but a meekness tugged at his features.

Olivia's guts twisted in pity. "Don't hurt him," she said.

"Didn't plan to," Christmas said. They clapped Taggart's shoulder hard, and the candy bag drifted down his leg. "No guts, no heart, nothing. I can sort you out. Find me at the Sprinkle Shack later, slick, and I'll tell you my two rivers theory." Their head turned from Taggart to give Olivia a nod. "And you—guessing I'll find you later, come hell or high water."

Christmas then shoved their hands in jacket pockets and strolled toward the vehicle rows and Starry Wood Lane. The concession stand lights briefly stroked the skin on the back of Christmas's neck, where red hair stopped at a curving brown mark.

A crescent moon to match Sunflower's.

"Gina?" Olivia whispered.

That didn't make sense. Christmas didn't seem enough like a girl to be Sunflower's long-lost sister, or a boy for that matter. Besides, not even twins shared birthmarks, let alone siblings split by years. The mark had to be a coincidence.

Taggart braced an elbow on the concessions counter. "Knew you cared."

Olivia rolled her eyes. "I wasn't going to let them bully you."

Taggart beamed, regaining his voice. "That code for you kind of liking me?"

"You don't even like me, Taggart," Olivia said. "You're just lonely."

Taggart shrank beneath the lights. "Yeah. Aren't you?"

"It isn't the same." Olivia glanced past him, toward the drive-in rows. If she acted like someone else were coming, maybe he would drift away again.

Six bumpers down from the concession stand, a figure slumped low to the ground. A tangled hill of tarp and blanket climbed from her back. Gnarled, scraggly hair dragged at the gravel, split ends inspecting each pebble. Some vagrant, wandering the drive-in for change and discarded snacks. If she started to bother customers, Olivia would have to intervene, one more headache tonight. Hopefully the woman would leave on her own. This evening already stretched eternal, and the drive-in hadn't even started the second picture.

"Can you watch the front a sec?" Olivia asked. "I need to check the staff bathroom, make sure tall, dark, and growly didn't flood the toilet."

"You're deputizing me?" Taggart asked, standing tall.

Olivia ignored him. The black door opened without resistance, and she didn't realize Sunflower had never returned the key until it winked from beside the sink. No murky water pooled on the tiled floor, and no new carvings scarred the walls.

But someone had left a present. Black sludge stretched weblike fingers halfway up the far corner. Either a smoker's lung, or the vomit of someone who'd been eating cigarettes all day. Not Sunflower's. Definitely Christmas's doing. Where had that weirdo come from? Chapel Hill offered few reasons to swing through. Maybe Christmas was somebody here's friend, or maybe they'd hitchhiked off the interstate, much the way Olivia showed up three years ago.

Three years? She'd really been terrified of Hartford, yet resentful of Chapel Hill for that long?

That meant she'd been carrying this torch for Sunflower across three damn years as well. She'd known Chapel Hill had a way of keeping life stagnant, but to leave it that unmoving from age fifteen to eighteen? Math was cruel. Chapel Hill might be crueler.

And hearts were cruelest of all. Sunflower had to have met up with Roy and parked at Lookout to the west by now. Out there, the Starry Wood earned its name, no drive-in lights to pollute the cosmos. The night would shine beautiful from the cliff, distant towns lighting the northern counties, as if the starry sky had swallowed the world beyond Chapel Hill. He would have a hand on her breast this minute, his mouth to her neck. Her eyes would close in ecstasy.

"Good for her," Olivia whispered, retreating from the blackened restroom corner. "She deserves to be happy." Had Christmas known better, they wouldn't have asked for Olivia's heart—a barbed wire organ, long snagged on someone who couldn't feel the same.

Olivia needed a mop and pail from the utility closet. Maybe she could deputize Taggart into cleanup duty.

His arms waved overhead as she appeared from the restroom.

"Olivia, check this out," he said, his voice tensing with worry.

If he'd found a dead body in the popcorn machine, Olivia didn't want to know. She'd had enough tonight.

From the register, her gaze followed Taggart's pointing arm toward the vehicle rows. He aimed at the vagrant woman, still harmless. Olivia opened her mouth to tell Taggart off, let the poor woman be, but he wasn't pointing only at the woman. Shadows surrounded her where several people had left their vehicles.

The letter jacket crew had finished smoking their cigarettes, but few had returned to where they'd parked along the drive-in's vehicle rows. Instead, their shoes and boots crunched over gravel, forming a loose circle around the tarp-covered woman.

She hunkered low to the ground now. Her knees had to be bending far up her torso, and if she leaned any lower, she could easily crawl on all fours. Maybe her back was aching, but none of the letter jacket crew reached out to help her. They didn't even raise friendly arms to wave at her like they'd done for Sunflower. A humid stillness closed over them. The boys eyed each other with predatory sureness that they had found easy game.

Easy prey.

Olivia shoved up the counter's staff partition and marched onto the gravel. The counter creaked and then crashed shut behind her.

Taggart dogged her heels. "Should I come?"

"Stay," Olivia said.

"Am I still the concessions deputy?" Taggart asked.

"Just stay!"

Olivia hurried deeper into the drive-in. The movie ran on above her, Booth Bill oblivious to the trouble brewing between the rows. Technicolor men in gray military-style uniforms spoke against a background of red earth and black cosmos. Their cinematic universe seemed to stretch beyond the screen, where sudden clouds now blotted a section of the sky above Chapel Hill. A storm seemed to be coming after all. Above and below. Olivia could feel it aching in her head.

The graduated football boys weren't alone in circling the tarp-covered woman. Their girlfriends joined them now, along with some of last semester's juniors, and onlookers who hadn't really been watching the movie.

A bright red can of Coca Cola sailed from Devin Shipley's hand and crashed into the woman's hump.

Her arms jerked toward the tarp's underside like a turtle bucking into its shell. Hissing breath crinkled the tarp's front edge, but the letter jackets' cruel snickering drowned her out. Another hand raised a soda can, held by a boy with a blond goatee.

Olivia darted into the circle, arms outstretched. "Knock it off."

The goateed letter jacket—face familiar, name forgotten—might not have expected a big voice from a woman her size. He looked around with a sheepish *oops* smirk.

"Lighten up, Olivia," Devin said. His fingers twitched.

Olivia stepped between Devin and the crawling woman. Dark brown hair cropped to his scalp as tight as Christmas's. Shoulders tensed as he cracked his neck. He didn't seem out for blood tonight, just bored. Somehow, that was worse.

"No fighting," Olivia said, lowering her arms. "Drive-in policy. We'll stop the movie and send everyone home."

Warm breath wafted up her calves. The vagrant dragged her hands at the gravel to rise. Olivia twitched to glance back, bend down, and help the woman. But if she dropped her guarded stance, Devin or one of the others might rush in, and the rest would start snickering again, juicing them up to keep going.

Just go, lady, Olivia wanted to say. *Run while you can.*

"This is how we keep the wrong kind out of town." Devin thumbed at the concessions counter down the vehicle rows. "Don't you have snacks to sell?"

"She don't have a choice," another letter jacket said, younger than Devin. "Ladies of the road stick together."

One of the girlfriends whispered too loud, "Maybe she's Olivia's mom."

That set Olivia's teeth. "I'm on shift," she snapped. "Which means I'm in charge, or I get Booth Bill to kick you all out."

Another can hit the gray-haired woman with a sloshing metallic thud and then ricocheted against Olivia's leg. Laughter barked from every direction. Taggart lingered with the crowd, dwarfed by broader shoulders and thicker arms. He should have stayed at concessions. His eyes wandered the gathered teenagers and then the sky, as if watchful for thickening clouds.

Olivia strafed around the circle, arms spread. "Stop."

Devin chortled. "Look at that face, too. What a dog."

"Not a dog," another letter jacket said. "See her crawling? That's a lizard."

A raspy whisper sighed across the ground. "Yes," the woman hissed. "That's why she calls me Lizzie."

Olivia turned to kneel and help the woman up, but Lizzie was already rising, her gray head with its scraggly hair aimed at Devin. Maybe she'd confronted people like him before. She was hunched and bulky, a shapeless mystery beneath her tarp, nothing of a fighter in her thin limbs and bony hands. How long had she been living rough?

This mini-mob bullshit couldn't go on. Olivia would let Taggart cover the concession stand for two more minutes while she guided the drifter to Starry Wood Lane, a few more dollars in her pocket than she'd come with. No one deserved to be pelted by jackals.

"Ma'am," Olivia started. "Lizzie? Let me help you."

Lizzie didn't look at Olivia. Her unkempt gray hair parted in places, offering glimpses of leathery flesh and pursed lips stretching far back along her jaw. The tarp rippled off her back as she grew taller than Olivia, than Devin, than everyone standing at the center of the Starry Wood Drive-In.

There was no hump swelling from beneath her shoulders. Bent arms jutted from her upper body where long hands dangled, fingers tensing. A serpentine torso uncoiled from her bending legs, where vertebrae peeked through clinging blankets like a row of lumpy teeth prodding beneath Lizzie's skin.

Not like a lizard. Like a snake.

Lizzie's mouth opened wide as Devin's shoulders, and her unhinged jaw freed a flood of drool as white as Devin's blood-drained face. Her bulbous head stretched high over his, and sharp, narrow teeth peeked beneath thin lips.

A collective jolt sobered the crowd. The letter jacket crew, their girlfriends, and unrelated onlookers flinched back, or let their jaws go slack into black-holed mouths. Each of them stood frozen in shock, their cruelty broken a moment too late. Olivia held rigid beside them, paralyzed as if by a venomous snakebite.

None of them could stop the horror show at their circle's center, where Lizzie's mouth snapped down over Devin's head, shoulders, and chest in a sinewy crunch.

3. MONSTERS

Devin's short, muffled shriek smothered beneath shrill screams and clattering gravel. Onlookers broke their threat circle and made for car doors and truck beds, their panic an infection that rattled the drive-in.

Olivia didn't watch them. They were fuzzy shapes around her focus—Lizzie's engorged throat, where Devin's arms fought meekly inside. One hand pressed up from the skin, stretching it in a roadmap of crossing blood vessels, and beneath them, each splayed finger wriggled and clawed for freedom. For the moment, Devin was still alive.

Lizzie swallowed hard, urging him down. Her torso rippled with the muscly force of his descent, and then her head turned to one side. Strands of hair spread like Devin's splaying fingers, offering glimpses of now-pursed lips and flared nostrils over a blunt, almost snakelike snout. One white, bulging eye shifted Olivia's way, its dark pupil pregnant with her reflection.

Olivia staggered back two steps and then darted for the concession stand. Purse, car keys, get away fast as she could.

High beams whitened her world. An engine's roar chased the light and sent her ducking between two parked pickup trucks. The oncoming car snapped across one truck's bed in zipping past, its tires spitting gravel. If only they'd mowed Lizzie down, Olivia could have quit running.

She didn't look back, couldn't handle watching Devin's legs disappear into that gaping maw. The concession stand waited ahead, its soft yellow lights showing the steel register, aged popcorn machine, and the cabinet for staff belongings. Purse. Keys.

Sudden technicolor brightness dragged her gaze to the drive-in screen, where the red, drawn-in outline of a hulking monstrosity terrorized the actors. Maybe Lizzie was the movie's fault. Play a movie about aliens and monsters, and one was bound to show up.

A cold raindrop tapped Olivia's head as she lifted the countertop's partition and ducked behind the concession stand. Sudden thunder crashed over retreating engine roars, and then the drumroll of rain pounded overhead. She glanced over the counter, where just minutes ago the night had shined clear and starlit.

But she'd seen the clouds rushing in when she ran to protect Lizzie, and now they painted the sky black over Chapel Hill. A heavy rainwater curtain cascaded down the concession stand's rooftop. Olivia could barely make out Lizzie's approaching silhouette in the downpour.

Purse. Keys. Out.

Olivia crept on her haunches toward the cabinet. The white Motrin bottle jutted from her purse's mouth, a petulant tongue. *Easy to find now, aren't I?* She knocked it aside and shoved one hand between zipper teeth. Lipsticks, tampons, candies, and a thousand other things, but not her damn keys. She wrenched her hand out, dug through again, and then thrust the purse upside down, vomiting her life onto brown tiles. Lipsticks rolled and candies ricocheted.

Her keys clattered out. They slid across the tiles and into the shadow beneath the popcorn machine.

Olivia crawled over the mess and jammed her arm underneath. The metal rim bunched up her sleeve and scraped skin down her forearm. She patted fragments of stale popcorn. One fingernail scratched a petrified butter spill. No keys.

"Please," she whispered.

Airy breath answered, a snake hiss that slithered beneath pattering rainfall. Lightning warned of a thunderous peel, lighting the world blue and casting a serpentine shadow across the floor.

Olivia yanked her arm from the popcorn machine's underside, scraping another patch of skin, and ducked against the counter. Her hands trembled again. Silly of her to have let Christmas rattle her nerves when a genuine monster stalked the drive-in.

"You're still here," Lizzie said. "You left your taste in the rain."

Her breath echoed from every direction, mouth ready to swallow Olivia headfirst. The rain masked the monster's footsteps.

A harsh gasp sucked at the night, and then a guttural clicking rippled up Lizzie's alien throat. "Talk to me," she said, patient as a favorite kindergarten teacher. Gravel stones clattered against the concession stand's outer wall. "I won't hurt you, Olivia."

How the hell did this thing know her name? That damn nametag again. Olivia tugged and snapped sharp plastic free from fabric and set it silently on the tile floor. A frayed black dot stared from her red uniform shirt, a peephole for her racing heart.

"Help me," Lizzie said, voice swimming over Olivia's head. Open jaws might have stared from above, still slick with Devin's sweat. "The little one trusts you. Make her teach me how to call people from the moon."

This thing wasn't only dangerous and hungry, but out of her mind, too. She wasn't the only one gasping for air; Olivia's breath chugged in and out through her teeth. Her throat swelled, pregnant with a scream. Lizzie would hear at any moment.

Olivia stuck the meat of one palm into her mouth and bit hard, smothering her scream to a whimper. A copper taste brushed her tongue. She squeezed her eyes shut and listened to the rain, the gravel, and Lizzie's gasping. The next breath sucked closer, and Lizzie's clicking chased it. She didn't sound like she was struggling to breathe, more like she was smelling the air, or flicking her tongue through raindrops to taste them.

Tasting for Olivia.

She plucked her hand out of her mouth and stared at the bitemark. Blood dotted the outline of a crescent moon. She thought ludicrously of Sunflower's birthmark, how this curve of blood might give Lizzie a sharper flavor to follow.

Gravel swatted the counter again, and one gray pebble clattered under the partition. Lizzie had to be standing at the register, where customers ordered snacks and drink. *How much for a former high school football washout? Does butter cost extra?*

Her gaping mouth tasted the air again. If she craned that snakelike neck over the counter, she'd find Olivia. That jaw would unhinge and—

Olivia plucked up one of her fallen lipsticks and chucked it toward the staff restroom. It ricocheted off the tiles, struck the wall, and rolled.

Lizzie's throat clicked, more birdlike than snake, and she stamped at the ground. One foot swept past the partition's underside, the skin milky, nails long, the shape almost human. Olivia waited for the monster to pass and then crawled over spilled purse guts and under the partition.

Gravel chewed her palms as she scrabbled to her feet. No keys meant no car, but she knew Chapel Hill's every street and neighborhood as well as any local, better than some alien monster. She would run pell-mell through the drive-in to Starry Wood Lane, follow its curve through the woods until it turned into Ridgemont Road—better yet, she'd crash through the underbrush and fallen branches beneath the maple and pine trees, soppy with rain. Anything to throw Lizzie off her scent.

Headlights flared ahead, another vehicle bearing down. The public restrooms stood to Olivia's left, nowhere to go. She dodged right, and her shoes sent pebbles clattering. Lizzie had to have heard.

"Olivia!" Taggart shouted. His rust-red pickup truck cast twin golden cones into the night.

Olivia cut a shadow across the light to the passenger's side and hopped in as lightning forked above the drive-in. Thunder grumbled after her.

She faced the windshield just as Lizzie stalked into the headlights' range. Her body blurred and swayed beneath the windshield's rainwater sheet, a cobra dancing to a snake charmer's will. Clicking windshield wipers cleared the view. The rain plastered her hair down her face until it parted around her blunt nose-snout and gaping mouth, needle teeth dripping raindrops and drool. Blankets tangled around her back, chest, and legs, but patches of pale skin poked through.

Within those patches, a bulge squeezed against flesh in the shapes of limbs, torso, and head. Devin's face, pressing from the underside of Lizzie's skin.

Olivia slapped the dashboard. "Get us out!"

Taggart shifted into reverse and swung the truck around in a clumsy backwards turn. Most of the drive-in rows had emptied, other vehicles left abandoned, their owners having escaped on foot for Starry Wood Lane and the trees. The truck jostled forward and headed the same way. Starry Wood Lane, and then they'd hit Ridgemont, and then down one of the neighborhood lanes to Main Street, where the rest of town opened.

Olivia twisted around and faced the back window. The truck bed stretched forever into the rainy darkness, and no monstrous jaws opened in its red taillights. Tires eased onto the dirt road. Slow going in the rain, the road turning muddy, but faster than Lizzie could chase.

"I should've run it down," Taggart said.

The whites of his knuckles glowed where he gripped the steering wheel. Tension and bluster, nothing more. The truck couldn't have gained traction on the gravel to speed toward Lizzie. She would've side-stepped the hood and climbed onto the bed as the truck passed.

"You got us out," Olivia said.

She reached to touch Taggart's arm, but he seemed distant. She let one hand drop exhausted to the seat and looked to the other, the one she'd bitten. The rain had washed away the blood, leaving only tiny teeth marks in a crescent. Outside her window, streaking water warped sagging black trees. White clouds seemed to float in the raindrops, as if they'd had dreams of becoming snow but couldn't harden themselves to the world before falling.

"Is Shipley—you know?" Taggart glanced to Olivia as Starry Wood Lane curled around the bend. The trees would soon give way to open sky. "Is he?"

"Devin's dead." At least, Olivia hoped so by now. If he was still alive inside Lizzie—

Taggart threw his arm across Olivia's collarbone and slammed the brakes. Water sloshed from hood to windshield, splattering the already-strained plastic wipers.

Taillights glowed a few feet ahead, most white or yellow, a couple red, their brakes still pressed. Olivia counted at least ten vehicles clustered over both sides of Starry Wood Lane, leaving too little space between the road and trees for Taggart's truck to squeeze past.

"It's Devin's buddies," Taggart said, popping open his door. Falling rain matted shaggy hair down his scalp.

"Did they crash?" Olivia asked. She glanced over her shoulder—still no sign of Lizzie emerging from the dark. "Do you think they need help?"

"What they need is to clear the road. It's their fault that thing went wild at the drive-in." Mud sucked at Taggart's sneakers as he hit the road. He pointed to swell of taillights. "Look, they're just screwing around."

Olivia popped her door open and peered at the vehicle cluster. Someone's tires must have caught in a mud trap, and the others had been stuck when they stopped to help. Everyone might have to escape on foot. Olivia wanted to believe a large group would keep Lizzie at bay, but then the letter jacket crew would've fought her down when she dove for Devin's head. Instead, they'd abandoned their friend.

Now, with the rain softening from downpour to drizzle, the letter jacket crew paced past the taillights, each lost and confused. Either someone was injured or the whole group had fallen into collective shock. Far beyond the cluster, where Starry Wood Lane became Ridgemont Road, streetlights reflected off disconnected cars, likewise stopped, their occupants wandering in the rain.

Something wasn't right. Olivia slid out of her seat, into the road, and opened her mouth to call Taggart back.

He had already reached the car cluster and raised his voice to drown out the rainfall. "Hey, assholes? Out of the road."

No one looked at him. No one answered.

"Cole?" he asked. "Garcia? I'm talking to you."

He stepped into their shadows, cast by the taillights, and a chill sank into Olivia's skin. Former and future football kids in blue-and-gold jackets, their girlfriends, and one elderly man who looked out of place—together they formed a dazed mob between the vehicles. Not one seemed to notice Taggart.

Why didn't they glance up? Why didn't they speak?

"Taggart, step back," Olivia said. "They're not okay." Her voice came faint, as if she'd left it on the concession stand floor with everything else she owned.

Taggart reached one of the football boys—Harley Cole, Olivia guessed. "Move your car!" Taggart shouted. He craned his neck and stood straight as if to put himself at Harley's height, and then he pointed at everyone gathered. "What do you need, a jump? Talk to me."

Harley said nothing. The out-of-place elderly man mumbled something Olivia couldn't make out through the rainfall.

Taggart pawed at the top of his head. He probably had a headache and wasn't thinking straight.

Olivia edged closer. She needed him to stop.

Taggart's pointing arm swung back to Harley and struck him in the chest. The finger prodded his sternum. In high school, that would've invited a sucker punch through Taggart's middle. No rage, no resentment, just a quick shot to put Taggart in his place before the letter jacket crew moved along.

"Move your car," Taggart said. The drizzle ebbed to faint drops, the storm deciding it wanted nothing to do with Starry Wood Lane.

Harley's face curled into a sneer. Lips peeled from teeth, eyes narrowed with rain or tears. The boy beside him echoed the expression, and the girl beside him, and so on, miserable rage painting every face present. The elderly man flashed a pockmarked snarl.

A hoarse note clawed up Harley's throat. "I—" he started, dragging out the vowel. "I hate you." His shoulder thrust into Taggart and knocked him into the mud. "I hate you! I've always hated you!" He lifted one boot and stomped Taggart's upper leg.

Taggart fought to sit up, arms crossed over his face. "Wait—"

Or had he said *hate* like Harley? Olivia couldn't tell. A cacophony of furious sound swirled over the road as the small crowd parroted Harley.

"I hate you!" they shouted. "I've always hated you!"

The mob broke from its daze and swarmed around Taggart. He tried again to get up, but their boots rose and stomped down as if flooring a stubborn gas pedal. Flesh and bone gave beneath enraged heels.

Olivia forced herself to step forward at Taggart's pained mewling. She had to help him, drag him out from under them. Distract them. Anything.

The mob gave a pained roar, echoing each other exactly as if they'd rehearsed this whole assault. It sent Olivia flinching back, and she banged her spine against Taggart's truck.

"Why are you like this?" the mob shrieked. "You hate me so much, but I hate you too!"

One of the letter jacket boys dropped to his knees and clawed up Taggart's trunk, where he grabbed Taggart's right arm and yanked it back at a bad angle. The left arm jerked from his head at the next kick. Another boot crashed into his face, and a sickening crack snapped his jaw. His lips parted with a bubbling moan, and another boot crushed his nose, and another crunched down on his temple, and then the mob came slamming across his chest, gut, and groin. Blood caked skin, hair, and sole as they went on screaming and shouting in unison.

"I hate you!"

"I've always hated you!"

"Hate. You."

The scene blurred through Olivia's tears. She clamped hands over her ears and turned away. No more. She couldn't watch another murder. Even then, her thoughts wouldn't shut up—she knew Taggart was dying. They were killing him while she cowered here.

Rain softened across her head. She lowered trembling hands and turned, half-expecting the crowd to charge shrieking at her.

They had stopped. Letter jacket boys and their dates shambled between their cars, exactly as Olivia and Taggart had found them moments ago. The elderly man shambled behind the rest, his frailty holding him back from the melee, and yet he'd stood idle through the murder. Like he didn't notice it was happening.

None of the mob pointed fingers or screamed now. They didn't wipe the blood off their shoes and boots. Harley angled around Taggart, but Olivia saw no other changes in the crowd's paths.

No one else looked at Taggart. Like they had forgotten he was there, and what they had done to him.

Harsh breath hissed through Olivia's teeth. Her chest heaved, and her head dizzied under a what-the-fuck cloud. She couldn't inhale deep enough. Taggart might have said the same if he could say anything anymore. Olivia started toward him, and then she held in place. Her gaze followed the letter jacket crew and their accomplices. If she wandered too close, they might wheel around on her, too. What had set them off? How did they lose their minds? Why the hell was Taggart dead?

His head had lolled to face the vehicle cluster. Blood welled over the bare skin at the nape of his neck, which lay bent at an unnatural angle. No one touched him, not even the rain. Drops only fell from tree branches or slid from wandering people and the undersides of their cars.

The sky had swallowed the storm and filled itself with starlight again, as if to pretend tonight had never happened.

4. SICKNESS

Olivia couldn't keep her eyes from the body. She didn't want to look; she wanted to hide in Taggart's truck. No, she wanted someone to pinch her awake. She'd sit up gasping in her bedroom above the craft shop, run to the bathroom, and spit this nightmare into the sink in a splash of minty toothpaste.

But the night remained, and everything wrong with it.

Soggy earth squelched beneath twenty or so footsteps, the murderers neither looking at Taggart's body nor tripping over him. They didn't bump into their cars or each other, either. Only when Taggart touched Harley had the mob awakened together, each murderer one in a swarm of insects, or the limb of an invisible puppeteering centipede.

Or maybe they had been infected with a mysterious, trance-inducing disease.

Running into the woods would slow Olivia down, maybe enough for Lizzie to catch up. Starry Wood Lane was the only road between the drive-in and the rest of town. Olivia could try one of the idling vehicles, the keys still dangling in the ignition, but she would run into the same problem as Taggart's truck. No getting around from this end. The way could be clearer at the cluster's front, but Olivia had to make it there first.

She shifted to take a step and then settled back on her heels. Getting past them—infected or otherwise—meant getting near them. She could plan all she liked to keep her hands to herself, but what if she tripped and smacked into the mob? What if she breathed wrong? The elderly man hadn't joined the fray, but touching him might still enrage the others. Flawless movement seemed impossible.

Especially when she wanted to walk with her eyes shut from Taggart. His blood shimmered beneath the taillights. Ugly gratitude crawled over Olivia's thoughts—at least when they'd killed him, he faced their cars and hid his crushed features from her eyes—and she wished she'd been less annoyed with him. She wished she'd tried to stop the infected. Blasted the truck's horn, thrown rocks, anything. They might not have come after her next, too sickly and confused to remember that rocks didn't throw themselves.

She could throw rocks now and find out, but the knowledge wouldn't help. Taggart was dead.

Twigs snapped somewhere behind the trees. Their wet crackling echoed through Olivia's bones, and she remembered why she and Taggart had needed to pass the infected mob in the first place. Any moment, she would hear a breathing and clicking in the woods, the sounds of an enormous mouth tasting for blood in the post-rain humidity.

Olivia forced one leg forward, and then the other. One step at a time, they remembered how to walk, and she crossed to the far side of the road, where ferns and fallen branches tangled in the mud. At the front of the clustered vehicles, steamy breath rippled up a sedan's crimson hood, its radiator busted where it had slammed corner to corner against the front of a midnight blue pickup truck. Neither looked safe to drive, and they blocked the other vehicles in.

The derelict vehicles wouldn't hurt her, only their bloodthirsty drivers and passengers. Olivia turned to look over one shoulder in case anyone from the letter jacket crew lumbered after her. Car trunks and fenders partly blocked her view of the road, but the mob didn't follow.

She couldn't see Taggart anymore. One small mercy tonight.

She turned ahead just as the elderly man swept into her path. His expressionless face hovered inches from her nose, and she flinched back screaming hot in his face. Her thighs tensed, ready to bolt into the woods, Lizzie be damned.

Long shadows drooped down the elderly man's slack features. His face fixed on Olivia as if she'd grown antennae and bug eyes, but his stare was vacant, a psychological cataract hiding the world from sight. His thin lips worked together in a moist mumble as he shuffled back onto the dirt road and around the steaming car hood.

He wasn't the only mumbling voice. Olivia couldn't hear them before the screaming began, but the entire mob now spoke to themselves in an uneasy chorus of nonsense. If she listened close, the words might reveal themselves.

She didn't want to. Instead she picked up her pace past the next vehicle, where she glanced around its corner for another ambush—all clear—and then dashed another couple yards. Dirt gave way to pavement as Starry Wood Lane became Ridgemont Road. No cars blocked the lanes beyond the cluster, but they dotted the sides here and there, drivers and passengers orbiting them in shambling circles. The next pair of infected, two teens about Olivia's age, stalked behind their car, but no mobs. Olivia could keep her distance.

"Panic later," she whispered to herself, and her chest clenched tight. She forced a breath in and then a harsher breath out. "Later will come. You'll live to see it. Panic then." She had to repeat it a few times before she believed herself, but belief made the walk easier.

Ridgemont Road breached the tree line that blocked Chapel Hill's northern slopes from town proper, where Olivia caught sight of red and brown slanted rooftops, timber houses, and rain-wet lawns now glimmering bright from the glowing nearby streetlights. A fork opened south toward Newport Avenue, one among many narrow southward neighborhoods that branched from Ridgemont Road.

Olivia could follow any of them to Main Street. She would lose Lizzie easily there and maybe find help for the infected. That would mean dressing up tonight's catastrophe. Gas leak? Serial killer? Some excuse besides a monster, the kind to convince people they should help her.

There were already a few Chapel Hill residents outside despite the late hour. Couples dotted the sidewalks of Newport Avenue, their shoes and slippers slapping puddles left by the brief storm, streetlight reflecting in their surfaces.

Olivia raised an arm and shouted, "Help!" with a smile on her face. This night could finally end.

No one glanced her way. They studied the sidewalk and its fascinating cracks, their expressions dull, their gait aimless.

Olivia lowered her arm. She turned from Newport Avenue and darted farther up Ridgemont Road, neighborhoods to her left, trees to her right. Riggs Avenue opened at the next three-way intersection, a parallel suburb to Newport's, where more of the locals wandered its sidewalks and lawns, ripe with whatever malady had overtaken everyone on Starry Wood Lane. If she kept heading west, she could turn toward home at the corner of Cooper Street and Sedgwick Road, nearer to Main. Hide there with Shelly and Dane. Hope tonight might end.

But the farther Olivia went without seeing an uninfected, the more she wondered if she and Taggart were the only immune people in Chapel Hill—and now Taggart was dead. Even one other person might mean Sunflower was okay, and Shelly and Dane, and maybe more.

Olivia ran again, her thighs and lungs aching, to the corner of Van Buren Avenue. Someone, please. Anyone.

Van Buren Avenue echoed Riggs, and Newport, and Ridgemont. Houses stood in white or yellow siding, their rooftops black or burgundy, and if Olivia only stared at their colors and windows, the town would have looked the same as any other night.

But a bald man in a raincoat staggered across his driveway. He was one of the high school teachers, though no one whose class Olivia had taken, and she'd never learned his name. Two small girls haunted the lawn beneath the picture window of his next-door neighbor's house. They looked like twins in their blue dresses. Where were they headed tonight, and who was supposed to take them? Olivia had no idea, and there was no one to ask.

Whatever sickness had swept through Taggart's murderers on Starry Wood Lane had swallowed Chapel Hill.

"Like a storm," Olivia whispered. "Something in the rain."

That didn't make sense. All of these people down each of these streets couldn't have happened to step outside when the flash storm swept through. Not the water itself then, but the pressure, same as had given Olivia a headache this evening, the infection knocking on the inside of her skull and yet not breaking through.

She seemed immune. Taggart, too, until immunity quit doing him any good. What decided that? Genetics? Zodiac sign? Some citizens of Chapel Hill might have been luckier than others.

Lizzie could be immune. Olivia hoped she wasn't—no need to run from her if she was a staggering zombie like the rest—but Olivia doubted it. The monster and the infection had appeared one after the other, and she guessed they had to be related. No coincidence that two weird things had struck town on the same night. And if it was coincidence, and this sickness spread on its own, and by chance a monster had stalked her way into Chapel Hill—

Olivia couldn't finish the train of ideas. Her breath flew out and wouldn't fly back in, lungs bellowing overtime and yet desperate for air.

She squatted in the street and tucked her head between her hands. Fine, she was panicking. She could handle that if she figured out what a person who wasn't panicking would do. If Sunflower popped onto the street right now, that would make the chaos easier to handle. They could face it together.

Sunflower was probably a mindless zombie right now, same as her mother Hazibel, and Roy, and Shelly and Dane, and most everyone who lived in this godforsaken town.

"Don't think like that," Olivia said, louder than she meant to, but what difference did it make? None of these people could hear her. "Happy thoughts. Panic later."

She let her mind drift back to the time she and Sunflower had stolen Roy's BB gun. An afternoon shooting bottles, just the girls, Blue Oyster Cult blasting from a small portable radio, and somehow they never missed a shot. The boys didn't believe them later. There was the time Olivia tried to get Sunflower into knitting. Her would-be sweater sprouted octopus tentacles of yarn, and after two tries of tearing out stitches and reknitting them, Sunflower decided to gift the monstrosity to Hazibel as a hat. She didn't wear it, not her style, but Olivia had seen the knitted octopus stashed in the Mason House coat closet. Hazibel had kept it.

Olivia's heart thundered beneath her thoughts. These were too sweet, too tame. They couldn't fight a night that stabbed lightning through her veins.

Last Fourth of July, the drive-in had replayed *Jaws*. When the shark sloshed up from chum-filled waters behind Roy Scheider, Sunflower didn't cling to her boyfriend of the same name; she clung shrieking to Olivia. It was a friend thing to do, but it was also a girlfriend thing to do to a boyfriend, and although Olivia knew it meant one thing to Sunflower, she let herself pretend it meant another while they grasped screaming at each other's arms.

The moment had sent a brief thrill through Olivia's chest, her heart stuttering, almost as hard as tonight. She thought it over again, but the memory still couldn't override running from Lizzie and the infected. Think—wasn't there a time when her heart had beat as hard with delight as it now pounded with terror?

Of course. Gina Night.

That evening's every detail had stitched itself deep into her chest. That was the night Sunflower first told Olivia in full about her older sister, the brave and beautiful, the creative and incomparable Gina Mason. Like Olivia, she had run away from home, but away from Chapel Hill instead of finding herself here.

On Gina Night, Sunflower had sat herself and Olivia on Gina's bedroom floor, where they snacked on potato chips and marveled at the stained-glass panes Gina had left behind. She'd made them in some high school art workshop, pretty framed slices of abstract shapes in every imaginable color. Each gathered dust on the walls.

When Sunflower tired of snacking and sulking, she'd opened Gina's walk-in closet and torn the clothes from every hanger.

"Try them. It's a fashion show." She hadn't needed to say that she used to try on these clothes while Gina still lived in the Mason House. Likely without permission.

Olivia had hopped in headfirst. Away with the pajamas, on with the sleek dresses, gawdy shoulder-padded jackets, old holey leggings, and assorted hats as colorful as the stained glass hanging on the walls. She couldn't imagine what Gina had taken with her if she'd left these treasures behind.

Though Sunflower had smiled through the night, the fashion show felt more like grieving, maybe an exorcism, as if she somehow knew then more than ever that Gina was dead, and she needed to give her big sister some special little sister sendoff. She and Olivia had plucked up Gina's old Polaroid camera, taking photos in favorite outfits, between outfits, out of focus or too close, or sometimes just right.

Gina Night had set Olivia's heart racing down terrifying, wonderful roads, the butterflies in her stomach swarming at full frenzy. Sunflower would never feel the same, but Olivia hadn't cared that night. They were free and loving and having fun, at least until Hazibel's return home. By then, Gina's bedroom looked like Olivia and Sunflower had slaughtered and gutted the wardrobe, and they had to clean and hang up everything back the way they'd found it.

Olivia had grinned every minute.

She didn't grin now, but she lifted her head and looked to the star-filled sky. If Gina still lived, she might be looking at that same sky somewhere far from Chapel Hill. She'd escaped this town, same as Olivia had escaped Hartford.

Olivia could escape this town, too.

If she survived the night. No more stalling. No more excuses. She would grab a bus, or hitchhike, or walk if she had to; back to Connecticut, Hartford, her parents' house. Knock on the door, confront them, and forgive them. Even if they didn't apologize, even if they didn't deserve it, even if she didn't deserve it either. Deep down, she loved them. They likely loved her, too. They would find closure as a family, no matter what.

"Promise," she said. "If I get out, we'll make it work." She couldn't say for certain whom she bargained with, but she'd said the words and meant them. No turning back now.

She needed to escape Chapel Hill.

Sharp slopes surrounded town in every direction except the southeastern side, where the land rolled in a calm slope. Main Street let onto Main E, which led downhill to flatland, easy roads, and the new on-ramp to I-376. The easy way out of Chapel Hill.

Much harder, but closer, Sunset Pass formed a steep, narrow two-lane that careened down Chapel Hill's western side. A place of accidents and memorial ribbons.

Too much danger had already come hunting Olivia tonight; she didn't need any unnecessary risks. Crossing town wouldn't take her more than three hours, four tops if she kept a strong pace. She would make for Main, southeast, flatlands, and the interstate.

And hope hard in her heart that this storm hadn't infected the entire world.

5. GLASS

The infected wandered Van Buren Avenue's lawns, sidewalks, and pavement. Olivia would have to zigzag around them and keep wary against getting cornered at a tree or the odd street-parked car all the way to Main Street. Van Buren formed one branch of a residential tree, only a couple of people per house, but Main Street offered Chapel Hill's most popular bars and restaurants along its busiest throughway. If most of town had been infected, Olivia would find more people shambling along its sidewalks, roads, and storefronts than anywhere else.

A young, skinny guy about her age lurched from sidewalk to street. He wore denim overalls and had probably been coming home from work somewhere when the storm struck. His lips chopped up and down, spitting words Olivia couldn't discern from here. And she refused to get any closer.

She wouldn't turn out like Taggart. His final, grunting noises slithered into her ears, and she rubbed them to block the sound.

How would Roy take the news that his best friend was dead?

He would never know. He and Sunflower were together at Lookout, shambling around their cars and between trees, veering dangerously close to the sheer drop of Chapel Hill's northern side. If only Sunflower had stuck to the old plan and stayed at the drive-in. She might've been infected anyway, but at least there wouldn't be a cliff she could stumble off in her trance.

Olivia couldn't think about that. She shivered, her clothes still damp.

If she was going to lose Lizzie down Chapel Hill's streets, she might have time to check for survivors. The apartment where she lived with Shelly and Dane stood in the direction of Sunset Pass, a detour from the way to Main Street, but maybe they'd started heading for the interstate, too. Driving would risk striking and enraging the infected; the Kincaids would go on foot. The least Olivia could do was keep an eye out for them. In case they were okay.

She hoped so. They had fed and sheltered her these past three years when everyone else but Sunflower had turned Olivia away. No chance that Sunflower could have convinced Hazibel to take in another mouth; she had probably been relieved when Gina ran away and her single mom responsibilities dropped from two daughters to one.

Meanwhile, Shelly and Dane had welcomed Olivia and loved her, no obligation, no questions asked. Their warmth was nourishing, and when Olivia sat and talked and laughed with them, she couldn't blame herself so much for running away from Hartford. The town considered the Kincaids hippies or freaks, depending on which local you asked, but they were kind. No one in this town knew that like Olivia. Their weirdness was not a fault to be tolerated; it was part of their charm. They needed to make it through the night.

And on the unlikely chance that Sunflower had ditched the northern cliffs of Lookout when the storm rolled in, Olivia would keep an eye out for her, too. Maybe everyone she cared about walked Main Street, waiting for her. Shelly, Dane, Sunflower.

Impossible, but Olivia let herself entertain the idea anyway. Her heart might crack otherwise.

And if she didn't find them there, Main Street gave easy access to most of Chapel Hill's neighborhoods. She could stretch her three-hour escape to four or five in order to search Cooper Street. She might even try the Mason House again. There was time to find the people she loved, so long as she didn't hear Lizzie sucking flavors out of the air.

"Olivia," said a beckoning voice.

Olivia's heart jolted in panic. She darted ahead two steps, swerved left around a shambling gray-haired woman in a pink bathrobe, and made for the back end of a black sedan. Sitting tight there wasn't an option when Lizzie could track tastes and scents, but Olivia could crawl. She wouldn't be snake food.

"Olivia," the voice repeated.

She froze halfway around the sedan. That voice sounded too high-pitched and bright for Lizzie, meaning Olivia wasn't the only uninfected person to walk Van Buren. She scanned every house, their lights dim behind curtains, and then turned to the road.

The young man in overalls had wandered her way. "Olivia," he said, his voice lilting.

Olivia practically skipped toward him. She didn't recognize his face, but he must have known her. Why wouldn't he? He might've blended with the rest of Chapel Hill High, but she was the outcast. Best of all, he wasn't infected.

"You're okay?" she asked, disbelieving. "Thank God, I thought I was the only one left." She reached out to pat his arm, like she didn't believe he was real.

Her fingers froze inches from his skin. Glassy nothingness haunted his eyes, same as Harley and the rest of the infected she'd seen too close on Starry Wood Lane. His gait came shambling, awkward.

Olivia drew her fingers back. "You said my name, didn't you?"

"Olivia," he mumbled again, and a half-smile creased his vacant face. "That's a pretty name. I've always liked that name."

Ice stabbed Olivia's spine, a chill that froze her skin. Her teeth began to chatter. "What did you say?" she asked.

The overalls man swerved hard. His breath brushed Olivia's cheek, and every nerve in her body screamed, *Get back, don't let them kill you*. He lurched, crashing toward her. She scuttled back and struck the nearby sedan. It jostled against her, but it didn't scream hatred and come pummeling with fists and bootheels.

The overalls man shambled past, head doddering to one side. "Oh," he said. "I'm Sunflower."

Olivia's frozen bones would have shattered had she fallen on the pavement. This man shouldn't have said those words. No one should. He was mumbling, out of his mind with sickness, and yet his recitation couldn't be coincidence. Olivia remembered that conversation beat for beat. Through classes, homework, and drive-in shifts, thick and thin, that conversation stayed. She would keep it when she was gray and toothless, her mind turned to mashed potatoes, should she live so long.

Only she and Sunflower should have known the words, and yet the conversation had fallen into this guy's head with the sickening rain, at least Sunflower's side of it.

What did the infection have to do with her? She was special, one of a kind, but she couldn't influence infectious storms and draw monsters to Chapel Hill. Connecting her to tonight's phenomena made no sense.

But then, nothing tonight made sense. If Sunflower had anything to do with the storm, then maybe she hadn't been infected. She could be okay.

Olivia smashed her forehead against her palm, a fresh headache beating down. Taggart's body and Lizzie's mouth had consumed every thought. Scared out of her mind, desperate to escape Chapel Hill and reach Hartford, she'd written Sunflower off as doomed.

What kind of friend did that? A shitty one, and Olivia was not a shitty friend.

She turned from the overalls man toward the way she'd come. Seeing Sunflower wandering and blank-faced might break Olivia's heart, but she'd have to take that risk. Better to be heartbroken than to escape Chapel Hill and always wonder if there was something she could have done. Especially if Sunflower had anything to do with the storm.

"Keep an open mind," Olivia muttered. "Otherwise I might as well be infected."

A dry voice answered. "Really ain't smart to bug the zombies."

Blood-red hair gleamed beneath a streetlight down the sidewalk. The figure flashed a peace sign Olivia's way and then lifted a fiery eye, cigarette smoke snaking between the two raised fingers.

"You still normal?" Christmas asked. The rest of their fingers stretched into a flat hand that waggled side to side. "Relatively?"

An annoyed twitch tugged at Olivia's mouth, but she couldn't help smiling. Only the weirdos seemed to have been spared the sickness, the infection as unwilling to touch them as the rest of town. Christmas was nowhere close to Olivia's favorite person, but she would take a stranger's company over walking alone right now. Especially if she had to reach Lookout while Lizzie prowled the northern woods.

"I guess you've seen what they do when you touch them," Olivia said.

Christmas stepped closer, their shoulders hunched, and an ashy cloud overpowered the rain's humid stink. "Could fight four, six," Christmas said, jacket sleeve wrinkling around one flexed bicep. "But more than that came at your friend. Like boxing a nest of wasps."

Olivia's forced smile fell. "You followed me."

Christmas sucked hard at their cigarette and let gray smoke trail between their lips. "Had an epiphany after I left you. Why walk all the way to the Sprinkle Shack for ice cream when the projection guy keeps those chocolate and vanilla sandwiches in a cooler? Soggy as Chapel Hill, but tastes the same. He wasn't right anymore though, nothing upstairs. I had to get lost."

Olivia would've liked to believe she'd assumed Booth Bill had fled from Lizzie and begun wandering Starry Wood Lane like the letter jacket crew, or that she'd hoped he would've hidden in the projection booth. Really, she hadn't considered him at all. Her thoughts had bent first to survival, and then to Sunflower.

"But yeah," Christmas said. "I was in the woods, saw what that snake lady did."

"And what that mob did to Taggart?" Olivia blew smoke out of her face. "Why didn't you help?"

Christmas's gaze and the cigarette's end formed a three-eyed stare. "Why didn't you?"

Olivia shrank beneath their gaze. "I'm not strong like you." She slid her arms around her chest and shuddered.

"Nah, that isn't why," Christmas said, flicking ashes into the street. "You ran at those clowns once tonight to help that snake lady, and boy, did that choice bite you."

Olivia looked past Christmas, up Van Buren Avenue. She didn't have to hear this; she had to reach Lookout.

Christmas's voice drew her gaze. "That's why you stalled when they came after Taggart. You wanted to help, but you remembered what happened five minutes before, and you won't make that mistake again. No, tonight's poisoned you. Might think twice next time life asks you to stick your neck out for anybody."

"That's not true," Olivia snapped. She'd been wrong; walking alone would be better than walking with a fork-tongued devil when getting flustered meant making mistakes. She couldn't afford one wrong twitch that might send her stumbling into the infected.

Christmas made that sucking noise again, too similar to Lizzie's gasping. "We'll see when it's your blond friend roaming like a zombie, or dead in the road."

The thought made Olivia's heart skip a beat. She glanced down the street, where the overalls man now orbited a streetlight's golden cone. Was he still mumbling? Olivia's private moments with Sunflower seemed cast on display tonight. There were few people left in Chapel Hill capable of hearing those echoes.

What was going on inside infected minds? Did they see Sunflower's memories? That didn't seem possible, but how else could they know these private moments? How much did Sunflower have to do with them, or the storm, or Lizzie, or any of it?

Olivia turned again to Christmas. She was getting nowhere fast, but she felt geared to fight, and if she couldn't do it physically, she would shout and cry.

Words rotted in her throat. Her gaze drifted up the length of Christmas's body, higher than their head and the houses, into the starlit sky.

A misty geyser climbed from the northwestern side of Chapel Hill. Blue light flickered in its smoke, a cloud brimming lightning before it unleashed a storm. Olivia heard no thunder, the misty column silent as it filled the sky, but her skin tightened, squeezed again by sudden pressure in the air.

Tonight's storm was again building to burst.

Christmas followed Olivia's stare as the geyser formed a cloud. "Rain?" they asked.

The cloud sagged, front-heavy as a poorly built toy. Its path formed a gentle arc through the air. Olivia had to twist toward Main Street to watch its descent, sinking and sinking until it hit the ground somewhere past Van Buren's curve, behind the lawns and houses. She couldn't find her words; the concession stand had run out, no more syllables until next weekend, thanks for your business. She could only wait for an impact tremor that never came.

"We should get back," Christmas said, their footsteps clomping up the sidewalk. "Better if we travel together, yeah? Safety in numbers. We might even live." They sounded unnerved now. Whatever had landed hadn't shaken the hill, only the people on it.

Olivia held still, watching down Van Buren Avenue. The clinging chill now prodded its fingers through fat, muscle, bone, into her marrow, and became one with her cells.

Christmas clacked their teeth around their cigarette. "You feel that cold?" they asked. "I sure as hell do."

A cool blue settled through the air. First the streetlights winked at Olivia, and then their reflections winked, too. Lawn grass and parked cars glistened with reflected light. That sense of blueness broke into bold violet, pale yellow, vibrant green, cardinal red, and streaking white.

A rainbow of frost crept across every surface, reconfiguring metal, pavement, and grass to sheets of stained glass.

Had the transmogrification been one of town hall's projects, Olivia might have laughed. Church windows to dress Chapel Hill. Too on-the-nose to be taken seriously.

Except the rainbow frost crept her way.

It crawled up a parked car, merging its door and window into one glassy pane. Shards jutted up from sidewalk cracks and lapped a nearby lawn's edges into rising glass crystals. Shapes haunted every surface, but Olivia couldn't make out clear images. No saintly depictions or gospel truths, only abstract patterns, as if nature had grown these gleaming colors as part of Chapel Hill's geology.

Down Van Buren Avenue, the mumbling overalls man slumped onto the twinkling street, and rainbow glass teeth latched around one brown boot. His next step hit the same, and the glass clutched from sole to ankle.

He didn't notice, and when he tried to take a third step, he fell on his hands and knees. Rainbow teeth snapped at skin as easily as boot. Colorful shards clamped at his wrists.

Olivia's skin chilled as if she'd scraped her teeth on an ice cube. Like she could feel that glassy bite. She couldn't look away, her neck frozen stiff.

The overalls man shifted forward, shoulders tensing. He meant to keep moving, one symptom of the infection. He would crawl if he had to, and without a mind to tell him to stop, he tried moving his right arm.

A wet, bony crack echoed across the glass. Flesh pressed into shards, and his forearm bubbled thick and red.

Olivia at last shut her eyes and stumbled backward. Her shoulders slammed into someone's sternum. She flinched, her memory caught in the mob's roaring hatred on Starry Wood Lane, but her eyes opened on Christmas's gaping face. Their cigarette had fallen to the street.

Olivia ducked around Christmas and started up the sidewalk. The infected staggered in their uncertain paths, oblivious to this new infection, a rainbow scab stretching from the intersection of Main Street and Van Buren Avenue and onward toward Ridgemont, the woods, and perhaps to streets south, east, and west, too. How far would it spread?

Christmas strode at Olivia's side. "Back to Ridgemont, yeah?" they asked, coughing, their eyes twitching every which way.

Olivia didn't argue. She wouldn't stay here and watch rainbow frost recycle these mindless infected into glass sculptures or listen to their bones crack as they fought to keep moving. She'd seen too many horrors tonight already.

Christmas nudged her arm while fumbling in their jacket for another smoke. "You heading somewhere particular?" they asked. "What's your story here?"

Words piled in Olivia's mouth, but she didn't answer right away. She glanced back at the creeping frost. Its colors offered no obvious pattern, only slats of deep blue here, harsh yellow there, in too many right angles to feel natural or random. Anyone else might have stuck with comparing them to church windows, even if they'd only seen them in photographs, but Olivia knew these shapes from a forbidden room's walls upstairs in the Mason House. In Sunflower's sister's room.

These stained-glass patterns could have been Gina's art.

6. THE GIRL OF MIDNIGHT SUNSHINE

"I know, it seems like a big if," Olivia said. "But if I get out, I have to go back. Unfinished business. My parents and I need to straighten things between us."

She couldn't be sure at what point in the walk up Van Buren she'd opened herself to Christmas, but she felt aired out at least to have thrown the whole mess off her chest, even to a stranger. Christmas had replaced their fallen cigarette with a new one. If Olivia didn't keep up conversation, she'd have nothing to distract her from the chill of spreading glass behind her and the sound of two lungs puffing a dragon of smoke in and out.

Behind them, the crystalline rainbow trapped the infected. Some of them would bleed out and die, Olivia guessed. She didn't expect them to attack the glittering street itself, but she couldn't be sure. They might charge Van Buren Avenue in a glass-hating frenzy.

At least Ridgemont Road hadn't changed. While she couldn't make out the street's every detail between the darkness and distance, nothing twinkled at her in the light. Pavement, trees, infected people, but no glass. The rainbow infection must have slowed from Main Street and would hopefully run its course before it overcame the entire town.

"Let me see if I understand correctly," Christmas said at last, tapping their cigarette over the sidewalk. "Your father saw you kiss some girl you didn't even know at the carnival, and then what, you just took off? No shouting match, no throwing you to the wolves. He saw it, and you up and left Hartford without a word? Didn't even wait to see how he'd take it, just skedaddled off to Nowheresville, Pennsylvania?"

"I was fifteen," Olivia said in a playful, defensive whine. "We didn't talk then, but before that night. Well, not us together, but there were things he's said, Mom nodding along to him, vice versa—it wouldn't have worked out." Her head slumped toward her chest. "At least, that's what I thought three years back. I'm not sure anymore."

"Not been sure for a long time, yeah?" Christmas's shoulders stiffened from blades to spine, as if tensing their neck to stretch as long as Lizzie's when she'd eaten Devin.

Olivia eyed the spaces between houses, where the lawns stretched from yard to yard, and expected a gasping mouth and bottomless throat to come lumbering from the shadows. She'd seen and heard nothing of Lizzie since Starry Wood Lane, but the absence didn't comfort her.

"And you?" Olivia asked. "Your story?"

"Grew up in a lot of places," Christmas said. "Best place was White River Valley, northern Ohio. Wet and cold, sure, but we never got weather this manic. The rain was normal, no glass. Came passing through Chapel Hill on a road trip and got stalled up. Little thing like you can stick out her thumb, get plucked off the roadside, but hitchhiking comes kind of hard when drivers size you up as the type to grind their bones to make your bread."

Olivia wouldn't have called it easy. Rides came willing, but every time a car or truck slowed to the highway's edge meant rolling fateful dice. Any wrong choice could have been the one to make her regret leaving Hartford.

"Still, got to see the sites," Christmas went on. "Devil's Tower, Badlands, big beautiful places, not too many people. No one cared how far I strayed. Never had a family, really." They turned to Olivia, somber now. "But if I did, I'd sure as shit give them a chance before I ditched them. Have their say, and fight back if they deserved it. Give them my piece of mind. You can't stay in Chapel Hill."

"I didn't mean to," Olivia said. "I've been wanting to talk to them, at least visit, but I can't remember their phone number, and the chance never comes up." A chill beat at her back, but when she glanced over her shoulder, the rainbow glass winked at least a block away. "This town seems to catch people."

Christmas nodded, cigarette smoke chasing their lips. "Always an excuse not to move on."

Steps ahead, one stunted figure made shambling circles around a faraway streetlight. An infected little girl, maybe eight years old. Chapel Hill had caught her, too, but she had lost any understanding of the outside world. None of the infected felt any sudden pressure to resolve unfinished business hundreds of miles away. No understanding of anything anymore.

A thin hand settled onto Olivia's shoulder. She glanced up at Christmas's smoky, resolute face.

"We're getting out," Christmas said, cigarette clenched between their teeth.

"I'm trying," Olivia said, her voice faint.

"No." Christmas's grip tightened, and they drew Olivia closer. "It's not a plan; it's a promise. We're getting out."

Olivia trembled in Christmas's grasp. Despite the spreading rainbow glass, and the infected mumbling out her past, and the too-real chance that a monster might spring from the shadows any second with jaws as wide as the world, for this one moment, she believed they could escape Chapel Hill.

Ridgemont Road opened to the right and left. Olivia glanced back the way she'd first come, past Riggs and Newport and toward the trees that led to Starry Wood Lane and the drive-in. To Taggart.

No sign of Lizzie.

Olivia glanced west. No glass stretched up the streets, at least none she could see from the corner of Van Buren and Ridgemont. No Lizzie that way, either. She must have wandered down the wrong lane, an alien creature lost in Chapel Hill. Its many small streets would keep her busy.

The Starry Wood filled Ridgemont Road on the north side, spreading west all the way to where Sunset Pass descended Chapel Hill in a steep, winding trail. Lingering clouds climbed beyond the northwestern trees. The highest limbs glimmered in a colorful sheen where the rainbow mist's bombardment left traces of stained glass sharpening the treetops. Beyond the mist and foliage, the cliffs of Lookout formed another of the hill's boundaries.

Where Sunflower had meant to meet Roy. She might still be there.

Olivia darted across Ridgemont and trailed the trees on the far side. She couldn't wait another moment to learn Sunflower's fate. Infected or immune, she had to know. Even if it crushed her.

Christmas stomped at her heels. "What gives? See something?"

"Detour," Olivia muttered.

Sticking this close to the woods where Lizzie could be lurking out of sight sent Olivia's hands shaking, but she hoped Christmas's presence might help. Christmas stood taller than Devin and seemed stronger. And, maybe superstitiously, Olivia felt safer around someone whose name Lizzie might not know.

She chased the line of green foliage, careful to give the sparse infected their own space. They seemed attracted to the streetlights, and twice as many dotted Ridgemont Road's residential side as its wild north. Trails cut through the trees from the drive-in to Lookout, too, but Olivia saw no benefit in traipsing through damp underbrush, especially if sudden patches of grasping glass might hide among the roots. A dirt trail opened to her right, formed by countless tires' comings and goings, and she followed. Lookout would have been an empty place tonight had Sunflower not made romantic plans. Tangled, dripping tree limbs soon overtook the sky.

"Not like I've spent much time in this one-horse town," Christmas said, ducking their head beneath waterlogged branches. "But I'm pretty sure this is no way out."

"Sunflower came here with Roy tonight," Olivia said.

She peered through the undergrowth for signs of headlights, taillights, a dome light, but both Sunflower and Roy would have kept their cars dark. Tonight offered no moon, and Lookout had no streetlights but the distant glow of northern towns.

"Right," Christmas said. "Roy."

Olivia slowed. "You know him?"

"Seen him. That is good business." Christmas's hand found Olivia's shoulder again and pulled at her. "Girl, that cloud popped from this way, and we don't know what it left behind."

Olivia shrugged out of Christmas's grasp. "Sunflower's up here."

Christmas grabbed harder this time and shoved Olivia to one

side. Her spine struck the nearest tree trunk, and wet bark sank across her shirt. Christmas's gaze hid in the wooded gloom, only their cigarette's eye glaring in the dark, piercing and judgmental.

Olivia took Christmas's hand and shoved back. A harsh grip closed around her wrists and pinned them over her head to the tree trunk. Olivia fidgeted, and the grip tightened. Her muscles stilled under the cigarette's glare. She stared long into its tiny fire, a light that faded and brightened with Christmas's frustrated breath. Her heart pounded again, would soon find its own way out of town if Olivia kept overworking it tonight. Another tremor flowed through her muscles, not entirely unpleasant.

"Does a cloud that turns the world to glass sound normal?" Christmas asked. "No, it sounds weird. We don't trust weird tonight. It's dangerous, yeah?"

"You're weird, too," Olivia said. Heat stroked her face, its scent filled with ashes and impatience. "Are you dangerous?" She watched the cigarette's glare slide to one side as Christmas smirked. "I'm kind of weird, too. Am I dangerous?"

Olivia couldn't move yet, but Christmas's grip no longer made her wrists ache.

She twitched her head toward Lookout. "If that cloud started here, Lookout might be the source," she said. "We could stop it, and everyone will go back to normal."

"Another excuse to stay," Christmas said. Their cigarette darkened and then tumbled to the damp earth. "Ending tonight won't bring anyone back. Won't straighten things with your parents, so to speak."

Their hand fell away, and Olivia's arms dropped to her sides. She resisted rubbing her wrists in case Christmas could see.

"Fine," Christmas grunted. "Blondie calls."

A match flared in the dark, and Olivia wondered if she'd only been let go because Christmas needed another smoke. She wouldn't look a gift horse in the cigarette-clutching mouth as her back lifted from the tree bark.

Foliage spread apart as she and Christmas neared the cliff. If she were to step too close, Christmas would stop her again. They had a warm touch.

Olivia shivered from skin to bone. "At the drive-in, why did you ask for my heart?"

Christmas hummed an *I don't know* tune. "Didn't want buttered popcorn." They exhaled hard, blowing smoke harsher than they needed as if they didn't want to admit something. "Seems like an okay heart. You're coming after Blondie, after all."

"She has a real name," Olivia said. "Sun—"

A low moan cut her off, and she turned ahead. Black trunks spread apart where the trail widened into a clearing, and then the earth fell in a sheer drop several yards past the woods. Two cars parked side by side, their steel and glass cast blue by the starlit sky. The world glowed in the distance.

A hunched silhouette teetered at the cliff's edge against a thousand faraway lights. It moaned again, and Olivia almost believed she'd found Lizzie.

But she knew better. "Sunflower!" she shouted.

Sunflower swayed back. And then forward, like she was about to fall.

Olivia rushed toward the cliff. Vertigo scrabbled cold up her legs as she neared the edge, where she wrapped her arms around Sunflower and hauled her backward from the several hundred-foot drop.

Olivia pictured the letter jacket crew's faces beyond the woods, a patient transformation from placid to vengeful, and wondered if Sunflower's face looked the same in the dark. She hadn't stopped to think she might be touching an infected. Concern for Sunflower had filled her mind.

"I'm sorry," Olivia whispered. "I love you, and I'm sorry."

Her arms trembled, waiting. Would Sunflower become like the placid elderly man who hadn't attacked Taggart, or would she be more like Harley, who'd led the mob?

"I heard a girl crying beneath the hill," Sunflower said. Air hissed through her chattering teeth, and she swallowed hard. "I wanted to see her. Don't you know? Listening to someone crying when you can't find them will drive you nuts. I didn't want that." She lolled her head back against Olivia's chest and stared up. "I puked off Lookout. Don't tell anybody."

Olivia nestled her face into Sunflower's hair and squeezed tight in a relieved, bone-breaking hug. Through wavy blond strands, she looked out on the counties north of Chapel Hill, filled with the twinkling lights of distant towns, romantic highways, and black mountains that blotted out the lowest stars.

Sunflower wasn't infected. The world was still out there, and Sunflower wasn't infected, and that was good, but Olivia had almost written her off, too scared to check Lookout. What if she'd never come here? Would Sunflower have plummeted? Would Lizzie have found her?

Olivia forced the what-ifs to the back of her mind. They hadn't come to pass, and now they couldn't. She held Sunflower again, and everything would be okay.

"Liv?" Sunflower slumped out of Olivia's grip and pressed her skull to the earth. "My head hurts."

Olivia rubbed between Sunflower's shoulders and then let her fingers climb up the back of Sunflower's neck, past the unseen crescent birthmark, where they began to stroke her scalp. Her muscles tensed at the soft touch.

"Where's Roy?" Olivia asked. She noticed his red-and-black jacket was missing from Sunflower's shoulders.

"Don't know," Sunflower said. "Don't care."

Olivia couldn't be hearing that, not after everything. Sunflower could be self-focused at times, but Roy mattered, didn't he? Olivia let the comment slide. If Roy had been infected, she couldn't help him. Better to focus on those she could.

Sunflower shook her head and tugged free of Olivia's fingers. "I blacked out. Couple times. I thought Mom was here and cried for her, but I guess she wasn't around after all."

Olivia hadn't seen Hazibel since idling outside the Mason House, when she'd heard the hill screaming. If only strange noises were the worst tonight could offer.

She drew her legs from beneath Sunflower's torso and stood. Even with eyes adjusting to the gloom, she couldn't make out any tracks in the earth. No sign of Roy or Hazibel. No sign of any crying girl, either. Had Roy wandered off the cliff? And Sunflower, waking from a blackout, maybe hearing him fall—had she mistaken the sound for someone else? Olivia peered through each car's back windows, but no one sat in their darkness.

Sunflower shuffled against the ground. "Who's that with you?"

Another cigarette's eye glared from the woods, and then Christmas took form, tall as trees. They sighed a stream of smoke.

"That's Christmas," Olivia said. "No one to be scared of."

"Beg to differ," Christmas said, but they didn't sound like they cared.

A gleam caught Olivia's eye. On the north side of the nearest tree, tangled in moss, starlight reflected in the surface of damp, black sludge. Olivia thought of the gunk she'd found in the staff restroom's corner at the Starry Wood Drive-In, moments before the letter jacket crew had attacked Lizzie. Olivia had blamed Christmas at the time, and she glanced their way now.

"Did you do this?" she asked.

"I'm not an animal," Christmas said, almost offended. "Why?"

"Nothing." Olivia turned from the sludge. If Christmas hadn't slopped it here, then likely Lizzie had. She'd swallowed Devin whole, perhaps digested him already, and now the waste had come vomited up, an unrecognizable mess of horror and bones.

A thick gasp stirred the leaves somewhere in the woods.

Olivia hoped she'd only heard the wind. More than anything, she wanted the noise to have come from harmless Sunflower, her lungs desperate for air in the middle of a hard cry. Both she and Olivia had cried that hard before, too many times. She turned to Sunflower, a silent girl with her head in her hands.

The woods went quiet, and then another gasp pulled air into an unseen throat, harsher, louder, closer. The sound of clacking branches rattled down Olivia's spine.

She stumbled toward Sunflower, eyes on Christmas. "Lizzie's here," Olivia said.

Sunflower plucked her head from the earth. "Who?"

"Big mouth, bigger throat, lots of teeth, snake lady," Christmas said. Their cigarette spun through the air and into the trees. "I can take her."

Olivia pulled Sunflower to standing, light as a wicker basket, and led her toward the trail. "She ate Devin Shipley whole." She felt Sunflower twitch at her side. "Her mouth's big enough for you, too."

"Not me. I'm all hard edges and packing heat." Christmas raised their fists as if ready to box and then kissed one bicep.

Olivia tried to turn and argue, but Sunflower clung to her shoulder, part of her weight propped on Olivia's, a responsibility no one else could take. Christmas didn't seem the charitable type. Fine, but Olivia couldn't take on babysitting for two. If Christmas wanted to die, that choice was their own.

Except Chapel Hill didn't have many uninfected survivors right now. Doubtful Christmas would find anyone else on their own. More likely, they would find the bottom of Lizzie's gullet.

Olivia ground her foot into the dirt. "We're getting out. That's what you said." Over her shoulder, she watched Christmas's boxing stance soften. "You said it's not a plan, it's a promise. We're getting out. Slower with Sunflower in tow, sure, but we're doing it. You promised."

Christmas let their fists drop and stretched to full height, their hair cresting somewhere between the clouds and the stars. "What are you, a parrot?" they asked.

Another gasp tasted the woods, and Olivia tugged Sunflower and Christmas back into the dark foliage. One arm slung over Sunflower's shoulder while the other crossed Christmas's chest and grasped their arm. Too late to give either of them instructions; Olivia had to hope they understood as the shadows spat a monster onto Lookout.

Lizzie's silhouette climbed against the night sky, a hunched form stretching snakelike into a bulbous head of shaggy hair. Each lock ended in a fang-sharp point. She looked gigantic now, her neck having reached out with anaconda thickness, and the sucking from her mouth seemed to swallow the wind. The dimness must have shifted her proportions like a funhouse mirror. Or was Olivia's fear doing the work?

Sunflower's chest heaved, and tiny frightened breaths escaped her mouth, growing louder as her heart and lungs climbed her throat.

Olivia clamped her hand over Sunflower's mouth and then pulled her head down, face to chest. She didn't need to see this.

A chilly rhythm writhed between their bodies and spread into the woods. Tucking Sunflower close wouldn't help her. She would only hear the hammers in Olivia's chest and realize how right she was to panic. Their heartbeats would quake through the trees and earth, into Lizzie's ears or whatever equivalent hid beneath her shaggy gray hair, louder than the storm still deciding if it wanted to hurt Chapel Hill again.

Lizzie had already made her choice when it came to causing harm. She shuffled along Lookout, neck coiling back toward her shoulders. A wet smacking noise chased her next gasp, and her tongue's silhouette curled around distant stars as if she were licking constellations, ready to swallow.

Christmas tensed beneath Olivia's hand, her arm, and she tightened her grip. If Christmas meant to charge, Olivia wasn't strong enough to stop them, but she had to hope some of her urgency breathed through her fingers. There would be no winning a fight here. Couldn't Christmas understand? If they cared, they might notice Olivia's thundering pulse, and then maybe grow a brain for two seconds.

Lizzie inhaled hard again, and then again, deeper and quicker. A frustrated sigh rippled up her coiled throat.

"You're still here," she whispered.

She had said the same at the Starry Wood Drive-In, but this time she left out any word on taste. The glass cloud had probably thrown off her senses, leaving her clueless on where to find Olivia, or Sunflower, whichever Lizzie wanted most.

"You can help me," Lizzie said. "Don't you want to help me?"

She waited a moment, expectant for volunteers, and then she growled and stamped along Lookout, into another black wall of trees. Her footsteps faded, but her breath swelled in Olivia's ears. She still felt Devin falling down that monstrous throat.

Sunflower slipped from Olivia's chest, her breath rattling. "What was that thing?" she asked. "What did it look like?"

"Like a nightmare." Christmas filled the world, smelling too much of cigarette smoke, and their insistent hand urged Olivia toward the trail through the woods, back toward Ridgemont Road. "You wanted no fight, you got no fight, but we'd better move or else she'll huff and puff along this way again, maybe a little more hate in her heart. Don't want to see it, don't want to be here for it. Got that?"

Olivia got it. She tugged Sunflower's weight onto her again, stumbled at first, and then her burden eased as Christmas helped take up Sunflower's other side.

"What do we do?" Sunflower asked.

"Leave Chapel Hill," Olivia said. Her breath rushed out. Carrying a friend made for heavy work. "That's the plan. The promise."

"But what if it follows?" Sunflower swallowed loud in Olivia's ear. Her voice dropped to a whisper. "What if that thing leaves too?"

Olivia had no answer. Tonight had twisted in so many ways she couldn't have foreseen that any more complex a plan seemed destined to fail. They could only take on Chapel Hill's storm and sickness and monsters one step at a time. Even if those steps went struggling over fallen twigs and underbrush. No matter what Lizzie did, the rest of them had to leave Chapel Hill.

The woods closed around their group, and their stagger broke into a jog as Lizzie breathed darkness behind them.

7. SAFETY IN NUMBERS

Ridgemont Road welcomed Olivia back, an invitation she didn't want. Her drive-in uniform clung stiff at her joints, and she needed a shower and change of clothes more than another trek south. She wanted to see Main Street by now, the interstate. She wanted to find herself in the world she'd glimpsed beyond Lookout. If not for the roaming citizens of Chapel Hill, she might have suggested circling back around Lizzie to Sunflower's car and driving across town.

Impossible without running someone down. Not only did Olivia have zero plans to hurt anyone, the rest of the sickened mob wouldn't forgive such a mistake.

"My town," Sunflower said, gawking. "What's wrong with them?"

"I don't know," Olivia said. "But if you touch them, they'll kill you."

Sunflower pressed a hand to her forehead. "Tonight was supposed to be special."

Olivia slid her arms around Sunflower and held her. "We'll help them."

Christmas scoffed, ruffled their hair, and took the lead onto Ridgemont. They didn't believe Olivia. She wanted to mean it, and even if the hope of getting everyone back to normal was a fantasy, Sunflower needed to hear it. Optimism would keep her going. Christmas didn't understand because they had probably never had a best friend before, someone both difficult to love and yet impossible to do otherwise. Likely Christmas took up the difficult side of their relationships.

Olivia kept her ears perked for another gasp in the trees and heard only rustling leaves and clacking branches.

She nudged Sunflower. "We can't stay."

Sunflower took two shuffling steps from the sidewalk and then paused. It was a start.

Streetlights reflected off derelict cars, orbited by wandering infected. Clusters of them shambled at the mouths of each neighborhood. Either the spreading glass had driven them toward Ridgemont or they happened to be migrating north. If Ridgemont filled up, dodging them while guiding Sunflower might soon become impossible.

Olivia nudged again. "Remember Gina Night?" she asked. "I never had a big sister, and I'll never know what it's like for one to run off, but that night was special for you. For me, too."

She tried to guide Sunflower another step. At this snail's pace, the road stretched eternal. Christmas had stopped ahead, their ear turned to the conversation, unwilling to abandon Olivia. None of the group would escape Chapel Hill unless everyone did.

Olivia leaned close to Sunflower's ear. "My heart was racing, and remembering that helped me get oriented again. You can do the same, at least until the interstate. Save the panic for later."

Sunflower turned to Olivia and blinked hard. "Was mine racing that night?"

Olivia shrank back, realizing she'd messed up. Of course Sunflower's heart hadn't been racing. To her, they were two friends playing dress-up in Gina's clothes, an almost childish memorial, both already older than Gina when she disappeared. Sunflower had been understandably focused on her own feelings.

And she wouldn't have felt the same toward Olivia as Olivia felt toward her. She had no reason for a racing heart on Gina Night.

"I forgot to check yours," Olivia said, forcing a smirk that made Sunflower giggle. "Ignore me. I don't know what I'm saying."

She glanced back at the trees and watched them for movement. Lizzie could appear while they stood here laughing, perfect time for an ambush, unhinge her jaw and charge the street, tarp and blankets billowing off her back. Devin was long gone, and she would be hungry again.

Nothing appeared from the woods. Olivia couldn't hope that would stay the case. She drew Sunflower forward and pointed up Ridgemont Road, where another neighborhood awaited down Westland Lane. Christmas lingered on the sidewalk.

"We'll make the next turn toward Main and hope the way's clear," Olivia said. "Can you try?"

"I'm not hurt," Sunflower said. That would have to be good enough. "Just the headache. Any more Motrin?"

"I lost it." Olivia almost mentioned Taggart and then swallowed her words—not now.

"It didn't really do me any good before." Sunflower shuffled another couple steps up Ridgemont. "My head was still pounding when I met up with Roy. When the rain started, the pain got so bad that I blacked out. Roy wasn't right when I woke up and then I blacked out again, and when I woke up, everything went misty. I thought I saw Mom heading through the trees. She was calling for me, and I wanted her, but she couldn't hear me. She might've been messed up, too." She chinned across Ridgemont, where two men in jeans and jackets stumbled circles around each other.

Olivia couldn't stare at them for long. Roy was infected. Hazibel might have been infected, too, although Olivia couldn't guess how Sunflower's mother would have known to find her at Lookout.

Blacking out. Olivia dredged up the same question she had wondered on Van Buren Avenue before her reunion with Christmas— what did the infection have to do with Sunflower? If she'd blacked out, she might have been infected herself. Snapping out of infection might explain why the overalls man had repeated one of her memories, some misfired neuron in whatever hivemind connection remained between the infected after losing one of its swarm.

Could that explain the glass, too? It had looked so much like Gina's art. The storm might have reacted to Sunflower's newfound freedom and produced a piece of her memories, impossible as that sounded. Chaos ruled the night.

Or maybe Sunflower was central to everything. Olivia could understand that. Her life had revolved around Sunflower since that first day they'd met at Chapel Hill High. The storm might have been the same, locked in some psychic tether to a headache that wouldn't go away.

Olivia couldn't bring up any of that right now. Every thought sounded like nonsense. Everything that had happened tonight sounded like nonsense too.

And yet tonight lingered, its events as real as the stars above. The heavens seemed unshaken by the troubles of Chapel Hill.

Christmas started up the sidewalk, their patience evidently running on empty. Olivia followed with Sunflower in tow. If Christmas wanted to play forerunner and bodyguard, power to them. They seemed to be craving a fight. Not everyone could handle a racing heart, and strong people like Christmas didn't seem used to frayed nerves. In normal circumstances, they would never fear the ordinary people of Chapel Hill. Tonight had become strange for everyone.

Even the infected, Olivia supposed. She watched one of them turn the corner a few steps past Christmas, a lithe woman in a pale dress, her dark hair streaked with gray. She paused at the sidewalk's center, long enough to become a new obstacle.

Long enough for Olivia to recognize her. Usually a cigarette jutted between those lips, the teeth vaguely stained by nicotine and an unkind tongue. Her pale blue eyes scratched icily wherever they looked.

Sunflower's mother, Hazibel Mason.

Were Sunflower to see that face, she would run ahead and throw her arms around that waist. Mother and daughter were rarely on peaceable terms, but tonight Sunflower craved intimacy. She wouldn't understand that her mother was not herself.

Christmas steered off the sidewalk, out of Hazibel's way. The infected didn't usually stand still, and Christmas couldn't know what to expect. Olivia had only seen one infected freeze in place, the overalls man when the rainbow glass caught him. Even then, he'd tried to move. The memory made her shudder.

She nudged Sunflower into the street and tried to block her line of sight. Her eyes glued to Christmas's shoulders. She hoped Sunflower kept the same unwavering stare.

Sunflower slowed at the curb. "Mom?" She pushed at Olivia.

Olivia pressed Sunflower's shoulders. "She's not right. Remember Roy?"

But Sunflower had only seen the infected, not what they did, and she fought against Olivia's arms. Bringing up Taggart might have stopped this. Olivia looked to Christmas for help, but they didn't seem to notice the squabble.

"Sunflower, you don't understand," Olivia said.

Hazibel's stern, sandpapery voice said, "Olivia, let her go."

Olivia trembled loose, and Sunflower dashed for the corner. She didn't understand that the infected echoed her own memories. Something bound them to her, and now they were luring her in.

Olivia couldn't manage more than a useless shout: "Don't!"

Sunflower collided with her mother so hard that Hazibel staggered back. Hazibel wore a perpetual scowl, but in moments, it would twist into a furious sneer and tearful eyes, mimicking the infected that had murdered Taggart, and the same rage would spread to every infected nearby.

Hazibel's lips instead parted in a frustrated sigh. "I had a hunch I'd find you on this side of town," she said, no tenderness, but no fury either. She rested hands on Sunflower's shoulders and shook her head. "I've been searching for the better part of an hour." She didn't seem to realize Sunflower was hugging her, but no hivemind dictated her thoughts and actions.

Olivia stared in disbelief. "You're not one of them."

"Them?" Hazibel eyed the street. "Certainly not. I'm made of sharper stuff."

This seemed too much a miracle for Olivia to hope for, and yet the proof stood at the corner of Ridgemont and Westland. Immunity might be inherited.

At last, Hazibel noticed the hug and patted her daughter's back. "Anything to say?"

"Sorry," Sunflower muttered. Her eyes were closed, her face nestled into her mother's shoulder. "I'm glad you're safe."

Hazibel softened. "We're not safe in the least, but good to see you, too." She slipped her arms from Sunflower and glanced around. "You were supposed to be with Olivia tonight. Where's the boy? Ryan, was it? Dashing through the woods with his pants around his ankles, no doubt." Her gaze shifted to Olivia and then to Christmas. "You have your pity friend and a stranger. Anyone else?"

"Monsters. Sick people." Sunflower began whispering into Hazibel's ear, and if Hazibel doubted anything she heard, her face didn't show it.

Monsters. Olivia glanced to the woods again, where a gap of darkness haunted the trees across Ridgemont Road. She couldn't remember if the gap had been there when she last looked. Lizzie might have stood and watched from that spot, studying her prey. But why leave then? Hell called, said she'd left the oven on?

"Big mouth, bigger throat," Olivia said, and realized she'd parroted Christmas. She caught their side-eye and ignored it. "Lizzie should have found us by now."

"Monsters catch up when you take on stragglers," Christmas said. They glanced over Sunflower and Hazibel. "Four of us. Five, really, since I count double. Safety in numbers could keep her off our heels."

Numbers hadn't saved Devin, but Olivia didn't argue. The sooner they moved on, the better.

Hazibel broke Sunflower's hug and looked her over. "You're not much worse for wear; there's that," she said. "Come along then. Keep a good pace, and we'll reach Sunset Pass soon."

Olivia recoiled at the name. If they followed Ridgemont Road, they would find the turnoff to Sunset Pass. They would also find steel guardrails dripping with now-wet memorial ribbons, their undersides covered in flowery wreaths old and new, signs of tragedy and death. Sunset Pass had seen too many accidents, but there was no way to widen the road without shaving off parts of the hillside, which would lead to greater threats of rockslides. Town hall could either shut the road down or leave it open. The latter was cheaper, and the guardrail grew more ribbons and wreaths every year.

"Sunset is garbage driving on a nice day, and you want to walk it on a rainy night?" Olivia asked. "I don't think it's a good idea, Ms. Mason. We're on our way to the interstate."

Hazibel had already half-turned to follow Ridgemont Road. "South across town."

"It's not that far," Olivia said, though in truth, she could use a rest first.

"On foot." Hazibel narrowed one pale eye. "Every street choked with sick neighbors."

The words opened a sinkhole in Olivia's gut. "You've seen it?" she asked.

"I have," Hazibel said, almost smug, and then her demeanor turned grim. "Main Street's a hellhole. Every block is a minefield of people gone out of their minds. Two intersections have been chewed up by colorful glass that no one's equipped to walk, least of all me." She stamped one shoe, its narrow heel tap-tapping on the sidewalk. "We won't make the main thoroughfare."

Olivia felt the world pitching her off-balance. Dodging the scattered infected of Ridgemont Road had been doable, but worming through crowds would be risky, especially when the group had to watch out for stained glass teeth, too. Worse, if Lizzie reared her head at the wrong moment, she could split the group and drive someone between glass and a mob. One elbow nudge, a single stepped-on toe, and the horde would rain down on them, leaving each survivor as bent and broken as Taggart. No forgiveness for mistakes; only death.

"Or," Hazibel said, and she jerked her head west, "we stick to this one road past the neighborhoods, follow the curve around Cooper, and we take the empty pass down. No more town and whatever toxin the Russians have dropped on us."

Olivia's mother could've made that last comment. She'd had endless theories, pulled from newspapers both reputable and otherwise, about what Russia might be up to, among other problems and conspiracies in the wider world. Olivia never paid much attention, but her goal tonight shined brighter. Mom was in Hartford with Dad, beyond the slopes and madness of Chapel Hill. Did Olivia want to die here, or did she want to see them again?

She looked to Christmas, who shrugged.

"Shouldn't we call someone?" Sunflower asked, sounding small. "Hide and wait for help, right? That's what we're supposed to do, I thought. We could head home."

No one answered. Olivia guessed their thoughts echoed hers. State troopers wouldn't answer reports of vaguely weird shit. Emergency personnel couldn't cure this infection. Chapel Hill's four police officers were probably wandering circles around their cars, chasing red and blue lights they would never catch.

If this storm had a solution, the group wouldn't find it standing here. Few seemed as lucky as Sunflower to have kept her best friend and mother intact. Hazibel was a pill, but better she was okay than not.

Maybe that luck wasn't their last.

"If we're heading west anyway, the craft shop's off Cooper," Olivia said. "I want to check on Shelly and Dane. They might be immune, too."

"The Kincaids?" Hazibel set her jaw. "Those hippies weren't too many strokes from this state in the first place."

Olivia chewed arguments off her tongue. "I need to know. It's a short detour."

Christmas scoffed, this time with a chuckle. "You're big on those." Their hand settled on Olivia's shoulder and steered her west.

Olivia let herself be led. "A detour took us to Sunflower. The shop's on the way, one quick turn before we hit Sunset Pass."

"Young lady, they aren't your parents," Hazibel said, turning to follow. Sunflower shrank beside her. "You're not responsible."

Olivia knew that; why the hell did everyone feel the need to say it? Of course they weren't her parents. No one in this town could imagine how keenly she knew the Kincaids weren't her parents when she'd run from her father after the carnival that day three years ago, still tasting that other girl's lips, after the hitchhiking, the turning here, the boundless and unconditional generosity she'd found with Shelly and Dane. Of course they weren't her parents, message loud and clear.

Despite everything, Olivia was headed to see her parents now. Wasn't that good enough? Wasn't it reasonable she wanted to see Shelly and Dane were okay first and take them along if they were? Didn't it matter that she loved them?

She lowered her head. "Will everyone make me go alone?"

Christmas released Olivia now that she was following, likely satisfied the group wouldn't split and leave stragglers for Lizzie. Hazibel marched ahead, eyes likely envisioning the long way down Sunset Pass toward a world oblivious to Chapel Hill's pain.

To she and Christmas, they had already escaped. Shelly and Dane weren't thoughts in their heads.

Could Olivia blame them? Every lingering moment brought danger. Infected footsteps now drowned out crickets. Bright blue mist, the kind that had tossed rainbow glass down Van Buren Avenue, now crawled high over Ridgemont, watching the group and not yet finished with them.

Cold fingers slid around Olivia's hand. She glanced over, where Sunflower beamed for the first time since the drive-in. Her hand squeezed Olivia's, and warmth flooded her cheeks as she squeezed back.

No, she wouldn't have to do this alone.

8. PSYCHIC CONNECTIONS

Main Street kept town hall, family restaurants, the library, and Chapel Hill High. Cooper Street, tucked aside, offered the nicer bar, the sandwich place, a few other oddities, and most importantly, the craft shop.

Shelly and Dane ran Kincaid Krafts and lived in the apartment on its second floor. Olivia sometimes minded the counter, but business slowed during summer, and Shelly and Dane mostly had it covered by themselves. One of them might have kept the shop open tonight before the storm struck. If infected, they would likely wander Cooper Street.

But if they were immune, Olivia worried they would have stepped outside anyway. They weren't the type to let neighbors wander lost in the road. The same compulsive kindness that had opened their hearts to welcoming, sheltering, and loving Olivia would have sent them to the sidewalk. She'd never seen them hold back a helping hand. Those hands would have touched their neighbors. *You okay?* Dane might have asked, grasping one shoulder. *Let's get you out of the rain, dear,* Shelly would add, cradling the arm of an infected.

Those same neighbors would turn and scream, *I hate you! I've always hated you!* at the sweetest people in Chapel Hill.

And that would have been the end of them.

Olivia's face pulled too tight against her skull, and tears blurred Cooper Street from sight. She couldn't make out the intersection where Kincaid Krafts faced the corner. One hand covered her face.

Sunflower still held the other, and she squeezed again and again as if to pump all the tears out. "We're turning here," she said. She couldn't have meant to sound bossy, but Christmas slowed, turned, and crossed their arms over their chest.

Hazibel's heels clacked the pavement in a short stop. "Really?" she asked, turning. "You're going to drag us into this, Sunflower?"

Sunflower didn't answer, but she didn't let go. Olivia could have kissed that squeezing hand.

"They want to go, and I don't care, long as it's quick," Christmas said, rolling their shoulders back, eyes on Hazibel. "You're outvoted. Or, you could wait for us here. Might throw the big-mouthed people-eater off our scent." Christmas opened their mouth wide and sucked in an airy gasp.

Hazibel turned toward Cooper, her face curled in a disgusted sneer.

Olivia's free hand slid from wiping tears to covering her mouth against a sudden giggle. This wasn't funny; she was horrified at herself. Her clearing eyes watched Christmas and Hazibel take the lead down Cooper Street. Christmas had their hands full with a cigarette pack and a match, as if mimicking Lizzie's gasp had made obvious the lack of smoke in Christmas's lungs.

Hazibel drifted close. "Got a spare?" she asked.

Christmas stuffed the pack into their black jacket's pocket. "Nope."

"Have a heart. It's been a long night." Hazibel reached out.

"Not into sharing," Christmas said, swatting her away.

The group approached the intersection of Cooper Street and Sedgwick Road, a brief side street that led between backdoor parking lots.

"What are you again?" Hazibel asked. "Boy? Girl?"

Christmas dragged at their cigarette. "Nightmare," they said, breathy and smiling.

Hazibel recoiled. "What does that mean?"

"It means I'll never make anything easy for you." Smoke blew through Christmas's lips and crossed Hazibel's wanting face.

Olivia and Sunflower caught the blowback. They waved the cloud away as Hazibel stepped aside. She ran frustrated hands through her dark hair, piling it atop her head and exposing the back of her neck. A growling sigh let loose as she let her hair drop.

But not before Olivia caught the crescent birthmark.

She had never noticed it on Hazibel before, not that she'd ever paid much attention. Hazibel was the Mason House's grouch, appearing in doorways to tell Olivia and Sunflower to quiet down or find someplace else to raise a racket. Her neck wasn't Olivia's business until tonight.

Sunflower, Hazibel, and Christmas had the same birthmark on the same spot. Had a crescent moon marked Gina's neck, too, inherited from mother to daughters? Christmas didn't fit. They weren't Gina, that sweet-faced girl with dirty blond hair, fifteen the last time her family had seen her. Besides, Hazibel had called Christmas a stranger. Would she do that to her own child? Maybe in better circumstances, but not tonight.

"Your mom has your birthmark," Olivia said, and she immediately felt silly.

Sunflower would already know that; it wasn't worth mentioning. She stared at her mother's hair but said nothing. Who cared about birthmarks on a night like this?

Olivia would have blamed tonight's strangeness, except no moon shined in the sky, crescent or otherwise. It had abandoned them. Darkness instead crept at the edge of starlight in the shape of seething clouds, the storm swinging back for another round against Chapel Hill. Rain and thunder were on their way, and maybe new monsters and infections with them. Olivia watched a falling cloud of blue mist disappear behind rooftops close to Main Street. She couldn't see the new scab of rainbow glass, but she felt its chill in her teeth.

Christmas paused at the intersection and waved one arm in a sweeping, smoky arc. "Which way, Liv?"

Had Christmas used that nickname before, or had they picked it up from Taggart and Sunflower? Olivia couldn't remember; tonight had stretched too long. She led Sunflower by the hand between Christmas and Hazibel.

The craft shop faced the intersection from the corner across Cooper, its outer walls painted cream from bottom to top, where a slanted, cardinal red roof faced the sky. Small windows gazed from the second-floor apartment, their wooden shutters patterned by white lattice. Green, almost treelike letters formed KINCAID KRAFTS against the wall between floors. Wider windows offered a view of the first floor, where crafting supplies of all kinds and colors sat behind the glass, and a green placard read COME INSIDE in friendly letters. A wooden door stood closed beside the widest window, but Shelly and Dane rarely locked it.

Farther down Cooper, Olivia made out the faint lights of Main Street and the myriad of black silhouettes that roamed there. Hazibel was right. Infected people swarmed Chapel Hill's main thoroughfare.

"We'll be a minute," Olivia said. "Less."

She didn't look to Christmas or Hazibel for acknowledgment, just pulled Sunflower up to the glass windows. Inside glowed alive with ceiling lamps, but Shelly and Dane had broken the little craft shop into so many narrow aisles that no one peering from outside could see around every corner.

Plenty of places to hide, even for a monster.

Olivia crept toward the door, turned the knob, and opened it a crack. The air held still within. No Lizzie, at least Olivia hoped. She pushed the door open, rattling the twin bells overhead. Any other time, Shelly might have popped out from behind a shelf to greet a customer, only to find Olivia. Dane would have sat behind the register, where he clutched a paperback novel and greeted the new guest whenever they approached.

There were no greetings tonight, only silence and emptiness where Shelly and Dane should be. Olivia didn't know where to start looking or whether it mattered. Vertical wood paneling peeked from the walls where they hadn't been draped in knitted blankets of violet and rainbows. Nothing in the store gave her a hint on what to do.

Sunflower squeezed her hand one last time before she let go. "We'll check down each aisle, the back," she said, drifting along the windows. "If they're not here, maybe it's a good thing. My mom wasn't at my house because she'd come looking for me. They'd look for you."

A glass bowl sat by the register with a white paper taped to its side, telling guests to either take a penny or leave a penny. A face-down paperback beside it showed a gray photo of the author's face, some white-haired bearded man who looked like a wizard. No Dane back there. He and Shelly were probably upstairs, staggering in circles and muttering Sunflower's memories.

"Do you remember the day we met?" Olivia asked.

There was a pause before Sunflower answered, as if she had to dredge up the memory. "Sure," she said. "You were so sad, all alone."

"My hero." Olivia smiled and then slipped around the counter toward the backroom, where stuffed cardboard boxes lined the shelves from floor to ceiling. Nowhere to hide, no one inside. "The sick people remember, too. One of them recited exactly what you'd said that lunch period, that you'd always liked my name. Remember?"

Only Sunflower's footsteps answered this time, pacing the craft shop's aisles.

Olivia shut the backroom's door. "It's been bothering me. No one could've known what you said. Even if you told someone, they wouldn't have memorized it word for word."

Still no answer from Sunflower.

Olivia pressed on. She couldn't ignore the tiny connections anymore, the curiosity of whether the storm and its every horror came tied to Sunflower. "Did you feel it when you blacked out? Maybe you saw through their sick eyes, touched their memories?"

Sunflower appeared from an aisle near the back. Behind her, beaded curtains covered a stunted doorway where a staircase led to the second floor.

"You know, emotional psychic connections," Olivia went on, "Anything like that?"

"Where do you get this stuff?" Sunflower asked, dismissive.

Olivia could have said, *In this house, in this very room.* Tucked behind scrapbook paper, paint bottles, skeins of yarn, and a hundred more varieties of crafting supplies stood a modest bookcase. Battered paperbacks and dogeared brochures lined its shelves; expert texts on clairvoyance, positive thinking, places of power, astral projection, spectral communication, and UFOs of every breed. Too many ideas to fit in such a small shop, but Shelly insisted they offer what she called *informative literature*.

Olivia swept the beaded curtains to one side and held them for Sunflower to pass underneath. Three years living here, and Olivia still smacked her face into them at least one groggy morning each week. The ascending steps creaked underfoot. Darkness swelled above.

"When we leave Chapel Hill, we'll have to find help," Sunflower said. "Maybe lie about what's wrong, if there's still a town to save by then."

She seemed to have judged Chapel Hill as damned already. Every other friend, her boyfriend, the people she'd known her entire life—scratched away, eraser to pencil marks. And could Olivia blame her? Tonight weighed too heavy to think on much further than survival, and survival wasn't promised unless they got off this hill.

"What about you?" Sunflower asked. "Back to Hartford?"

Olivia slowed at the top of the steps. No, she couldn't blame Sunflower for trying to put tonight and Chapel Hill behind her when Olivia meant to do the same.

"You've been meaning to go," Sunflower said.

She strode almost fearless past Olivia and into the shadows. Of course she couldn't understand Olivia's hesitation—Sunflower had only heard about Lizzie and had barely been lucid at their close encounter by Lookout. Between them, only Olivia had seen the face of a former classmate bulging up from beneath Lizzie's skin.

But no monstrous throat sucked at the air from the second-floor hall. Olivia forced herself to follow.

Beyond the stairway banister, the apartment opened into the kitchen, den, and bedroom hallway, where one bathroom took up the heart of the home. Another set of beaded curtains hid the den, where baskets of yarn and books filled the paths between furniture. The kitchen needed cleaning, nothing new.

"It's been years," Olivia said, scanning the apartment. "My parents and I never had it out. We need to. There might be something to salvage if I see them again."

"I think they'll hurt you." Sunflower plowed toward the bedroom hall, new cheer overtaking her tone. "Mrs. Kincaid? Mr. Kincaid?" They hated how old those titles made them sound, likely why Sunflower said them. They would have been quick to correct her.

No one answered.

Olivia drifted into the living room, her shins bumping against yarn baskets and paper stacks, and pried the end table's banana-yellow phone off its receiver. The cord coiled around itself, but she fought the handset to her ear.

No dial tone. She tapped the receiver, but the earpiece kept silent. Her hand dove for the TV remote, but the blocky television's screen offered only hushing static, not even the rainbow columns of an emergency broadcast.

She switched it off. Had the storm sawed Chapel Hill off the map, no one getting in, no one getting out?

Sunflower lingered in the bedroom hall, a black blot in the darkness. "No one's here," she said. "They could be okay, yeah?"

Olivia wanted those words to warm her, but she couldn't keep from shivering. "I'm going to change out of my wet uniform," she said. She made for the hallway and hoped that Shelly and Dane had left of their own will and with sound minds.

"Let me borrow a couple things," Sunflower said. "I need dry clothes, too."

"Check Shelly's closet," Olivia said, pointing to the bedroom Shelly and Dane shared. Olivia's clothes rarely fit anyone else, and Sunflower knew it. She steered herself toward the Kincaids' bedroom door.

Olivia flipped a light switch at her bedroom doorway. The room used to be backup storage, but Dane had moved everything downstairs three years ago when Olivia moved in, insisting she needed her own space. A basket of yarn nestled beside the trash pail between bed and dresser. Her bed's underside slobbered school notebooks she hadn't gotten around to throwing away. She dug through her drawers.

Sunflower appeared with a heap of Shelly's clothes, each slightly longer than Olivia's. Once upon a time, Olivia had hoped to grow closer to Gina's shape, but only Sunflower had finished that journey of longer limbs and a flat belly.

They tugged on dry jeans, tank tops, and knitted sweaters. Sunset Pass ran down the hillside, the winds cool even in August, and sweaters would keep them warm if not dry. Soft red yarn looked lovely against Sunflower's hair. She tossed blond locks aside and flashed a crescent-marked neck again before turning around.

Olivia had seen that birthmark on Gina Night, at the drive-in, and dozens of times between. Nothing psychic or supernatural about it—Sunflower's birthmark, plain and simple. Anything weird about Hazibel's and Christmas's necks fell to them. Coincidence or tattoos, nothing more sinister.

Why then did she have to fight this hard to convince herself?

Sunflower straightened the hem of Olivia's sweater for her, knitted with forest-green yarn. "We're dressed ready for

Christmas," Sunflower said, pressing red and green sleeves together. "I'll poke around for scarves and umbrellas in case Mom and your friend want them." She skipped down the hall, her mood bright and hopeful. They might manage to survive this.

Olivia gazed down at her green sweater. Ready for Christmas? No one seemed ready for the redheaded stranger outside. Christmas had sprung from the darkness as unexpectedly as Lizzie. Between a protective devil and a man-eating beast, Olivia would choose the devil every time.

Sunflower shouted down the hall. "Liv, I found them!"

Olivia lingered in her bedroom a moment longer, trying to think of anything she wanted to take. Nothing came to mind as her muscles caught up with her thoughts—Sunflower didn't mean she'd found scarves and umbrellas.

She'd found Shelly and Dane.

Olivia darted to the kitchen, where Sunflower stood beside the staircase. Squat square windows faced the backlot, where customers and residents alike lined two rows with vehicles. Tonight, only a few scattered cars dotted the lot, likewise joined by scattered infected. Olivia knew most faces, neighbors or staff from other shops, a few of the thousands of people who had been broken under Chapel Hill's bizarre storm.

She knew Shelly and Dane better than the rest. A shawl covered Shelly's back and shoulders, and her lengthy graying hair flowed down her broad blouse and skirt. Dane wore only sweatpants and his tan bathrobe, damp chest hair poking through the trim. His bearded face gazed thoughtlessly at the pavement as if he were chasing to read a book that wouldn't sit still.

Sunflower's touch came gentle yet firm. "You don't need them anymore," she said. "You're going to Hartford."

Olivia's skin cooled beneath those comforting fingertips. Sunflower had reacted the same at Roy's vanishing, no sign of him in the woods at Lookout, no despair from the girl who earlier tonight had been smitten with him. From glee at the drive-in to near indifference, past intent absent. Olivia wondered if the storm might be affecting Sunflower, a side effect of the infected mumbling her memories and the rainbow glass that echoed Gina's art, each syphoning from her mental state.

More likely, Sunflower's coldness protected her. She knew this town better than Olivia ever would, and tonight she had to watch it bleed away. Walling off her emotions seemed best. If she opened her heart now, the monsters, infected, and otherworldly glass might cut it out, raw and beating. There was nothing she could do. Best she harden herself to the night.

But not to Olivia. "I wish it was different," Sunflower said. "I'm really sorry."

Thunder groaned across the sky. Drumming rain beat the rooftop, gentle now but likely not for long. An airy fist squeezed Olivia's head, and she doubled over, almost smacking her face against the window glass. Sunflower cringed beside her, the headache striking them both.

They needed to leave, no more detours. If they didn't escape Chapel Hill soon, they wouldn't escape at all.

The headache waned, and Sunflower straightened up. She gave Olivia's hand another squeeze and then darted for the staircase. Christmas and Hazibel were likely wondering about the holdup.

Olivia lifted her head to the window again and took one last look at Shelly and Dane. She didn't expect to see them again after tonight, and though the storm had broken their consciousness, she owed it to them that she burn this last moment into her mind. It measured small against years of their selfless compassion and warmth, but Olivia had nothing else to offer.

A bright blue glimmer blinked past the upper window and faded before Olivia looked up. The sky hung all dark now, the stars erased. The storm had thrown something into town, hadn't it? A chill ran down her spine, and she eyed the backlot a moment longer before she felt the cold above her head.

Daggers of yellow glass sliced through the plaster above the windows. Across the apartment, green and red glass surged above the entrance and rattled the beaded curtains, the panes cutting the ceiling into their own little territories of rainbow. The blue mist had struck the roof and now bled inside the craft shop. Shards reached sharp fingers toward the walls' edges.

Toward Olivia. The glass would turn toothlike and bite her then. When it reached the lot, it would bite others.

Time to go.

Her eyes turned again to the window and the people outside. She kissed the tips of two fingers, aimed them at the backlot, and then left the apartment, shop, everything she'd called home the past three years.

Out front, Christmas and Hazibel had huddled beneath the shop's meager awning. Sunflower stood behind them, holding open the front door with one hand and hugging three sea-green umbrellas with her free arm.

"It's just one smoke," Hazibel said, pleading.

"You'll soggy it up," Christmas said.

Both turned as Sunflower let the door clap shut behind Olivia, and then Christmas tossed a shortened cigarette to the sidewalk. Hazibel's face fell with it.

Christmas eyed the craft shop and then studied Olivia. "You okay?"

Did Olivia know the meaning of that word anymore? She couldn't remember. On some level she had needed someone to ask the question, but the answer seemed lost. She glanced toward Main Street, and then she looked back toward Ridgemont.

"You haven't seen Lizzie?" she asked.

"Nope." Christmas cracked their neck to one side. "Probably scared."

Olivia and Sunflower exchanged concerned glances. Just because they couldn't see or hear the monster didn't mean she wasn't here, following, tasting Olivia in the air.

Christmas went on theorizing. "Messed-up townies could've killed her. Or they're chasing her still."

"Would she give up?" Sunflower asked. "Cougars and wolves keep their strength for when they know they can kill."

"I don't think she's like an ordinary animal," Olivia said. "She just ate someone earlier tonight, but she's chasing us. Still hungry, and she probably can't chomp the infected or they'll swarm her. We might be the only people left in Chapel Hill she can safely eat."

"Speak for yourself," Christmas said.

The storm did its own speaking. Rain pounded in earnest, and thunder shouted with renewed fury. Its vibration shook the craft shop's windows in their frames, the glass overtaking its roof, the houses up and down the street, a quake that jostled Olivia's bones as if the hill itself might soon wake up.

"No more stalling," Christmas said, eyes widening, almost fearful. "Don't figure we've seen the worst tonight."

They were right. The storm had come in phases since the beginning. Lizzie, the memory infection, rainbow glass, and now a tremor in the ground too gargantuan for thunder. How many more strange waves could the group survive?

Olivia nodded—yes, she was done here.

Hazibel's face settled into relief, and she turned to follow Christmas toward Ridgemont for the last time. Sunflower smirked at Olivia and then set on her mother's heels, one arm outstretched to offer an umbrella.

Olivia thought to glance over her shoulder, but she couldn't let herself do that. One step, then another, following their group's small train with Christmas again taking the lead. Sunset Pass wasn't far now. They were getting out.

Not a plan. A promise.

Beneath Olivia's sneakers, the hill rumbled again, more fiercely this time, as if it knew they were trying to get away and would have none of it.

9. SUNSET PASS

A red stop sign glowered at the end of Ridgemont Road, Chapel Hill offering futile protection from the world's edge. Steel railings hugged the steep slope to the road's left.

Olivia laid her hands on the upper rail. Rain and time had washed away the most recent wreaths from where she stood, but a pair of white and yellow ribbons clung to the lower rail, twin warnings to head back.

The hill rumbled a warning of its own.

"See anything?" Sunflower asked, one hand latching onto the railing beside Olivia. Raindrops pounded their umbrellas.

"Nobody," Olivia said. No streetlights below, no headlights. Darkness would have to be a good omen for Sunset Pass.

Glancing back, Chapel Hill showed pine peaks rising behind maple foliage and a smattering of brown buildings muddied by night and rain. Hardly a fitting last look at the town, but what would be? Chapel Hill had been a break from the road, but then it had refused to let Olivia go.

Until now, tonight, and she was taking the best part with her. At least to the bottom of Sunset Pass.

She looked to Sunflower, who forced a hopeful smile, and then to Christmas and Hazibel. Christmas shifted from foot to foot, two steps from beginning their descent. Hazibel huddled beneath the last umbrella, her dark hair fading around graveyard-gray locks.

In the distance, a scream tore across town, and a flurry of familiar shouting said that someone else immune to the storm had collided with the infected. The voices were somewhat muffled, but Olivia had heard them clearly before. Her mind filled in the blanks, insistent she relive every word. *Hate. You.*

Christmas approached the guardrail, folded their fingers around a cigarette butt, and flicked it over the edge. It tumbled down Sunset Pass, swallowed by blackness. Christmas stood resolute, their body unreactive even to the rainfall, but a stillness held their eyes, and they snickered with breathy disgust.

"What's funny?" Olivia asked.

"Don't know that I can explain," Christmas said. "I was trying to count the seconds it fell before I couldn't see it, and for a moment I forgot how to count to five. Weird, yeah?"

Olivia thought so. And she wondered if Christmas was afraid. She wanted to give some encouragement, but that sounded like the kind of sentiment Christmas would rebuff.

"Sad last words," Olivia said. "*I forgot how to count.* You can do better than that."

Christmas raised a bewildered eyebrow and then barked out a genuine laugh. "Yeah, all our dreams are piss down the universe's leg. Same as this hillside."

Olivia laughed with them. Her body jostled, chilly but also relieved, and then she caught Sunflower's stare. She was looking at Olivia and Christmas, but Olivia couldn't read her face.

Another infected outcry climbed from town behind them, louder now. Olivia didn't need her mind to fill in the blanks this time—every word rang crystal clear.

"Why are you like this?"

"You hate me so much, but I hate you too!"

"I've always hated you!"

Sunflower's expression broke into obvious shock. Olivia guessed her face looked the same. One of the voices sounded almost like an infant, clumsily forcing up babble to mimic the word *hate*.

Olivia didn't want be here to see that or hear it. She slammed her palms over her ears, but the shouting ended mercifully fast this time. She glanced to Sunflower, Hazibel, Christmas, as if expecting one of them to lie as dead as Taggart, ambushed by a sudden throng of infected. Everyone stood stunned, yet alive.

"Why do they say that?" Olivia asked, lowering her hands.

"Hazarding a guess," Hazibel said, "I'd say it's hatred. I'd rather we leave before they hate us, too."

Olivia and Sunflower followed the guardrail to the top of the pass. Christmas took that as a sign to move, and Hazibel followed. Sunflower rubbed at her scalp. Her headache clearly lingered. She would feel better once they escaped Chapel Hill and the storm's pressure. Not that Olivia could tell where that ended. At least they would leave the infected behind.

Sunset Pass wove a steep, lengthy zigzag down the carved-open western hillside, its first stretch heading south, the next north, over and over until the pass reached the hill's foot, where normal roads resumed.

"It isn't so bad," Hazibel said, as if she'd read Olivia's thoughts. "Steep and snaking, yes, but at each curve there's a pull-off for cars if they're in trouble or if they need to let others past. Places we can rest."

Or duck out of the way from an oncoming car. If headlights climbed the hillside, they would cut amber warning cones through the darkness below, and the group would know long before the vehicle reached them. They might even warn the driver to turn back.

Olivia's nerves weren't in a listening mood. An intrusive impulse ordered her to jump, as if she could fly, aiming her attention across the pass's two narrow lanes, where asphalt ended in open air. Her nerves didn't have her best interests at heart.

Neither did the road. Thin, arcing waterfalls spilled down from Chapel Hill's top and loosened debris from the hillside. Mud spilled across both lanes, and water pooled in trenches of soggy earth. Sunset Pass would soon become Sunset River. The wind swept raindrops under Olivia's umbrella. They spattered her clothes and skin, everything both too warm and too cold in her sweater. She was both grateful to have changed out of her work uniform, but she was going to get soaked anyway.

One sneaker skidded in the mud, and she tumbled forward. For a stretched-out moment, she thought the water would sweep her over the edge, but instead she landed on her umbrella. Two spokes snapped beneath her.

Sunflower didn't notice. One hand still grasped her head, and she could barely hold her umbrella straight. The storm was going to split her skull in two.

"You can't stay," Christmas said.

Olivia glanced ahead to where Christmas paused, their skin and clothes now drenched and dripping.

"You got to tell your parents where to stick it, right?" Christmas asked. "Who else will?"

Where to stick it, or who they'd made, or why they should love her, or hell, Olivia would make excuses if she had to, hide everything the way she'd hidden it from everyone except Christmas tonight. A talk with Mom and Dad, an embrace, one moment when they could be a family again, much as Olivia had ever known one—she'd take any version of reunion she could get. Whatever awaited, Sunset Pass would bring her there.

She pushed her umbrella against the mud-caked asphalt and scrabbled to her feet. The umbrella's tip slipped, and she almost fell again, but her hands dug into the dirt and launched her to standing.

"It's not just me," she said. "We'll get you to White River Valley. You'll get home, too."

Christmas gave both an exaggerated nod and exaggerated shrug, as if their home meant less than Olivia's, and then turned downhill again. They were a giant against the storm. Sunflower and Hazibel might sink deeper into darkness as they drifted farther from the lights of town, but Christmas could light another cigarette and give Olivia a torch to follow. Tonight had taken its toll, but both travelers had sacrificed their complacence, too.

No more stalling. Off this hill was their way home.

Olivia spread open her wounded umbrella, for all the good it would do, and skidded downhill to catch up with Sunflower. She and her mother would need more encouragement than anyone. They were leaving behind everything they had ever known.

A white forked tongue lashed the clouds and bathed the hillside in flickering light. Maybe Christmas wouldn't need to light a tiny beacon.

In the brief illumination, Olivia spotted shoeprints dotting the damp soil, soon to be washed away—Christmas, Hazibel. One set became barefoot where Hazibel must have taken off her heels.

But there were other bare prints, closer to the rocks, pressing odd shapes in the mud, sometimes forming crescent smears, sometimes walking on front pads. Olivia doubted anyone else had escaped Chapel Hill this way.

She wondered briefly what Lizzie's footprints looked like.

Above, the lights of town shimmered over the hill's edge, but they couldn't illuminate the hillside. Olivia almost expected a squat silhouette to appear against that light, watching her. Downhill, the light was gone, leaving only a murky blue-blackness. There might have been no sign of Lizzie since the group met Hazibel because she'd chosen an ambush over a chase. Sunset Pass could end in a trap.

They were here now, and climbing back would run them ragged. What choice did they have but descent?

The first stretch ended in its sharp turn, and as Hazibel had mentioned, a muddy pull-off jutted from the roadside where cars could pull over. Christmas hadn't waited to see if anyone wanted a break; they plowed ahead down the second stretch and toward the next pull-off, the next stretch of the pass's zigzag. Olivia's thighs ached, but she didn't want to linger on the hillside either.

No one protested. The quicker they went, the sooner they'd be free.

Mud pooled worse along the second stretch. Every step came slippery, and Olivia had to brace her free hand against the hillside's boulders and slick soil. Wasn't there a yellow, diamond-shaped sign that warned of landslides somewhere along the road? She couldn't remember, and no sign stood out from the dimness.

Another vicious lightning bolt cut the night, followed by temperamental thunder and a round of residual flickering. Hazibel's dress seemed to soak in the light, turning her ghostlike ahead where she and Christmas blazed the trail. Sunflower walked at Olivia's side. No one else wandered the pass that she could see.

Yet a few steps down, the boulders and soil broke around a vertical crevice, taller than Olivia and slightly thinner, like a dark eye in the hillside. Chilly air puffed from within, a draft that suggested tunnels wormed through the hill's depths.

Wouldn't a snake hide inside such a hole?

Olivia and Sunflower paused when they reached it, and Olivia listened for a gasp, footsteps, the sound of jaws that might come snapping out at first movement. Still no sign of Lizzie. Olivia hurried past.

And she hurried alone, she realized. "Sunflower?" she asked, turning back.

Sunflower had stalled at the crevice. Her face leaned into its draft, stuck in a staring contest with the hill's dark eye. Her fingers slackened, and her umbrella plopped into the mud. Rainwater soaked her hair and sweater.

Olivia glanced downhill, where Christmas and Hazibel had almost reached the second pull-off, and then climbed back to Sunflower. "What's wrong?" she asked.

Sunflower didn't break eye contact with the darkness. "She's crying under the hill again," she said. She raised one hand toward the gap and curled her fingers around the raindrops. "She's crying everywhere."

Olivia listened, but rainfall, flowing water, and another thunderous rumble drowned any sound outside hers and Sunflower's voices. She couldn't be sure she would hear Christmas or Hazibel call from this distance.

"There's nothing," Olivia said.

Sunflower didn't answer. Her raised hand reached into the hill.

Olivia snatched Sunflower's wrist. "We can't stay." She was parroting Christmas again, but she didn't care. The command went for Sunflower, too. No one would be left behind.

The next lightning flash thrust its tongue across the sky as thunder shouted down the hillside and through Olivia's skull. She let her umbrella drop and grasped both sides of her head. Her brain split in two, each side hating the other.

Sunflower squeezed her hands against her head, too. Near the second pull-off, Christmas and Hazibel cried out in unison, the group headache ripping down the hillside. Someone else wailed in the storm, maybe the infected, maybe Lizzie. Pain thumped too hard through Olivia's head for her to tell. The pressure only trickled free when the lightning's flicker ended.

A new glow lit the night in its place. Sunflower's hair had soaked up the stormy flare, same as Hazibel's dress.

No, not her hair. A shining line rippled down the center of her scalp from the back of her neck to her forehead, a white-hot grimace in the night.

Olivia reached for it. Had Sunflower been struck by lightning, or was she infected with some new wild condition?

A strained wooden groan tore Olivia's attention skyward.

Faint light still crept over the hilltop's edge, where dark chunks of debris were tumbling with the rain. They looked almost like wooden shrapnel, but Olivia couldn't tell for sure from two stretches down the pass. Harsh wind rumbled from above.

And then the light broke around an enormous black block, falling as if dropped by a giant's hand. A surprised shriek fought up Olivia's throat, but she couldn't get it out, even when she felt the impact as the dark intruder slammed onto the guardrail looking down on Sunset Pass, buckling steel and crushing memorial ribbons into the yielding damp earth.

Olivia had stood in that spot only minutes ago, wondering how she and the others could survive this descent. A tremor rocked the hillside, shooting up her legs.

Lightning lit the world again, briefer this time, but enough for her to make out what had crashed into Chapel Hill.

A two-floor, split-level house teetered on the ledge above. Dark wood formed its outer walls, and black shingles covered its divided roof. There should have been a short set of steps climbing to the low porch, but that part of the structure must have shattered in the fall. Olivia only knew because she had visited this house countless times on the far side of Main Street. Her car had idled outside it tonight while she called for Sunflower. She'd spent Gina Night on one side of the upstairs, and every sleepover there in Sunflower's bedroom on the other side, each sister's room facing the other.

The Mason House.

The sky went dark, again turning the split-level into a black, blocky silhouette. Its corners tipped over to glare at Sunset Pass, the house too unwieldy to hang on the hill's edge.

Olivia grabbed Sunflower's arm and tugged her downslope. Sneakers skidded underfoot, but Olivia didn't care.

Sunflower's teeth chattered. "I want to go home," she said.

No need—somehow, home was coming to her. The Mason House groaned again, and then a wood-cracking roar echoed down the hill. Its frontside weight tipped the balance, tearing its underside from the ledge, and the house came hurtling out of the darkness.

Outer walls crunched across boulders. The house roared downslope, spitting soil and pebbles at every scraping inch. It struck the first stretch of Sunset Pass with an earthshattering crunch and then went rolling over the next ledge, down the rocks.

Splinters pelted Olivia's head, and she skidded screaming along the mud. Sunflower ambled behind.

The house splattered where Sunflower had been reaching into the crevice, its timber shrapnel blocking up the opening in the hillside. The collision blasted louder than thunder.

Olivia slowed and twisted to face the house, her heart caught in her throat. Sunflower stood petrified beside her, unpanicked. The light had faded from her skull.

Broken walls growled over mud and water. Olivia would have run to the shattered Mason House and shoved it over the ledge were she strong enough. Tumbling below and ahead of them, the ruin would be no threat.

Here, the storm had greased its path and aimed it down the same stretch where they ran. Wood snapped in an unsteady rhythm, as threatening as a rattlesnake's tail.

Olivia grabbed Sunflower's arm and sloshed downhill again. Christmas and Hazibel stared from the pull-off, shocked into stillness.

"Run, fucking *run*!" Olivia shrieked, her throat cracking.

They must have got the message; both of them dashed from the pull-off and started down the third stretch of Sunset Pass.

The growl snapped into a wooden roar. Cracking and breaking, the house came sliding down the second stretch, a beast with a mouth of muddy gums and shattered wooden teeth. The pull-off lay bare ahead except for its guardrail. Olivia would hit the mud and swing around the turn, Sunflower in tow. A few more yards and they'd make it.

Chunks of snapping wood batted at Olivia's legs as the roaring house swallowed the world. Its walls cracked open, mouth widening. The house would scoop them in, chew them up, and drag them through the pull-off's railing, down Chapel Hill.

Olivia's sneakers hit the curve, and she skidded to turn.

A wooden beam struck her back, and her hand wrenched free of Sunflower's. Splinters hailed around her. She landed hard in the pull-off's soil, caking her clothes and hair with mud.

The house roared past her, slammed face first into the steel railing, and poured itself over the ledge.

Olivia scrabbled to her feet. Where was Sunflower? Wooden chunks littered the pull-off, but no body. Olivia darted for the ledge, where the twisted guardrail leaned into the drop.

Sunflower dangled over the cliffside. Only her desperate two-handed grip on a jagged steel beam kept her from plummeting behind her house, but the collision had unmoored the guardrail's remains, and rain slickened the metal. She was sliding, the rail was sliding. Everything would chase her house down the drop.

Olivia dove after her. Chilly terror shot from toes to skull, but vertigo couldn't hold her back at Lookout and not here either. She grabbed Sunflower by the forearms and pulled hard. Rain and mud spattered their skin.

"Dig your shoes in," Olivia said through clenched teeth. Her heels sank into uncertain muck. "Grab my clothes, grab anything!"

Sunflower slid one hand up the guardrail, and then her head wrenched to one side with a pained squeal. "Make her stop crying," she said.

"Grab onto me!" Olivia pulled, but damp skin slid through her fingers. Gravity was winning.

Sunflower contorted her face. Renewed light shined down her scalp from neck to forehead in a sickly pus-white glow.

Olivia tugged harder. "Don't do that," she said. "Focus on me."

Sunflower couldn't seem to hear. Her face squeezed tight, teeth bared, eyes shut.

Another wooden groan broke the night. Olivia gritted her teeth and glanced up, where a tremendous silhouette caught the hilltop's high ledge.

No, it couldn't be another one. Sunflower had one house, and it had already tried to kill them.

Except the Mason House that came rolling down Sunset Pass to crush them hadn't been the same house Olivia idled outside when the night began. That house sat on the other side of town. No way it could have wandered here. And if one mimicry of the Mason House could burst out of this dark storm and try to kill Olivia and Sunflower tonight, why not a second?

It came trying to kill them now. No stretches of Sunset Pass would slow it down. The house dropped in a free-fall toward the second pull-off.

Olivia dug her nails into Sunflower's skin and yanked as hard as she could. She heard footsteps pound the mud, either Christmas or Hazibel rushing back up the pass to help.

Olivia turned her head, mouth open. "Don't get close—"

She yanked Sunflower one last time before the house crashed into the ledge. The impact sent Olivia flying down the stretch and over its lip. Her fingers clawed uselessly at muddy pavement, and then just mud. Where was Sunflower? Safe?

Olivia didn't see. Soil crumbled under her fingers and sent her slipping down the steep slope between stretches. Wooden shrapnel chased after her. Her shoulder struck asphalt, and then her hip slammed against a boulder. Sky, ground, house, and stone all blurred together in a swirling roll down the hillside. Lightning sent Olivia's head screaming and turned the world white.

Until her head struck a hard surface, and the world went black.

10. THE TIDE

Consciousness never ended.

Or Olivia was dreaming; she couldn't be sure. Her legs bobbed up and down as if caught in an outgoing tide. She'd never been to the beach, let alone the ocean, but her body seemed to grasp a primal memory, passed down maybe from her parents, or their parents, some inherited terror at being dragged out to sea. Her head lolled back, seeking any landmark, seeing nothing.

In the blackness, she felt Sunflower. The shore lay distant behind Olivia, and she couldn't see or hear what she'd left there, but she knew Sunflower stood watching, tears rushing down her cheeks. Olivia tried to call out, but saltwater spat in her mouth as the waves gulped at her face. She had no power in this shifting place. Only the ocean decided her fate.

It decided to let go.

Her head struck hard earth, and the blackness finally let her eyes flash open. The world drowned in mud for a split-second, and then light broke through.

Stars dotted the sky. Dark clouds drifted over the lower constellations, the storm maybe on its way out forever, maybe readying its hateful fists for round three against Chapel Hill, but distant for now.

Olivia tried to sit up, but everything ached and her clothes weighed heavy and damp. Her left leg throbbed beneath the knee. She let herself lie a moment longer, fingers toying at her sweater's new frayed ends, and then she shut her eyes and rolled to one side, onto the leg that didn't wish her dead. She guessed she'd landed on another pull-off some ways down Sunset Pass. The others would come looking. Hopefully Sunflower was okay.

They were getting out. Olivia was going home. Not a plan; a promise.

Warm breath wafted down her mud-caked hair and clothes, blowing raindrops from her skin. Someone loomed over her, unseen behind her eyelids. She paused another moment before she forced them open.

A realization chilled her bones—she was never going to see her parents again.

Ahead of her, thin lips curled back from needle teeth, and a fat maroon tongue flicked up and down in the gaps behind them. Did it remember the taste of people? Behind it, a stretching throat gasped hard, drawing odors and flavors over every tastebud, and then some unknown organ inside made an odd clicking noise, familiar from the drive-in while Olivia cowered behind the concessions counter. Raindrops and slobber dripped down her chin. Everything smelled of wet leather.

"Sweet Olivia," Lizzie said. Her voice came thick and breathy. "Always making it easy for everyone else. Always eager to help."

11. NO PAST

Olivia shut her eyes, waited a moment, and opened her eyes again, hoping the mud and rain and the monster might disappear.

But the world persisted around Lizzie. Olivia kept blinking, and nothing changed. She could only stare at the world as it was and take everything in.

Another crumpled Mason House leaned behind Lizzie and glared over Olivia. It was too intact to be one of the houses that had chased her down the hillside. This one must have formed here, or fallen a shorter distance. That left one Mason House sitting where it belonged atop Chapel Hill, three for Sunset Pass. Were there others yet to be born? Others already existing that Olivia hadn't seen? How far had she tumbled, and then how much farther had she been dragged?

Wooden steps descended from the front door, almost like the real Mason House. Lizzie sat on the lowest step, a wart grown from the front porch. She seemed as unhurried as the shining stars beyond the rooftop. Their light outlined boulders which formed the walls of Sunset Pass, only pausing where vertical crevices blotted the hillside. They watched Olivia, sure as Lizzie's white eyes.

"I saw you and that Hazibel together," Lizzie said. "I listened to you decide on this dangerous path, but here is the place where secrets are buried, always in the hill, and I knew then how to convince you to help me. Telling is only half. I have to show you what's real." Her jaw slackened the way it had before she'd swallowed Devin at the drive-in.

Olivia tensed every muscle from head to throbbing left leg. Lizzie had been watching up on Chapel Hill. Not a mindless animal charging from the brush, but a calculating monster who had overheard the plan to head west, turning the pass into her trap after all. How much else had Olivia guessed right only to talk herself into the wrong conclusion?

Lizzie clicked her throat and turned to the porch. "Do you want to see?" she asked. "When the house appeared, I brought her inside, out of the wet. Best thing for her, next to resurrection." Her neck coiled against her body, crinkling the tarp that draped her back. "Resurrection isn't so fine a thing."

Olivia almost asked, *Who?* but with the monster's back turned, now seemed the time to run like hell and never look back.

Except Olivia could hardly sit up. "I hurt my leg in the fall," she said. "It might be broken. I can't follow you."

"It isn't broken, and you didn't hurt it in the fall." Lizzie half-turned from the house and stretched one foot, toenails gnarled and cracking, down the porch steps, where she ground her heel into Olivia's left shin. "The pain is mine."

Fire roared up Olivia's nerves, and she bit her cheeks against screaming with them. A frustrated squeak escaped her lips. "Stop."

Lizzie lifted her foot and grinned needle teeth. "No more running," she said, her tone patient, almost encouraging. "I expected you to come with the others, but this is easier. Fortuitous me. Now, follow."

Olivia took a couple harsh breaths and then shifted up onto her right leg. She could bear the weight despite the ache down every muscle and joint, but running would be impossible when her twinging left leg meant she could scarcely hobble. If she tried to escape, Lizzie would catch her, and their rapport might spoil from conversational to late-night snack.

Better to do as Lizzie said for now. And just who had she dragged into this cracked clone of the Mason House?

Olivia grasped the porch handrail and hopped one-legged up the steps. The front door hung open on a small foyer, where an end table held a dish for keys beside the coat closet. Dark wood brooded from every surface. Beyond the foyer, the main hall led to kitchen and bathroom on the left, living room on the right, stairs at the hall's end on the left, and a turn opposite the stairs that led to a briefer hall and then Hazibel's room.

Olivia had crossed this threshold a thousand times. She knew its wall paneling, the photo frames of Sunflower, Gina, and Hazibel, with any picture of Hazibel's ex carefully removed. The yellow-painted kitchen always seemed to judge when you stepped inside alone. There was the teal bathroom with its ripe green porcelain, spacious enough for sisters.

The one piece of Gina's stained glass that Hazibel had allowed into the living room hung framed above the sofa. Its colors always looked prettiest when the fireplace roared, as Olivia heard it roaring now. Dust often coated the underside of the furniture. Neither Hazibel nor Sunflower saw much need to clean here after their family of four had dwindled to two. Olivia couldn't tell whether Sunflower's father having wandered off and never come back still mattered much to those left behind, but Gina's absence haunted the Mason House.

Something felt wrong about watching Lizzie creep through its halls.

Rainwater dripped through cracks in the ceiling and tapped down her tarp. She turned as she reached the living room entrance, where flickering firelight cast an orange glow. Her saliva-damp teeth shined in the new light. She opened her mouth as if to taste Olivia in the air.

Lizzie's body deflated in a heavy sigh. "I have no past," she said. The fireplace growled and flickered, and the shadows deepened around her.

Olivia grasped the kitchen doorframe to keep that sudden gravity from dragging her down.

"Once upon a time, Sunflower played on the kitchen table," Lizzie said. "A dance she doesn't remember. She toppled the table and came out with only bruises and scrapes, but the table leg snapped. She didn't mean to break it, only wanted to dance, but too late. It was broken. And since she didn't want to have broken it, she decided someone else had."

Lizzie turned to face the living room. Her white eyes soaked up the firelight. They seemed wider now, and Olivia realized she'd crept closer against her will.

"She slid herself out of place," Lizzie went on. "Remove tab gold, insert tab gray. Hazibel punished her anyway, but Sunflower told herself she wasn't to blame, and she buried that righteous knowledge deep inside. She pardoned herself and let that gray idea inherit the sin. Do you understand?"

Olivia didn't answer. She wanted to turn and hear nothing, but Lizzie's gravity wouldn't let go.

"I am the inheritor of sin." Lizzie curled her lips at Olivia in a needle-toothed grimace. "Not only for the kitchen table. I inherited years of sins. In time, I grew a face as she gave me shape. *It wasn't me,* Sunflower would say. *Lizzie did it.* And when she grew too old to say it, she thought it. Even in the excuse she'd made of me, she believed."

"Are you another sister?" Olivia asked.

Lizzie tapped a nail through her hair. "Only of the mind."

A suggestion slithered across Olivia's mind, Christmas's sarcastic reply to Hazibel near the craft shop. *Nightmare.* Olivia wouldn't say that to Lizzie.

Her breath quickened. "Just what are you?"

"An inclination," Lizzie said. "It starts with an idea. Ideas are temporary unless we think them through. Think of them often, and they become memory. I broke the table because Sunflower remembered that I broke the table."

Olivia bit her lip. That wasn't how the world worked. Blame didn't decide reality.

Lizzie's lips slid into a smirk, as if she'd read Olivia's thoughts and found them amusing and childish. "Memories are powerful, even when they're wrong. Believe a memory, and it becomes the past. Past shapes present, bound in a chain. The memory becomes real."

Olivia's fist curled, knuckles scraping the wooden wall. "You can't just make people up."

"Not yet I can't, but she can." Lizzie lowered her head to the floor, and her matted hair flopped forward. She dug at gray roots until every lock peeled from the back of her neck. "Do you see it? The mark?"

Drops of rainwater tapped Olivia's head, urging her closer. She hobbled deeper into the house to escape them. Not to look. It wasn't because she needed to see what the firelight revealed in Lizzie's skin. What she knew she'd see.

A brown crescent curled over the back of Lizzie's neck. The same as Sunflower's birthmark, as the blemishes that marked Christmas and Hazibel.

"She calls people from the moon. She makes us real." Lizzie raised her head, her face as close to Olivia's as they'd been outside. Hot breath whistled through her teeth. "I want to call them, too. If the little one figured it out, so can I. She can teach me."

Little one. How was Sunflower the little one? Olivia glanced at the foyer's photo frames, the pictures hidden in darkness while their glass glinted firelight. Sunflower had always been taller than Olivia, the headstrong leader between them, popular, but for all of Sunflower's grandiosity, she was the youngest in her family. The little sister.

"Does this have anything to do with Gina?" Olivia asked.

"Everything's about Gina," Lizzie said.

If Sunflower made people—that couldn't be real, but if it was— did that begin with Gina's disappearance? Gina had left many scars.

Olivia couldn't guess how deep. "How do you know any of this?"

"The rain told me some." Lizzie licked her upper teeth. "It can't help telling. Some of us, it tells too much, and they dream of memories forever. You've seen them. The memory sick."

The infected. Olivia nodded through a trembling sigh.

Lizzie lifted one hand toward the ceiling, and raindrops dribbled down her fingers. "I dreamed, too. The big storm comes down in tears."

"But I saw you in the rain," Olivia said. "You're immune, like me and—" Her words died away. The others. What had happened to them? Was Sunflower okay?

"Tolerant," Lizzie said, jarring Olivia back to this moment, this unreality. "If you have no tolerance, you dream forever. But don't fool yourself into thinking tolerance is immunity. I tasted the memories, sipped the poisoned rain, and dreamed the Night of Sunfall, the first Hazibel, every truth. She cries it from the sky, over the hill."

A memory screamed from the back of Olivia's mind—a noise she'd heard idling outside Sunflower's house when the night began, before the monsters.

Olivia didn't understand *Sunfall* and *First Hazibel*, but *poisoned rain*? When riding in Taggart's truck, a white mist in the raindrops had reminded her of tiny snowflakes. She'd known that something in the rain had infected Chapel Hill. Could it be memories? Lizzie's explanations sounded outlandish, but so did everything Olivia had seen tonight.

"So much pain, all breaking at once," Lizzie went on. Her hand fell, splashing rainwater across the foyer floor. "You can almost hear the raindrops scream."

She turned again to the living room and crossed its doorway. Firelight flickered down the coils of her neck and across her tarp, where raindrops glittered like lost starlight. Maybe everyone who came here had lost their way.

Her voice beckoned from the living room. "Tonight told me of the time before myself, but I always knew the truth. There is no avoiding your gestation when part of your memory is to see yourself being invented. I learned who I was while she slowly thought me up. A stark difference between being born and being hers. She didn't mean to call me into the world tonight, but either guilt or the storm forced me out. Same with the other inheritor of sin, for each thought that embarrassed her, each night with that boy she liked. She broke the world to shed her sin. Merry Christmas indeed."

The bottom dropped from Olivia's stomach. Christmas knew Chapel Hill, had been there, and yet Olivia had never seen them. Christmas wore Sunflower's birthmark. Another creation like Lizzie, called from memory, branded by the crescent moon. But that would mean—

"And this one, too," Lizzie said. "A replacement for secret sin."

Olivia hobbled to the firelit doorway. New, crackling warmth soothed her damp skin, and she would have liked to sit on the sofa, or in one of the soft seats, and doze in the fire's loving air. She knew better. There would be no love tonight, not in this house.

Lizzie formed a black blot where she crouched in front of the stone fireplace, across the living room from its doorway. To the right, the bulky TV set perched on a wooden stand between two windows, one red curtain still hanging, the other shaken loose. To the left, the seats and sofa formed a crescent of their own beside an end table. Its lamp had toppled over, and bits of lightbulb glass now dotted Hazibel's ceramic ashtray. Gina's stained-glass art somehow clung to the wall despite the damage to the rest of this Mason House.

On the sofa's far side from the fireplace slouched a corpse, head hanging chin to chest, face covered in dark gray-streaked hair. Much of the skin had shriveled, but that hair, the body's frame, the way Olivia had seen someone sit that way in this very room so many times, chastising and scolding, often gripping a cigarette between two fingers.

Unmistakably Hazibel. Exactly the woman Olivia knew, the

one accompanying her in a desperate escape from Chapel Hill, except this Hazibel sat baring the back of her neck.

There was no birthmark. No crescent patch. Her skin showed a new moon of nothingness, echoing tonight's sky. Had there never been one, or had the mark faded with decomposition?

"Old Hazibel," Lizzie said. "First Hazibel, from the day when Sunflower swallowed the fallen sun, before she called people from the moon. Sunflower put her down, and I dug her up. Righteous knowledge, buried deep."

"Sunflower wouldn't have done this," Olivia said. She didn't need to think about it.

Lizzie snaked her head over one shoulder. "Will you blame me, too?"

Olivia's lips moved without words. She'd seen the mark on Hazibel's neck on Cooper Street. Another person from the moon, as Lizzie put it, built from Sunflower's memory. Half-hearted, a thing like Hazibel, but not.

"But when?" Olivia finally asked.

"Sunfall," Lizzie said. "First Hazibel, house Hazibel, walking Hazibel."

Olivia gaped. "There are three?"

Lizzie stuck out three fingers. "First Hazibel, dead. Second Hazibel, you've met her before, but she is sickened with rain. Sunflower wanted her mother in the woods, so she made an extra tonight, the one who walks with you. There might be more unknown even to me. So many houses, so many Hazibels. Who can keep track?"

Olivia fell into the seat farthest from the sofa. Her wet clothes sank into the cushions, and her head slumped into her hand, a fresh headache coming fast.

"Does Sunflower know?" she asked.

"The little one dips in and out." Lizzie swept a hand over her head. "The bloody-haired one doesn't know. The new Hazibel can't. Only one of us figured it out. I am the nightmare that knew what it was and knew what the dreamer could dream."

Lizzie's mouth wrenched open and gasped hard, sending a shock through Olivia. Her maroon tongue lapped at the air, and then she bolted for the curtainless window. Hot breath clouded the cracked glass.

"There, that taste," she hissed. "She's made it."

Olivia held stiff. "Who, Hazibel?"

"Sunflower." Lizzie sprang from the window, knocking the TV set's corner, and grabbed Olivia's arm. Her cold fingers tensed, and then she yanked Olivia out of the seat, onto two legs.

Olivia cried out, but Lizzie didn't care. She dragged Olivia limping back through the foyer, toward the open front door.

"You'll help me now," Lizzie said, her breath frantic. "She'll listen to her best friend. Tell her to teach me how to call people from the moon, same as her. We small ideas can birth ideas of our own. She didn't think of that, did she?"

As they hit the porch, Olivia tugged her arm free and glanced at the outside world.

Beyond the porch railing and beneath the blue-black sky, Sunset Pass sloped to one side and climbed to the other. Puddles of rainwater reflected the night. A figure descended the pass, a few inches taller and thinner than Olivia. Her blond hair caught the starlight.

Sunflower walked unencumbered, uninjured. A white line of light no longer divided her head.

Tonight had started with headaches, guesses at psychic powers that neither Sunflower nor Olivia had taken seriously.

For whatever reason, the storm had sparked something inside Sunflower, a force erupting in word and memory and a sister's glass. A force that birthed houses and sent them plummeting from the sky. Each phenomenon had seemed random chaos, but deep down, the madness grew from Sunflower's roots.

Olivia had made too many assumptions, each of them wrong. Monsters, infection, birthmarks. She couldn't be sure she had every detail straight even now, her head reeling with revelation.

But the important things never changed. Her eyes fixed on Sunflower, best friend, impossible crush, the greatest person in Olivia's world. Lizzie didn't need help. Sunflower did.

Olivia lurched onto the porch and limped as fast as she could.

12. PEOPLE FROM THE MOON

"Olivia?" Sunflower's voice swept in as Olivia stumbled off the porch. Her left leg shouted at every step, but Sunflower raced closer, her soles pounding the ground in a harsh rhythm until she slammed against Olivia's chest and swallowed a choked sob.

There wasn't time for hugging, but Olivia held on tight. She needed this. Sunset Pass had tried to kill them under dark rain and summoned houses, but now the night glowed warm and bright. When Olivia glanced back, the Mason House doorway stood empty, and she let herself cling to a little hope that Lizzie might have disappeared into shadows again.

"What about the others?" Olivia asked.

"On their way," Sunflower said. She coughed hard over Olivia's shoulder and slipped back, her pretty face flecked with mud and tears. "Liv, don't scare me like that. You can't disappear like Gina." Her hand slid down to Olivia's chest as if checking for a heartbeat.

Olivia felt its thrum against Sunflower's fingertips. Steady at first, and then faster, disturbed by the groaning of an unsettled porch.

Lizzie darkened the Mason House doorway. One hand grasped the doorframe while the other lingered in the foyer's shadows. She hadn't grinned so wide all night.

"There she is," she sang in whisper.

Sunflower took in a sharp breath. She tugged hard at Olivia's arm, dragging her a step too fast. Her left leg buckled with pain, but Sunflower didn't seem to notice. She tried to drag Olivia toward the slope.

"We can't just leave," Olivia said.

Sunflower turned to Olivia, eyes wide, and then to her house. "We have to."

"You want to," Lizzie said, nearing the porch's edge. A dry scrape followed her, as if she were dragging a tail. "Olivia always helps, and you always do what you want. That's why you needed more of these."

Her trailing arm swung forward, hauling a limp burden—a desiccated corpse with no crescent moon marking the back of her neck. The body rolled down the porch steps, joints and head beating a wooden thump-thump until she hit the ground. Her face aimed at the house, but same as inside the living room, she was unmistakably Hazibel.

Even Sunflower had to see. She shook her head hard and aimed one hand up the hillside. "That's not my mom. Mom's coming."

"A memory comes, little one," Lizzie said. "First Hazibel has been dead for some time."

Sunflower crumpled beside Olivia. Her teeth clenched visibly through bared lips, hands against ears, another headache rolling through. Olivia glanced up, but the storm's blackness hugged the sky at some distance, not yet rushing back to Chapel Hill for another onslaught of strange misery.

That didn't stop the light. A chalky glow sparked at the back of Sunflower's neck, shining so brightly through her hair that Olivia made out the crescent moon birthmark. The light chased up and over the center of Sunflower's head, a line drawn that dared ideas to cross.

"See?" Lizzie's bulbous head aimed at Olivia, and her feet clung to the edge of the porch's top step, a terrible vulture awaiting opportunity. "She always does what she wants. And right now, she wants to see her mother alive and well."

Olivia reached for Sunflower and then whipped both hands back. The air itself trembled between them, boiling and apprehensive. A rich, green-wood crack filled the night, and Olivia scanned the sky for another plummeting Mason House.

Nothing hovered overhead but the stars themselves, their luminance fading as Sunflower's light sharpened to unrelenting sunshine. The brilliance stung Olivia's eyes, but she couldn't turn away. Milky light breached Sunflower's head, a sickly thing desperate to escape its skull prison.

The glowing line widened by sinewy inches with another harsh snap. Light pulsed wetly, widening its fissure to an alley, and then a canyon, laced by threads of tissue and bordered by cracked-open skull.

Sunflower's groan surged into a high-pitched scream. White, glowing pus bubbled out between flesh and bone.

Olivia shrieked and scuttled backward. Sunflower needed her, but every organ and bone held back, wouldn't go, wouldn't touch another monster if they could help it. A best friend had become one more infection Olivia didn't want to catch.

Glowing sludge slopped through the gap in Sunflower's head and struck the earth, pooling inches from her knees. An umbilical cord of light bound the inside of her fissure to the roiling mess in the mud. The cord pulsed with stars like shining pale blood. White tendrils lashed in every direction, and their cooked-spaghetti texture thickened with bone and muscle. Meaty appendages split into fingers and toes.

Olivia couldn't be seeing this. Couldn't accept it. Footsteps patted down Sunset Pass, an excuse to wrench her gaze away.

Christmas jogged down the slope, red hair plastered to their head. Hazibel ran behind them toward the pull-off, where a copy of her house slouched against the hillside.

Some child of a scream and a moan surged through her lips. "Sunflower!"

Sunflower didn't look her mother's way, but her head twitched as if she could somehow hear beneath the sloshing meat and fusing bones. The light wormed through the air above her head, disturbed by interruption as it stitched a solid form out of its raw glow. A wet snap slammed the fissure down Sunflower's skull shut, and the umbilical cord of light flaked to powder.

Light faded around a solid figure, rising from a puddle of black afterbirth. Gray roads cut through her dark hair, and the locks parted at the back of her neck, revealing a crescent mark. She wore a white dress and heels, more intent on having a fun night out than traipsing down a hillside. Familiar steely eyes cut from her face.

Another Hazibel.

Any shred of doubt left inside Olivia dropped dead. Lizzie had told the truth. Memories made real, people from Sunflower's personal moon. It was all real.

"Mom?" Sunflower squeaked, raising her head. No light shined from within her skull anymore. She looked like herself again, Olivia's friend, except for a line of blood that now trickled down her ear.

Olivia's gaze shifted from the still-bright Hazibel that stood over her, to Lizzie's dead First Hazibel below the porch, to the running Hazibel who'd found the group on Ridgemont Road. Were there more? The Hazibel who'd met them might have climbed out of the black sludge on that tree at Lookout. And the one Olivia had known these past three years? That Hazibel could still be stumbling around Chapel Hill, sickened with her memories like Lizzie had said.

How many mothers had Sunflower made? How many had died?

The Hazibel who'd suggested they travel Sunset Pass staggered onto the pull-off and slowed beside Olivia. Her fists trembled at her hips.

"I want to know what's happening," she said. Her glare turned to Olivia and then Sunflower. "I want someone to tell me."

Olivia would've explained. She just needed everyone to head back to her house and gather in the apartment's living room, where she could focus on knitting that scarf she should've been working on at the drive-in. They would all drink tea, both living Hazibels, Lizzie, maybe something stronger for Christmas. They could talk it over. Olivia would have felt comfortable enough to tell everything in the kindest way.

"You're dead," spilled out instead, each word a toneless, rotting carcass shoveled off her tongue. "Sunflower made a new one. And then another new one."

Light faded from the new Hazibel. She wobbled on new heels, her feet pressing into black sludge. Fifty seconds old, but she looked identical to the Hazibel who stood at Olivia's side.

Who could keep track of Sunflower's endless supply of mothers? Tonight's Hazibel would be Sunset Hazibel, for leading them down Sunset Pass. They would have to come up with a name for the new one, too.

"I'm not dead," Sunset Hazibel said, and then she pointed at her fresh lookalike. "I don't know what's happening here, but no one slapped me together like that. I would know." Her accusing finger aimed at her daughter and then dropped to her side. She kneeled down, her face in Sunflower's hair and her voice rattling. "Tell me everything."

Sunflower shook her head, batting back her mother's chin. "Why are there so many?" she whined.

Porch steps groaned. "Because you want your mother," Lizzie said. Her serpentine neck uncoiled in inches, and she leered closer to Sunflower. "Now you have her again. And again. All the mothers you want. You always get what you want."

Sunset Hazibel stood fast, her mouth snapping open. She probably wanted to know what the hell Lizzie was, if she'd been the thing chasing them. She fit the description, a big-mouthed people-eater like Christmas had said.

But the new Hazibel opened her mouth faster, and a bestial screech scraped up her throat. Her head cocked sideways, a bird sizing up the world for bugs and worms, and then she hunkered close to the ground, bow-limbed, almost apelike. Teeth flashed between pale lips.

Sunflower struggled to her feet. "Mom?" No telling which Hazibel she was talking to.

The new Hazibel bounded from her birthing sludge and pounced on Sunset Hazibel in a storm of dress and hair. They rolled into the dirt, the wild one's nails scratching, jaw snapping, as furious as the provoked infected, except no one had touched her. She'd gone feral all by herself.

Olivia started to stand, but she didn't know what good she could do on two legs, especially with one still throbbing.

Christmas shouted, something like *hey* or *stop*, but the noise muffled them. Only the words "Fuck it" came clear from their mouth before they charged for the two near-identical Hazibels.

Sunset Hazibel lay flat on her back, feet kicking as she tried to get away, while the feral Hazibel thrashed in a tornado of fists and teeth. Christmas grabbed one bony wrist and caught sharp nails raking at their arm and then their face. They said something else, but the feral Hazibel's screech drown it out.

Olivia's limbs twitched, desperate to help, but how? She was weak. All she had was the truth, terrible and useless. Christmas wanted to talk this feral Hazibel down, but they didn't understand the trouble here any better than either Hazibel. No way for Christmas to know they were yet another creation, one of the people from Sunflower's moon. And Sunflower herself couldn't have been more lost. Only Olivia knew what was really happening tonight.

And Lizzie. She crossed the black sludge, eyes fixed on the flurry of Hazibels, now with Christmas trying to pull the two apart. She stretched her neck and scratched her throat, eyes focused in fascination, as if a wild animal version of Hazibel meant more to the world than a chain-smoking judgmental one. Gray hair rippled in the open air, flashing the crescent on Lizzie's neck.

Two hands wound around Olivia's arm and tugged her from the chaos. She turned to face the only person left to drag her along—Sunflower, the summoner. Olivia's injured leg seemed readier this time, still throbbing but willing to follow.

"Where?" Olivia asked. Not like she had a plan, but she hoped Sunflower might.

Sunflower stared ahead as she led them stumbling up the porch steps. "The monsters will get us," she whispered. Like they were little girls at a sleepover who'd stayed up too late watching scary movies. Like they'd ever known each other that young.

Like the monsters weren't real.

13. STITCHING

Sunflower pulled Olivia through the front doorway and into the foyer, where she slammed the front door and hurried down the hall. Wet marks dotted the floor, and Olivia couldn't tell whether they had pooled from the rain or been left behind when Lizzie dragged First Hazibel from the sofa to the porch.

Firelight flickered through the living room's entrance. Its soft crackle invited Olivia to sit and warm herself by the fireplace, but Sunflower steered them toward the opposite side of the hall, into the dark bathroom. She forced the door shut without turning on the light and then locked them inside.

Near total blackness engulfed them. Only an orange line lit the bathroom door's underside, and it wavered with the inconsistent firelight. Raindrops dribbled from the cracked ceiling and tapped inside the bathtub with the rhythm of a leaky faucet.

"This won't help, will it?" Sunflower whispered. "I've trapped us."

"It's not your fault," Olivia said.

She didn't have it in her to explain how Lizzie had watched them, planned her ambush, stolen secrets by drinking the rain. How could Sunflower begin to understand?

Olivia felt hands at her shoulders, and she let them draw her toward the back of the bathroom, onto the floor between the toilet and the tub. Cold tile pressed through Olivia's jeans.

Sunflower was cold, too, trembling against Olivia, and they clung to each other in the dark. Crying would have been easier than anything else right now, one long bout of conjoined sobbing to let everything out.

But there wasn't time.

"Do you remember what happened?" Olivia asked. "On Sunset Pass?" The shivering darkness beside her said nothing. "What about right now, when the other Hazibel came up? Do you know where she came from?"

"What am I supposed to know about it?" Sunflower asked. "Whenever it happened, I didn't see it. I must've zonked out, and then I opened my eyes and she was there, and Mom, and there were two Moms, and it, she—that thing!"

Olivia nodded against Sunflower's head, chin to hair. Her scalp felt solid, as if light had not come crawling to life from inside. Of course, the split left no evidence. Had there been a fracture line, Sunflower would have wondered about it after Christmas first poured out of her. Likely she had blacked out in the drive-in's staff restroom, and Christmas had climbed from the dark sludge in the corner. And hadn't Sunflower mentioned blacking out at Lookout? Olivia had assumed the infection had come and gone, but Sunflower must have made Sunset Hazibel then, leaving that same residue against the tree as she'd made here in making the feral Hazibel.

Lizzie must have crawled up from a similar stain, elsewhere at the drive-in. Born sometime between Christmas and all these Hazibels, a symptom of the storm rather than its cause, a memory of an idea now stitched into reality as surely as yarn became a sweater or scarf.

Hinges squealed somewhere outside the bathroom. Someone was opening the front door. Floorboards creaked beneath hard footsteps, first in the foyer, and then stepping closer to the hall. A wet gasp filled the house as a familiar throat sucked at the damp air.

"Olivia, it's time to help me," Lizzie said. "Make her do it. Tell the little one to teach me."

Olivia's fingernails plucked at frayed sweater bits. The knitting had snagged and torn on rocks when she tumbled down Sunset Pass. Clothes didn't last forever. If she wanted it undone, her knitted sweater could be ripped apart.

Many things could be.

Olivia pressed her mouth into Sunflower's hair and tasted mud and rain. "I won't leave your side," she said. "But I need you to accept everything I say right now, and fast."

Lizzie inhaled again. Was she still stalking the hallway near the foyer? Or had she wandered into the living room, sucking up fireplace smoke, rainwater, and the decay of a dead Hazibel in hopes of finding her prey?

Olivia felt Sunflower nod against her in the dark, and that would have to be good enough. "You have a gift," she said. "The kind of psychic thing you'd laugh about if Shelly and Dane tried telling you about, but bigger than they ever dreamed, and better, because yours is real. When you zonked out, you made that wild Hazibel. Dragged her up from dreams. Same for Christmas out there and the other Hazibel who isn't dead. And that monster."

"You're not making sense," Sunflower said, too loud. "I couldn't." A tremble in her voice suggested she wasn't sure one way or the other.

Olivia needed to make her sure. "They all have your birthmark." She dug her hand underneath Sunflower's hair and stroked the back of her smooth neck. "Every weird thing tonight comes from you."

"But how?" Sunflower pawed at the back of her neck, and her fingers crossed Olivia's. "Why me?"

"For the same reason as every other part of you," Olivia said, almost laughing. "Because you're the most amazing person in the universe. I always knew you were special, but now? You're everything, Sunshine."

Floorboards creaked, closer now, and a shadow broke the orange line beneath the bathroom door. Would Lizzie taste the air within, or would she assume Olivia and Sunflower had taken refuge in the bedroom upstairs, same as too many days and nights before?

Olivia lowered her voice to a breathy hiss. Her lips felt sticky, her tongue dry. "You stitched them into the world. Now you need to rip out her stitches. Do you get it?"

Sunflower swallowed. "Unstitch them?"

"Yes, exactly that." At least, Olivia hoped. Sunflower had made the idea real; maybe she could unmake it. If the light touched Lizzie again, she might poof out of reality, an overlong magician's trick finally coming to an end. "You start with an idea, same as when you made her. But this time, we do it the other way. Coming up with a non-idea, okay?"

Sunflower bobbed her head at an uncertain angle. A nod for *yes*, or a shake for *no*?

Olivia couldn't tell, but she kept going. "First you need the thought to unstitch her, and then you have to think of it, remember it, want it. Instead of thinking about a finished piece—" She tugged at her damp sweater. "—think about the skein of yarn."

If Lizzie was right. Olivia could only hope. The wild Hazibel had spilled out because Sunflower wanted her mother. The houses must have fallen because she wanted to go home. If Sunflower wanted to suck Lizzie back inside, flesh reduced to idea, maybe that would happen too. Olivia wouldn't want that monster inside her, but hers wasn't the skull Lizzie had spawned from. This was the only way she knew.

Sunflower's head sank into her arms. Despair, or another headache?

"I'm with you," Olivia said. She slid her arms around Sunflower's shoulders.

The door swelled inward, slid back, and then shattered open, its lock cracking between door and doorframe. Orange light swelled across Sunflower's tearful face, hers and Olivia's damp clothes, the cold tiles, and then darkness filled the doorway. A hulking shadow grabbed Olivia by the aching leg and hauled her out of the bathroom and across the living room's threshold, where fire baked the air.

Olivia caught a flash of Sunflower's wide-mouthed face, frozen upside down in a scream, before Lizzie tossed her sprawling toward the fireplace.

Lizzie's head snaked over one shoulder. "You can't imagine true loneliness. How could you when you can replace one, and another, and so on as you want? You can't care about anyone."

Olivia forced herself into sitting up. She would scrabble and crawl. That mouth would not swallow her whole.

"Prove me wrong, little Sunflower." Lizzie lurched toward Olivia and hauled her in both hands. Sharp teeth parted, and slobber ran down Lizzie's bottom lip.

Olivia kicked and slapped at Lizzie's long arms, but she was too weak, and the monster too strong as she dragged Olivia deeper into the living room, where the fireplace growled. Lizzie's hair and the dancing firelight cast flickering shadows over her face, like long fingers scratching at her eyes. Olivia made to reach for those eyes and claw them out, but Lizzie snapped her teeth, and Olivia wrenched her arm back.

"How many times have you helped this ungrateful Sunflower tonight?" Lizzie asked. "This week? Eternally? I want your help now. You told me when we first met, when those boys wanted to hurt me. You told me you would help."

She shoved Olivia over the hearth and closer to the stone fireplace. Hot air wafted around them, blurring the living room. The sofa, curtains, bulky TV, and Gina's wall-mounted glass all turned to fuzzy shapes in Olivia's gaze. Embers stung at her neck.

"Don't," she rasped, swatting uselessly at Lizzie's shoulder, her face. "Don't!"

"Now it's my turn. Help me." Lizzie thrust Olivia through the mouth of the stone fireplace. "Either Sunflower teaches me, or you die. Convince her she wants you to live, sweet Olivia."

Olivia's back thudded against warm chunks of wood, spitting a cloud of embers into the living room and spilling ash from the fireplace's lip. She felt nothing at first beyond Lizzie's grip.

And then pain came lapping on tongues of flame, white-hot and merciless. She didn't recognize her own desperate scream.

"Always making it easy for everyone else," Lizzie said. "Make it easy for me."

Heat climbed Olivia's back and sent her flailing. Lizzie didn't care, she was as strong as Christmas, maybe stronger, ready to let her fingers cook if Olivia would suffer too.

Somewhere far outside the fireplace, Sunflower moaned. She had crossed the entryway to the living room, lost again. Now wasn't the time to help. She should run.

Olivia choked on her own shrieking. Fiery fingers grazed her hair and invaded her thoughts. Her parents would never know their daughter burned to death hundreds of miles from home. The heat devoured thought, and she fought mindlessly. Kick, claw, bite, anything to run from this fire and never feel warm again.

"Teach me, little one," Lizzie said. "Save her."

Sunflower's voice trickled beneath the roaring fire. "Teach you."

Lizzie's fingers eased from Olivia's chest. The monstrous face shrank back, no longer filling the world, not even filling the living room.

Olivia flopped out of the fireplace and rolled over every bruise and scrape she'd earned dropping down Sunset Pass. She batted at the ends of her hair, beating out any embers. Her sweater felt stuck to her screaming skin, the flesh now cooked to peeling and blisters. She couldn't see the ruin that scarred her spine, but she wasn't burning anymore. Pain meant survival.

White light fought the fireplace's orange-yellow glare in shining spokes through the Mason House, a glow cast from the line down Sunflower's head. The fissure had cracked open again. Sickly tendrils bound the inside of her head to Lizzie's tarp and flesh, parasitic worms in search of pores. They found their openings and then dug inside.

Lizzie's head snaked back and forth, eyeing Olivia and Sunflower in turn. "You don't know loneliness," she said.

The worms of light bent into ragged hooks. Their ends curled back toward Sunflower, dragging flesh from Lizzie's frame, and a clicking cry choked up her snakish throat. Her body stiffened, trapped in the pull of Sunflower.

"I wanted more, that's all," Lizzie moaned. "I didn't want to be the only one like me."

Olivia's lips trembled. *Stop*, she tried to say, but nothing would come out, and she didn't know how to change that. Not after everything tonight. Not for a monster.

The white glow wrenched back, yanking a wordless cry up Lizzie's serpentine throat. Her hands sank together, almost in prayer, but there were no clasped fingers, no fingers at all, every digit having fused into a congealed lump of shimmering flesh.

Her tarp rippled over her back, its center deflating where her torso began to cave in. Skin stretched tight over muscle, plastering each contour in a map of blood vessels, and the subdermal lumps of flesh reminded Olivia of Devin Shipley, trying to fight his way out of being eaten alive.

But only Lizzie was being swallowed this time.

Her muscles squeezed inward. Olivia cringed, expecting the sinewy sounds of breaking bones, but the damp swallow, like mud sucking at a boot, was much worse.

Lizzie's bones had melted into slush. Her jaw unhinged for the last time, running loose beneath her mouth as if she were drooling it onto the living room floor. Her eyes ran in white tears, boiling down her cheeks. Gray hair flattened against her flesh as she sank toward the floor, her still-alive body folding into uncooked fat and grease. An embryo caught between life and death.

No more prowling, gasping, murdering. No more anything.

The last wet remnants slithered up a stretching umbilical cord, and the light of Lizzie drained into the pale abyss of Sunflower's skull. Her head fused whole, a mouth finishing its meal. The glow faded from her forehead to the back of her neck.

Olivia forced herself up from the floorboards, her back stinging, and hobbled across the living room. No pieces of Lizzie stained the floor, not even the black sludge left behind by Sunflower's stitching. The monster been swallowed whole.

Maybe that had always been her destiny.

"Did I do it?" Sunflower asked. Her voice sounded frail. She dragged herself up the living room doorframe and turned to Olivia, eyes hopeful.

Leg still throbbing, back screaming, Olivia lurched toward Sunflower and kissed her hair. "Yes," Olivia whispered. "Yes, you did it, yes, yes." Again and again until she was certain Sunflower had absorbed it.

Sunflower lurched unsteadily backward, and her gaze swept the empty living room. "I had no idea," she said. "Any of it."

"You couldn't have." Olivia took a breath against the pain, and then she took Sunflower's arm in gentle fingers. "But now you do, and you can unstitch the rest. The wild Hazibel, the houses and glass. Suck up all the memories from the infected. Every awful thing that came out of you can go right back inside."

Sunflower blinked hard, the mascara having washed from her eyes. "Okay." She sounded dull, a little broken, but she understood now. That was enough.

Olivia limped into the hall and led toward the front door. She needed ice, maybe burn cream, and definitely an endless nap, but relief and comfort could wait. Lizzie might have been right; Olivia seemed always ready to help. She couldn't be embarrassed about that, no matter how people from the moon felt about her. Half-formed ideas couldn't understand.

"So, I thought them up," Sunflower said, following Olivia toward the gaping front door. "And then I made them? And I can take them apart."

"Far as I understand," Olivia said. If she couldn't believe Lizzie's words, she believed her own eyes.

They reached the front door, where the cool night air breathed across Olivia's face. The rain had left a damp scent earlier, but now the world smelled cleaner. Down the slope of Sunset Pass, Christmas seemed to still be wrestling with the wild Hazibel. Tonight's work was far from done, but one problem at a time. Olivia started out the door.

Sunflower's fingers encircled Olivia's forearm so that each grasped the other. Olivia felt her arm tug behind her and go taut. Sunflower had stopped them in the front doorway, and the air stilled as if the world had stopped too.

Olivia glanced over her shoulder and a flash of lightning cast a brief white gleam over Sunflower's eyes.

"So." Sunflower cocked her head in thought. "So, I'm like God."

The stillness in her voice sent a chill across Olivia's blistered skin, nervous and tingling. Something inside her sank down the maw of a deep unknown cavern and went on sinking the longer she stood still. She hadn't realized human bodies could hold such endless darkness.

"Sunflower," she whispered, turning her body to face the doorway.

She opened her mouth to speak again, but Sunflower yanked them both back inside the Mason House. The door slammed shut on the Hazibel mess, Christmas and their struggle, the fighting, and the rest of the world. Its tremor rattled Olivia's bones.

14. THE KISS

Olivia in tow, Sunflower swept past the warm living room, its fire gentler now. The staircase to the house's upper split yawned open, and its rim dripped rainwater down cracked-open walls.

"What about Christmas?" Olivia asked. "The Hazibels? Chapel Hill?"

"Don't rush me," Sunflower said, waving a hand. "I'm figuring this out as I go." She slowed as they neared the back of the hall. "I made all this." A bright smile rose over her shoulder. "Me."

"You." Olivia's back ached; her everything ached. "That's why we have to go outside. To unstitch tonight's mess. Only you can fix it."

Sunflower looked ahead. "But should I?"

Olivia recoiled in shock. Her legs stiffened to slow Sunflower down, but she kept tugging, and Olivia didn't know how to resist. They reached the fork at the hall's end, where making a right would lead down a shorter hall to Hazibel's room. Sunflower eased left and focused on the stairs.

"That monster—Lizzie." Sunflower squeezed Olivia's hand. "I think she had it wrong. When you lose a left shoe, you don't go buy the same left to match the right. You buy a newer, nicer pair of shoes."

She planted one sneaker on the firm bottom step and led Olivia up. Fissures in the wooden walls exposed wire webbing, and behind them, a crevice in the hillside formed another dark eye to watch Olivia's ascent. Her shoulders shuddered with cold. She focused hard on the ache in her leg and skin, the sight of Sunflower's mud-caked back, her red sweater sopping wet.

"How long's it been going on?" Sunflower asked, cresting the top step. "Just tonight? Or longer?"

Olivia wasn't sure anymore. Had Sunflower talked this way before tonight? Which came first, the storm, or that sickly glow, or this brash mindset? Lizzie had thought she was explaining everything, and the mess of Hazibels and Mason Houses spun Olivia's mind, but she hadn't said what *Sunfall* was, or what else Sunflower might do with her gift. Olivia could only think to put everything back the way it was before tonight began.

But Sunflower seemed to have other ideas.

The small upstairs divided between a window wall at the back, Gina's room on the left, and Sunflower's room on the right. Sunflower took two steps into the meager hall and gave Gina's room a hard stare. Was she thinking of Gina Night, like Olivia had earlier? Or was she thinking of Gina?

"Wish I'd known," Sunflower said, the pep in her voice wearing down to melancholy. "When did you find out I could do this? Just now?"

Olivia nodded, but she didn't think Sunflower saw, too busy throwing open her bedroom door. Her fingers reached inside the doorframe, and a battery-powered lava lamp cast a warped orange-white glow. It had lit many sleepovers and at least one power-out.

Aside from a dented corner and the runny cracks in the ceiling, Sunflower's room looked largely undamaged by this Mason House's descent from Sunset Pass, if it had fallen at all. Maybe it had sprung here from Sunflower's head full-formed while they were still descending the pass.

Her fluffy bed fit against one corner, across from a vanity, its dresser split into a couple dozen slender drawers. Taped-up Polaroids circled the mirror. Some had broken free and now rested on the messy dresser, littered with spare purses and discarded makeup. Junk piles formed islands across the maroon rug—tattered notebooks, frayed ribbons, cheap plastic jewelry, empty cassette tape cases, clothes that should have been hung up in the small closet. Christmas lights, their bulbs darkened, ringed the back-facing window in dull green wire and spread along the bedroom walls, painted the faded pink of a childhood wish left to sour.

"God should make things better," Sunflower said. She waded into the mess and then spun to face Olivia. "But I've been making things the same, or worse, haven't I? If I'd known before, I'd have more practice."

"That's not it," Olivia said, her voice frail. "It's not your fault."

Sunflower squeezed her hand again. "You're right. Thank you for telling me. Nobody ever tells the truth about anything, not really. That's why everything's gone so wrong. But now I know the truth, and it's on me to make it better."

Olivia glanced back at the upstairs hallway. "By unstitching it."

Sunflower tittered. "No, no. Liv, no." She slinked deeper into the room.

Olivia could not remember a time she hadn't been eager to step inside Sunflower's room. Even during petty, bickering arguments, she'd craved this place. Close to Sunflower, laughing with her, having it out. Shelly and Dane offered a home, but Sunflower offered a temple.

Tonight, Olivia dragged her feet and had to force herself through the doorway.

"It's about making it better. Because I *can*, so I *should*. Right?" A light swelled in Sunflower's eyes, like she'd moments ago plopped behind the wheel of a monster truck, itchy to see what it could do. "Like the house. I'm the reason the house is down here. But why's it exactly the same? I could imagine a bigger one. I'm smart enough, creative enough, aren't I?"

Olivia almost didn't want to speak, but the words fought out of her anyway. "You are."

"How about a castle instead?" Sunflower's grin glowed orange in the lava lamp's light, her teeth turning to small pumpkins. "We could have anything. I can make anything. Anyone. Even the people we've lost. You said I just have to start with an idea."

Olivia chewed at the insides of her cheeks. She hadn't said that; Lizzie had. Olivia had just repeated it. A parrot, according to Christmas, good as any tape recorder imitating a real voice.

The skin flared down Olivia's back. The pain demanded she turn away, find burn cream, and then dash down Sunset Pass and at last escape Chapel Hill. She stood amid the rug's junk instead, staring at Sunflower.

Olivia paused, searching for the words, and they came in a disbelieving laugh. "Sunflower, you're not God."

"You can't see the scope of it yet. You're still freaked out." Sunflower waved a dismissive hand. "But I got all that out of my system earlier."

Olivia's plan to panic later now seemed silly. If she'd panicked earlier, she could have gotten it out of her system, too, and then she would share Sunflower's headspace.

"Doesn't it make sense?" Sunflower asked. "Tonight's not strange. I'm strange, I just didn't know it before. Now the pieces have fallen into place, and I know who I really am." She thumped onto her bed, comforter and sheets hugging her thighs. "The world makes more sense. You don't know what that's like, figuring out the truth about yourself. Especially this kind of truth. The kind that changes who you are, and you can't be the same."

Olivia's memories sank through Chapel Hill, back to Hartford, to the girl she'd kissed and her father who'd seen it.

"I do," she whispered.

"But did you accept it?" Sunflower's hair puffed behind her head. "Did you let yourself have it, or did you bury it?"

Olivia knew the answer. Burying that truth had been the only choice that made any sense. Her arms crossed her chest in a frail embrace. The mattress creaked as Sunflower stood and crept closer until her face hovered inches away. One hand stroked Olivia's hair.

Olivia flinched back, sending a fresh ache up her leg. "What are you doing?"

"I had an idea," Sunflower said. She kicked past a junk pile, her face in Olivia's again. "And now I'm making a memory."

Olivia tried to slide back, but Sunflower wrapped her arms around Olivia's shoulders and held her in place.

"I know what you've buried," Sunflower said. "Dig it up."

Olivia couldn't break free. Her back and leg stung, and she

didn't have the strength to fight even Sunflower's narrow limbs as they led her toward the bed and forced her to sit.

"Why are you doing this?" Olivia asked.

"I want you to get what I'm going through right now." Sunflower sat beside her. "I accept myself, but you haven't. Accept yourself, and you'll get it. Best friends, same page. Like we're supposed to be."

Olivia wanted to say she didn't understand, but her nerves said she understood perfectly.

"Come on, I'm not ugly now, am I?" Sunflower sounded almost like Christmas.

"No, but—" Olivia's head sank deeper.

A fingertip touched her chin, and then Sunflower drew her up so they could look at each other face to face. Her eyelashes fluttered in the lava lamp's glow, and her lips glistened nearer, nearer.

There had been less weight preempting Olivia's kiss with the girl in Hartford, a one-day friendship running helter-skelter through cotton candy, carnival rides, the kind of noncommittal joy she'd never found in school. The kiss had been sudden, an impulse. They hadn't even known each other's names.

Olivia had danced a precarious waltz of confused feelings around Sunflower since not long after their first meeting at Chapel Hill High when Sunflower said Olivia was a pretty name, that she'd always thought so. Here, on this terrible night, the confusion writhed warm and alive. It offered sweet promises hovering two inches away.

And Olivia shuddered to think of doing it. What was wrong with her now?

A smirk tugged the corner of Sunflower's lips. "What's your plan for heading back to Hartford?" she asked. "Let your parents decide how things go from there, right? Let them frame the conversation, I mean."

Olivia had planned for a non-plan. "Let them decide," she echoed.

"And then what, say you're sorry? Are you actually sorry?" Sunflower's scoff blew hair out of Olivia's face. "Whatever they say, you're ready to accept it, but you won't accept yourself. You can't understand why I'm not freaking out. It's because I know myself now, and I'd never run like you did." Her hands cupped Olivia's cheeks, fingers cold, palms warm. "You said you won't leave my side. Was that a lie? Would you run from me?"

Olivia tried to shake her head again, but Sunflower held tight. Yes, Olivia had wanted this, but not *like* this. Not tonight, muddy and cold, her back and leg crying, knowing that people suffered atop Chapel Hill, suffered right outside this house.

Always making it easy for everyone else, Lizzie had said.

"It's okay," Sunflower said. "You don't deserve the pain. All that shame over a little kiss, what good's it doing you? Accept it, get it out of your system."

That day came alive—the screaming kids on rollercoasters, the stink of fryers and taste of horrid, wonderful corn dogs, the sweat dotting Olivia's forehead, dotting the other girl's lips. Sunflower thought she understood, but she didn't. Couldn't. The kiss was a pebble beneath the mountain of what the kiss meant. Sunflower's mountain loomed larger. Greater builders, higher peaks, more meaning. How could she compare herself to that girl at the carnival?

How did she even know?

Olivia's head wrenched back, breaking Sunflower's hold. "I never told you about that day."

Sunflower shrugged. "I just know."

Olivia's legs wobbled as she stood from the bed. "You don't just know. I only told one person, and that was tonight, and you weren't there."

The steps pounded outside the room. Olivia's thoughts flew to Lizzie, as if she'd somehow only melted into the floorboards and was now crawling up from some black pit. But no, Lizzie was gone, unmade, an idea again and nothing worse.

Christmas lurched into the doorway. The lava lamp cast orange across their bruised limbs and split knuckles.

Olivia sprang from Sunflower's bedside and reached for Christmas. "You're hurt," she said.

"So are you," Christmas said, black pupils darting up and down. They looked as tired as Olivia felt. "I had to hurt that thing bad. Didn't want to, but our Hazibel's in a rough way. No choice."

The mattress groaned. "Olivia," Sunflower said. "Come back here. We're busy with bigger problems than this thing."

Christmas stretched to full height, and their head crested the doorway. Olivia hobbled back without meaning to, her gaze darting between doorway and bed.

"Bigger than me?" Christmas asked. Their arms coiled as if ready for another fight.

"Big as God." Sunflower stretched her back, and though she still overshot Olivia, she couldn't match Christmas's height. Disdain sharpened her voice. "You're nothing but a bad idea. Time to forget you."

Christmas pressed their arms to either side of the doorframe. "Not some vampire who steps out on your say-so."

"And I'm not some kid you can push." Sunflower strained to smile. "Hold on."

White light slashed down the center of her head. She hugged her chest and doubled over, aiming her glowing crown at the doorway. Grunting pain squeezed every muscle in her face. A harsh crack struck through the room.

Olivia didn't understand until the light pushed open Sunflower's skull. Sunflower had thought Lizzie up, stitched her into the world, and then unstitched her. Sunflower had thought Christmas up, stitched them into the world, and—

"Don't unstitch them!" Olivia shrieked. "They're not a monster!"

Sunflower's head jerked aside. Her knees buckled, and she landed in one of the rug's junk piles, tape cassette cases clattering like bones through catacombs.

White sludge poured down her head and pooled onto the floor. Fast and messy limbs slopped out. They twined and climbed into a white dress, gray-streaked dark hair, and a snarling face.

Another Hazibel, growling and wild as the last. Black sludge leaked into the rug.

Christmas shrank from the doorway, their exhaustion a chain around their neck. The wild Hazibel hissed, her mouth full of spit and clenching teeth. She charged, knocking the vanity's corner, and a snowstorm of Polaroids swirled behind her as she pounced onto Christmas. They fell from the doorway and clattered out of view against walls and floor. Were they falling down the steps? Olivia started to follow. Christmas needed help.

Her wrist snagged in Sunflower's grip.

"You're hurting them," Olivia said. She tugged her arm, but Sunflower's grip only tightened. "You're hurting me, too."

"Because I messed up again," Sunflower said. Her head had resealed, its light fading. "You can't interrupt me, not while I'm learning."

"But you were going to unstitch them," Olivia said.

"And? Unstitching would've been peaceful enough." Sunflower's face turned up in a shining smile. "That's not your friend, Liv. I am. That's just another thing I made."

Her left ear twitched, and a slender red bead trickled down her earlobe and neck. She rubbed the side of her head against her shoulder, and the blood smeared across sweater and skin. She loosened her fingers from Olivia's wrist and sank to the floor.

"Maybe you shouldn't be making anything else," Olivia said. She wanted to run for Christmas, but she couldn't leave Sunflower. Both needed help. Her knees hit the rug. "Stitching hurts you."

"When I get it wrong. When I'm interrupted." Sunflower scratched at her bleeding ear. "You've changed your tune since downstairs, huh? Unstitch one and not the other. Maybe that monster had a right to be here, too."

Olivia didn't know; that had never been her decision, and she didn't want it. She'd just been trying to make tonight better. Furniture clattered somewhere downstairs, and her needy heart reached for Christmas. The rest of her had to run, hurry, anywhere. Reality was crumbling, so what good was loyalty?

Sunflower stood shakily, feet kicking loose from debris. "Don't stress. This is for the best. You and me, together."

"I'm going home," Olivia said, but she didn't feel strong enough to go anywhere. Her left leg could hardly handle kneeling here. "To Hartford. I need to see my parents again."

"We could bring them to us."

Olivia froze in place. *Bring them.* "Here? To Chapel Hill?"

Sunflower's face filled with her smile. "Where else?"

"Do you mean bring them from Hartford?" Olivia asked. "Or do you mean from—" She couldn't finish the next part and instead chinned at Sunflower's head.

"Depends on your flavor," Sunflower said. "Think about it. You could tell me about them until I get the right idea, and then I can whip them up. Except they'll be better than before. The way everything will be better. They'll be parents who accept you exactly like you are. And what good's someone who can't see the specialness of my best friend?"

Olivia shuddered in disbelief, shame, and then again in disbelief for good measure.

"What'll they think of you?" Sunflower asked, beaming. "Olivia Abram, the right hand to—what did you call me? The most amazing person in the universe?"

"I was trying to help," Olivia whispered, voice catching in her throat. "To stop Lizzie." But she couldn't give Lizzie the blame for the words themselves. Those had come from Olivia, and when she'd said them, she'd believed them.

"You helped plenty. And now we're here, to this, and anything else I can do." Sunflower rubbed at her scalp as if she might grow a crown. "I'm everything, remember? I'm God, and my house will be my temple. And you'll be here with me, and we'll make everything right for us. Our perfect lives."

This couldn't be Sunflower; Olivia refused to believe it. Sure, Sunflower was self-focused sometimes, occasionally inconsiderate, but not arrogant to this degree, right?

But then, when else had she been given the chance? Not while scrambling out of Hazibel's way, or holed up in her bedroom. What would godlike powers have done for her then? In the heat of some moment months or years ago, she had been some poor girl who'd needed her mother to tell her that she was special. She likely hadn't been the first case of desperation to wander out of the Mason House.

Olivia knew one other.

She stared up at Sunflower. "Gina wouldn't want this."

Sunflower's smile died, and her eyes turned steely. "Don't do that," she said. "Don't say that. Ever."

Olivia shivered. Deep in her chest, her heart cracked, and no sickly light poured out.

Something thumped downstairs, and a choked cry chased across the floorboards. It didn't sound like Christmas. If Christmas were being strangled, Olivia doubted they would cry out, more likely to flip off their attacker and keep fighting.

"Sounds like Mom needs help," Sunflower said. Her pleasant demeanor cut across her face, sharp as a knife. "One more sec, please be patient, and then I'll make something for you."

For Olivia? That would only make things worse.

"Don't go anywhere." Sunflower retreated to the vanity, placing a stretch of junk-riddled floor between herself and Olivia. "Might not hurt me if I do it on purpose this time."

Her teeth clenched against a guttural groan, and she clasped hands to either side of her head, the white glow returning. Faint this time, as if fighting a thicker skull shield to reach Sunflower's hair, and beyond that, the world. Maybe she was running out of juice.

Olivia tried to stand, but the stress of the night weighed her down. She wouldn't let herself leave. Even if Sunflower ascended to the throne of some evil goddess, rewriting reality from the side of Chapel Hill, Olivia's barbed wire heart wouldn't unravel. Always ready to make things easier.

She couldn't leave, but she couldn't watch. Her gaze traveled the floor and its new layer of Polaroids, some pristine, others bent, most still wearing circles of clear tape on their white backs. She pawed at the little squares to gather them. Three years of memories didn't belong on the floor, mixed with the junk and the growing pool of sludge that now dripped down Sunflower's head.

Hanging around the school's hallway, gymnasium, and parking lot. Fooling around at the drive-in. A day trip to Lookout from two years back, as if they'd find any older kids necking in the sunshine. Snow-filled winter walks on the east side overlooking roads that would later grow an on-ramp to the interstate—if only tonight could have taken them there, far from Lizzie and her powerful secrets.

Olivia overturned a photograph of Sunflower wearing a denim jacket, its shoulders swollen with rhinestones. Gina's jacket. They had taken some of these photos on Gina Night.

At the edge of Olivia's vision, pale mud bubbled with half-formed limbs. She leaned deeper toward the floor and photos, trying not to see it. If she leaned close enough, maybe one Polaroid's borders would stretch wide and swallow her back to that heart-pounding, beautiful night instead of this one.

In another photo, Olivia had thrown her arm overhead, striking a pose. Short as she was, Gina's mini-skirt reached almost to Olivia's knees. She hadn't cared back then. An exhilarating evening cleared all anxieties.

Arms slapped boneless from the sludge two feet away. Another wild Hazibel, almost here. Olivia grabbed another photo, and another. One of them would slip her through the desperate cracks of time.

In this one, Sunflower wore Gina's chartreuse dress. Sunflower had struggled to zip the back, and rather than help her, Olivia had laughed and snapped another photo. Sunflower had her back to the camera, arms straining around shoulders and hips like a confused lover.

Her hair had parted around her neck, revealing the crescent moon. Pretty and innocent then, no curse that sent light from birthmark to forehead and stitched ideas into reality.

The newest Hazibel hadn't finished forming yet, but a growl already rippled in her throat. Would she charge out of the room, as Sunflower wanted, race downstairs to help her predecessor fight

Christmas? Or would she turn out even worse and instead savage Olivia's jugular? Dark hair swamped down an emerging head. A crescent moon flashed from her neck in the lava lamp glow.

Olivia leaned deeper, eyes straining, nose almost touching the photographs. In the next, her past body struggled with the same chartreuse dress, when it was Sunflower's turn to laugh and snap a photo. Same zipper, it refused to close its teeth around anyone but Gina Mason. She must've had long arms to grasp the tongue and pull.

Here, the dress flayed open in a peeling chartreuse skin, Olivia bunching her hair overhead so that it wouldn't catch in the zipper. She awaited Sunflower's help, sure to come as soon as she finished laughing. The teeth would close from the small of Olivia's back to the peak of her neck.

Where a crescent moon marked the skin.

Bones cracked across the rug, the new Hazibel finding a firm shape, but she seemed small and insignificant now. Olivia slid the photo from her face. She'd been looking too close, and the lighting had been off, shading Sunflower's blond hair to Olivia's brown. She was looking at a photo of Sunflower, not herself. That had to be the answer.

Except these arms looked too short to be Sunflower's. And the crescent remained.

The other photographs tumbled from Olivia's fingers as her hands formed claws around this Polaroid's borders, smudging the picture.

"No," she whispered. Her arms jolted, and she let the last photograph float feather-like to its sisters on the rug. "No, no, that can't be right." Her fingers traced from her throat to beneath her hair to the back of her neck. It ached to touch, kissed faintly by fire. If a crescent once marked her, Lizzie and the fireplace might have burned it away.

But there had been a crescent one year ago, on Gina Night.

Olivia dug nails into stinging skin. A scream snaked into her head, where she remembered a voice that was not hers.

No one slapped me together like that, one Hazibel had said outside. *I would know.*

An echoing whisper rattled through Olivia's lips. "I would know."

15. ANOTHER THING

Sunflower finished birthing a new nightmare from her skull. Another wild Hazibel climbed hissing from the rug on all fours.

She stared at Olivia a moment, gauging whether she was friend or prey. Maybe the wild Hazibel found stitched-together kinship in Olivia's eyes before she obeyed some unspoken impulse to charge out the bedroom doorway, white dress fluttering around her thighs. Her footsteps thumped down the stairs and into the main hall.

Christmas shouted something Olivia couldn't make out, and furniture crashed again. Had they beaten the other wild Hazibel, or were they now fighting two at once? Christmas was strong, but not immortal.

"I kind of like Mom this way," Sunflower said, gasping for breath. No blood trickled from her ear. "Never says a nasty word, never insults my friends. I might make more on purpose. Better than guard dogs."

Olivia scanned her arms for answers, bruised by the fall, the right forearm scraped by the drive-in's popcorn machine. Accident? On purpose? Why did *she* exist?

"I told you, don't stress," Sunflower went on. "I trance out, no pain. Or at least, I don't remember, and that's just as good." Her body shuddered, bucking off exhaustion. "Anyway, your turn."

Olivia turned to face Sunflower full-on. White light shimmered down her blond scalp. A sting crossed Olivia's hands. They'd formed fists without her realizing, and her fingernails left tiny crescents along her palms.

"No," she said.

The glow froze where Sunflower's hair parted. "You'll like her," she said. Her voice came slow, mind teetering at the edge of trance. "She'll look like me. A me you want to kiss, who wants to kiss you. It starts with an idea, and it's not like I haven't thought about this. One Sunflower, two Sunflowers." Her grin shone as bright as the sun. "Ooh, maybe more of us could stitch a new Gina!"

Olivia's teeth clenched. "You stitched me."

The glow shifted black, and Sunflower's head dimmed. Her eyelashes fluttered, but there was no charm in them anymore.

"You. Stitched. Me!" Olivia swept the Polaroids off the floor and thrust their cloud at Sunflower's face. "Your birthmark. It's on my neck."

Sunflower watched the photographs smack the floor, studied them with those cold eyes. Olivia had lost herself in that bright blue stare on too many afternoons. She glanced from the photos, and Sunflower's curious hands slid into dark hair.

Olivia wrenched away and dragged herself up the vanity, left leg complaining at every movement. "Why didn't you tell me?" she asked.

"How could I?" Sunflower's head sank between her hands.

"I didn't even know I could do this stuff before tonight. I had dreams, but dreams aren't supposed to be real, so how could I guess? You turning up back then always felt like fate."

"And you always thought Olivia was a pretty name." Olivia couldn't stop the tears. "I loved you. You made me up to love you."

Sunflower held out her hands to Olivia. "But now you're here."

Olivia flinched out of reach. "From what? A movie, a book? Where'd you hear about a girl who kissed another girl and ran away from home? What gave you the idea to make a messed-up life like mine?"

Sunflower grasped her head again, pained this time, but her mind was a Magic 8 Ball that always said, *Ask again later*. If answers existed, they didn't like to be known.

Olivia staggered back another step, injured leg bowing under weighty implications. She'd never come from Hartford, never been there. No parents had run a pet store. No mother had watched the news with a vice grip on details, no father had seen Olivia kiss another girl at the carnival. There had been no carnival, no girl. The memories swirled hollow, a void as heavy as Chapel Hill. Olivia crumpled backward onto the floor.

Sunflower reached for her again. "Don't take it personally. You're the perfect best friend. What's wrong with that?"

"Olivia's not your friend," Olivia said. She couldn't raise her eyes to Sunflower. "Olivia's just another thing you made."

"You're angry?" Sunflower's sneakers shifted; a junk pile collapsed out of her way. Her hands dropped again to her sides, this time curled into fists. "You should be grateful."

"I'm your mimicking parrot. Your dog. Why'd you do it, Sunsh—" Olivia clenched her teeth. No nicknames. No friends here. "You made me up to love you. Why?"

A dry, tired voice slunk from behind. "Because her sister wouldn't."

Christmas slouched against the bedroom doorway, their jacket ripped down the sleeves. Skinned patches leaked blood down their hands, and scratch lines striped their head, where nails had torn out skin and hair. Blood painted streaks around clover-green eyes. They'd seen horrors, and yet somehow they had survived.

Olivia wanted to reach out, ask if Christmas was okay, what she could do. She wanted to help, and she wanted help, and she didn't know what to do anymore. The world weighed too heavy.

"Everything's about Gina," Olivia whispered.

Sunflower stamped the floor. "Get out."

"Gina," Christmas echoed. The air itself hung weary around them, but their glare burned hot through a mask of blood. "Gina ditched your ass. She couldn't stand your bratty bullshit anymore, and she took off. Never looked back. Your sister left, so your sad little head coughed up somebody who never would."

"I said, get out!" Sunflower shouted. "Don't talk about my sister. Ever!"

"Probably the first time you fucked with what's real and what ain't, yeah? Liv might be worth that skull-splitter headache, I'll grant you." Christmas reached for Olivia. "But she ain't Gina. Never will be."

Olivia fumbled for Christmas's hand. She would have to crawl a little closer to the doorway.

Sunflower grasped her head and sank to the floor. "You stay, Liv!"

Her shout clapped icy chains around Olivia's legs. Where did she belong? Who did she belong to? Her gaze swiveled between Christmas and Sunflower, her soul torn in two.

Sunflower's head shined with blinding light, its halves tearing faster this time. It had conserved its energy by slow-baking the last Hazibel, but now Sunflower's skull couldn't keep the brilliance down. A crack quaked in the earth, the storm overhead rumbling thunder again, called back to Chapel Hill. Tendrils snagged the bed, vanity, pink walls, and junk piles, Sunflower's pale stitchwork lashing out in a luminous web.

No sludge puddles awaited Hazibel embryos this time. Knots formed in the webbing and grew bulbous pods, together a hatching nest of gnashing and snarling Hazibel faces. Each new mother crawled through the light, desperate to share birth's agonizing burden.

They wanted Olivia.

Her arm tugged back, this time caught in Christmas's grip. "No," she said.

"Don't got the steam to keep fighting them." Christmas pulled again, harder this time, and Olivia struggled to her feet. "Don't belong here, either."

Sunflower's face hovered inches from the rug, her light's reflection glistening in a puddle of black sludge. She steered her eyes to the door, white with rage. "Won't leave my side."

Olivia felt herself floundering. Hazibel faces grew heads and necks and claws.

"That's what you said downstairs, remember?" Sunflower asked. Her teeth gnashed in time with her wild mothers' jaws. "Said you won't leave my side. So, where the fuck do you think you're going? You're mine!"

Claws ripped through white webbing. The Hazibels were tearing free, a mob of mindless animals, forever enraged.

Olivia stumbled into Christmas's arms, and her legs locked

up. Why did they want to stay so badly? Time to go, every part of her, no matter what her creator wanted.

Sunflower's head rammed against the floor, spilling white fluid. Her bedroom's new web fattened down every strand, each tendril a thick spoke jutting across a wheel of light. At the center, the shine widened beyond Sunflower's skull, past her shoulders, swallowing the room, and another face emerged.

Blond hair, bright blue eyes. Another Sunflower.

This one didn't snarl or shout. Her face hung placid, and her eyes stared, as mournful as her meek voice. "I didn't mean it," she said.

The floor fell beneath Olivia's feet as Christmas swept her up. Her aching leg knocked the doorframe, but Christmas didn't pause. They barreled down the stairs, past the holes in the walls, over bloody, bruised corpses in white dresses, past the dwindling flicker of a distant fireplace, and outside into a fresh sheet of rain.

The cool drops soothed Olivia's back and nothing else. She watched the house shrink over Christmas's shoulder as they descended the slope of Sunset Pass. The ledge soon blocked it from sight, but not from sound.

Behind them, the Mason House screamed.

16. NO FUTURE

Christmas faltered halfway down the narrow stretch and dead-dropped Olivia into the mud. She stumbled against Christmas's chest and then toward the hillside. Her palms splayed over slick stone, where soil clumped with rainwater. The hill wouldn't hold her up, had never really cared for her.

"Need a breath," Christmas said, gasping. Red streams ran down their face and neck. "Left Hazibel ahead. The one that makes sense, but like I said, she's in a rough way. Not sure she'll make it."

Olivia pressed her forehead to cool stone. "I have no past," she whispered. Unseen hands rolled her sweater up her stinging back and pooled cold wet slop across the burns.

"This should help," Christmas said.

No mother had ever slathered sunblock down Olivia's shoulders when she was a little girl. There was no mother, and she'd never been a little girl. Fifteen out the gate. What a horrible age to start a hollow life.

"She made me," Olivia said. "Poured me out like the wild Hazibels."

Christmas grunted, maybe with effort, maybe with acknowledgment. Did they understand?

"Lizzie, too," Olivia went on. "And you. She made you. This storm, that glass, these Mason Houses. The memories that everyone's sick with, they're Sunflower's. Every awful thing tonight started with her."

"If she's doing everything you say, makes sense." Christmas tugged Olivia's sweater back down. "Fuck too much with reality, and reality fucks back."

Olivia's fingernails scraped stone as she whirled around, and wet hair snatched at her cheeks. "You're someone she thought she'd be, hot and tough, who goes to lonely places she's only seen in magazines. A persona to shrug off the world. You don't care because she didn't think you up to care."

"I've been caring all damn night," Christmas said. They wiped at their face, the rain having cleaned away most of the blood. "How many times have I stood up for you? Hazibel, too, and I don't even like her. Looked out for Sunflower on your account."

"No one's waiting for us out there," Olivia said. "There's no such place as White River Valley, no Hartford. Are Ohio and Connecticut even real? What if there's no rest of the world, and it's all something Sunflower put in our heads? We can't even be sure what year it really is!"

Christmas sighed mist into the rain. "She didn't invent geography. Or time."

"I don't know anymore." Olivia hit the ground, and damp soil soaked her knees. The earth hadn't sprung from Sunflower's head; it had more right to be here than Olivia did. "She made up these memories, our bodies, and forgot she did it. How do I know she thought me up three years ago when I landed in this town? You and Lizzie only popped out tonight, same as the Hazibels. I might be no different."

"That guy at the drive-in knew you," Christmas said. "Not the only one. She'd have had to make up all of Chapel Hill, and you know she didn't."

"I can't check their necks anymore." Olivia tried to remember the back of Taggart's neck, when he lay dead on Starry Wood Lane facing taillights and the memory sick. Had he shown a mark then? Could she trust even that memory was real?

"Ain't the only difference." Christmas gestured toward the top of Chapel Hill. "They're sick. We're immune."

Olivia shook her head. She'd believed that before, but Lizzie had said no one was truly immune, only tolerant. That monster had known better than Olivia, and Taggart had died before his tolerance could be put to the test. Christmas had made too many assumptions tonight, a flaw they and Olivia had in common, like being Sunflower's creations. Christmas's purpose was clear. Lizzie's, too. Another Hazibel popped out whenever Sunflower needed a mother.

And Olivia? Replacement Gina. Older sister swapped for surrogate sister, some weird, dependable friend who no one else would like, someone to worship the god that was Sunflower since before she could have known her godhood. A living accessory.

Christmas ground their heel into the soil, their eyes fixed on something distant and imperceptible. Memories, Olivia guessed. Whatever Christmas knew about Ohio had been stuffed into their thoughts, each living breathing manifestation constrained by the limit of Sunflower's teenage imagination. Only duplicates seemed whole, like Hazibel. If Sunflower had made anyone else in Chapel Hill, she'd likely copied them from other sources, perception made thought made real.

"Who cares who made us?" Christmas asked at last. "If it wasn't Sunflower, it'd be some parent, or a real god, or nothing we can figure out. Doesn't matter. You're just embarrassed you still care about her—best friend, crush, whatever. Listen, your heart will heal. Go on and grieve the feelings, bury them, move on. That's life, regardless where we come from."

An agitated shout climbed Olivia's throat, but thunder shouted louder, and she ducked her head. Christmas had only popped out tonight, had no real understanding of life, but they faced the same existential emptiness as Olivia. She had no right to monopolize it. Everyone in the world had to deal with their new god Sunflower in their own way.

The rain petered to a drizzle. Beneath it, a fresh cry echoed from down the slope. It sounded like Hazibel.

"Now what?" Christmas lurched downhill, a hand raised to Olivia. "Sort yourself out. We're leaving once I get her situated to move."

Olivia watched the rain thin around Christmas's black jacket and drenched red hair. Farther down, a white dress lay in the muck, wrapped around an unmoving figure. Christmas had moved Sunset Hazibel to the next Sunset Pass pull-off, away from her feral duplicates. Lying there, maybe dying. How many Hazibels had died tonight already?

Storm clouds receded from Chapel Hill, having finished another round of beating the earth with rain and wind. The storm couldn't seem to destroy the hill, not for lack of trying. Enough rounds of fighting, and maybe the hill would finally win. For now, the clouds weaved west, lightning still pulsing through their blackness. Stars retook the rest of the sky, stopping only where no moon graced the night. The only kind of moon Olivia had seen was the one that shined from Sunflower's neck.

From Olivia's neck.

She had never seen the back of her neck before. Had she stepped into a tattoo parlor asking for ink there, the artist might have noted the birthmark and checked whether or not she wanted to color over it. Her parents would have disapproved.

Except she had no parents. Either they were real people who lived in maybe-existing Harford, bound to made-up memories, or they were entirely figments of Sunflower's imagination. Olivia's home and history were a place built from bits of TV and books by a half-understood adolescent. The family-run pet shop was probably a chain store in real life.

Was there room in a Connecticut city for a carnival to set up shop? For an indiscreet kiss between adolescent girls? Olivia didn't know. Hartford's layout felt incomplete in her head, the fragments of a child who didn't pay proper attention, or the delusions of someone who'd never existed.

The more she worked the memories over, the more ludicrous they seemed. Sunflower hadn't put much thought into Gina's replacement.

Another cry stole Olivia's attention, where Christmas bent over Hazibel. Around the pull-off's curve, another Mason House had broken apart. Only the split-level remained, splattering Sunflower's room across the mud in a gory wooden wound. Each copy held the same furniture, same photographs. Olivia could search each one and find the same damning crescent on the back of her neck.

"I have no past," she said again. "No future."

Inches up the slope, rainwater pooled in a pothole, overflowing from the last torrent. Had Olivia carried Sunflower's lava lamp outside, she expected she would find the same misty whiteness of memories in the water that had sickened most of Chapel Hill.

But don't fool yourself into thinking tolerance is immunity, Lizzie had said.

Olivia ran fingers over her forehead, raindrops indiscernible from sweat. To overcome any tolerance would take more than droplets. The mud squelched as she inched forward, half-kneeling, half-crawling to the puddle, the knees and shins of her jeans turning brown with muck.

She lowered her hands through the soupy surface, let the misty water pool in her palms, and then she splashed it over her face.

The watery curtain seeped into her eyes, nose, and mouth. Memory drops trickled over her tongue and down her throat. They tasted like Sunflower smelled. Not her perfume or shampoo, but that distinctly human scent that clouded from her pores on sunny days.

The same scent flowed through her memories. Their sound and presence had drowned most of Chapel Hill into a memory-overdosed dream, but those people didn't have any tolerance. They could escape into oblivion. For tolerant Lizzie, she had sipped the memories down, blacked out, and then woken again with knowledge. Drinking only a little of the poisoned rain wasn't enough to be taken by memory forever.

What would drinking deeply of that poison do for Olivia? Would it let her forget she was a parrot? A puppet? A stitched-together dream of a lost sister and a made-up best friend?

Maybe Sunflower's memories would give some kind of peace. And if not, at least they were real. Not full of invented parents, or an imagined running away. Genuine memories, worth more than any fabrication.

Olivia leaned close to the puddle. It lay placid with Sunflower's poisoned rain, as toxic as cyanide in its own unique way. Reflected stars dotted the puddle's rim, blotted out only by Olivia face. She couldn't tell if she smiled or scowled. With any luck, she would become like the memory sick, and there would be nothing left inside to give either expression ever again.

Her face plunged through the surface. Water ran up her nose, mouth, ears, stinging with cold, hurting, overwhelming, smothering. She remembered when her dad had let her sink through a pool, unnoticed by every adult present—

Not real. She started to remember a lakeside, but she'd never seen one. None of it was real. None of it mattered. Nothing lost.

Through the water, she thought she heard Christmas shout. They weren't real either, and their exact words drowned in coming darkness. Sunflower's memories were taking over. Olivia forced herself to suck them deep. Belly, lungs, mind, everything soaked in Sunflower's past.

At the last moment, she saw the stars again, the world behind her eyelids glittering white.

And then she floated with them.

17. THE GIRL WHO SWALLOWS THE SUN

When Gina tells stories at night, she never brings up the girl born in a too-tall world on her own. She always has to be reminded. Ten reminders aren't enough. One thousand reminders might be close, but how can a girl born in a too-tall world ever count that high? Even Gina can't do that. On tired nights, she reads from flat, hardbacked books with golden spines, their covers colored in images of Disney's Cinderella, Snow White, Winnie the Pooh, and others. On lively nights, Gina tells her own stories of devils, angels, burned churches, and an evil witch who concocts potions to help little girls sleep.

Gina doesn't understand when she first hears about the girl in the too-tall world. "You mean *The Borrowers*, Sunshine?" she asks. "Those are long books."

Sunflower doesn't know what that is, and she shakes her head. "I mean me," she said.

Gina shifts her legs as if she's going to abandon the foot of Sunflower's bed, trudge across the hall, and shut her door.

Sunflower can't have that. She'll take Cinderella, Pooh Bear, anything for Gina to stay. The too-tall world can wait for another night; Sunflower already lives it.

A distant door slams, and shouting erupts from downstairs, Mom and Dad storming from their room to the living room.

Gina settles into the mattress, her smile hollow. "I'll see what I can do." She clears her throat. "Once upon a time, there was a girl born in a too-tall world. The furniture, the houses, even the people—they were all too tall for her. She couldn't reach them unless they bent and picked her up, and sometimes they would, and sometimes they wouldn't."

Sunflower wants to know how the girl felt, whether she cried, but Gina's soothing voice always melts the pink bedroom walls into a pond of dreams before Sunflower can ask even one question.

The dreamy waters don't let her surface until she hears stamping downstairs. She descends with loud footsteps, hoping that to show her face might stop the arguing. Sometimes it does.

Not this time. Dad fills the front doorway, where he casts the vague shape of a man lost in the night. One foot inside the house; the other presses onto the porch. The lights have all gone off outdoors, leaving the yard and driveway painted black by a cloudy, starless sky.

Mom stands inside, a teal bathrobe wrapped around her, a cigarette poking from her lips. She claws at her dark hair. "Because they both have vivid imaginations, Vic," she says. "You can't go filling their heads with sin and demons off the bat."

Dad's shoulders shift. Shadows and time have eaten his every detail. He might have been mountainous, or lanky, or a beast in between. Sunflower can't tell, as if the memory isn't hers, tucked behind a foggy store window on a winter's night, her purse too empty to buy it. She can only speculate what her father might have looked like.

"Can we drop it, Bel?" Dad asks, impatient. "You know my way."

"We can't drop it," Mom says. Her teeth sound gritted. "They're our little girls. They're important."

"So you say." The porch's darkness sweeps a protective blanket around Dad's shoulders and draws him out from the front doorway. "I don't feel like arguing."

He turns from house and family and lumbers into his only friend, the night. Sunflower has heard his excuses many times in the few years she's known him, the same answers to every family trouble.

An unexpected hand squeezes Sunflower's shoulder. She looks up to find Gina's face above, eyes carrying gray bags that might follow Dad out the door.

"This way, Sunshine," she says. "We don't need him."

Unsettled floorboards draw Sunflower's gaze. Mom has taken Dad's place in the front doorway, her cigarette a chip of light against the outer darkness, but she doesn't seem eager to chase him. Her fiery glare sweeps the night, as if responsibility falls to her to watch it burn.

Sunflower turns from Mom, her head sliding slow through heavy air, and Gina—

It burns.

—charges down the stairs, hot on Sunflower's heels. "I'll kill you," she says. No shouting, no shrieking. She just wants Sunflower to know what's about to happen.

But Gina doesn't realize Sunflower has bothered her for exactly this purpose. The chase, threats, and killing together make a love language only for sisters. And Gina probably doesn't realize that although a predator chooses to chase, the prey decides where they go.

Until the predator catches up.

Gina claps her hands around Sunflower's middle, thrusting her against the living room sofa. That should be the end of it, prey caught, hunt finished, but this afternoon brings a killing season to the Mason House, and Gina shoves Sunflower down against the cushions.

"Not me!" Sunflower cries. "Lizzie did it!"

"That doesn't work, Sunshine," Gina sang. "You're not a baby anymore, or a Lizzie, or even a Sunflower. Just a dandelion, and I'm blowing you to bits."

Her grasping hands roll Sunflower's shirt up from her seven-year-old potbelly, and Gina plants her face there and blows rude raspberries, stirring up half-hearted protests and giggling squeals. Sunflower tries to call for help, but no one else is home, Mom—

It's in my belly.

—sits in her soft chair to one side of the sofa, where long, yellow-ended fingers tap a cigarette over the ceramic ashtray.

"What the hell were you thinking?" she asks, her tone prodding and sharp.

Gina leans against a window beside the TV set. A cigarette smolders between her fingers, too. Like mother, like daughter. Its fiery end blends with the outside's orange sky, overcome with rust-soaked dusk.

Hazibel—no, Mom draws in smoky breath. "Do you think no one watches you?" she asks.

"We're nice-looking ladies," Gina says, blowing smoke against window glass. "Runs in the family. Of course people watch us."

"You're fifteen." Mom's head shifts toward the living room entrance. "A child."

Sunflower ducks back just in time to avoid Mom's gaze. She doesn't want to be seen, or be known, or be part of this, but she needs to understand it despite what she wants. She needs to smell the cigarettes and taste the airborne spite. After a moment, she tilts her head past the living room doorway and goes on watching the remains of her family.

A gruff sigh blows from Mom's mouth. "What would your father say?"

"Probably, *Who's Gina? Who's Sunflower?* Does he still know he has kids?" Gina turns from the window and perches both elbows on the sill. "What's with your fresh concern for reputation? Like half the guys in Hartford don't know our phone number."

Mom's attention slashes toward her wrist and its ticking watch. It's Friday night; she'll be meeting a date soon.

"That isn't the same," she says.

"Pretty much. What we do is nobody's business." Gina sucks at her cigarette. "So, I kissed her. I'll do it again. You'd rather I get knocked up?"

"I'd rather, if you're going to kiss this girl, that you don't get caught." Mom grinds her cigarette's fiery end into the ashtray, and her hand comes up trembling. "Christ, you'd think I taught you nothing." She leans forward, beginning to rise.

That's Sunflower's cue to tiptoe up the hall and pretend she's been hiding in her room for the entire conversation. She wishes she'd slept over at a friend's house, and she might have tried that now to escape this house, but Mom doesn't like her biking past sunset. After Mom drives off to meet her date, and Gina pounds up the stairs, Sunflower is glad she's stayed.

Had she left, she wouldn't have caught Gina.

Across the hall, door wide open, Gina storms into her bedroom and begins stuffing clothes into a maroon backpack.

"If you're sleeping over somewhere, can you drop me off at Stacy's?" Sunflower asks.

Gina yanks open a dresser drawer and piles underwear into her arms. She doesn't glance at the door. A green ball of cash slides up between her fingers. She wouldn't bring her socked-away money to a friend's house; there would be no reason.

The idea stirs itself frothy in Sunflower's head. "You're leaving?"

Still no answer. Gina slams the drawer shut, buries the cash deep in her backpack, and snatches at scraps of idle clothes that litter the bedroom furniture and floor.

"Like Dad left?" Sunflower asks. "To go live with him?"

"No," Gina says at last. Her eyes fix hard on the backpack's zipper, but she doesn't pull it shut yet. "No, not to live with him. Yes, leaving like he did."

Sunflower sinks against the doorframe. She would merge with it if she could. "Who's going to watch out for me?"

Gina scans the walls, her stained-glass artwork, her wardrobe. Her eyes fall on Sunflower. "You'll be a teenager soon. I was already watching out for myself by then."

"Is it because I took your jacket that one time?" Sunflower asks.

"Not that."

"What'd I do?"

Gina should soften now, Sunflower knows. The big sister has a responsibility to set down her pride when the little sister needs pity.

But Gina doesn't look like she remembers having a little sister. "It's not about you, Sunshine. Never was."

Memory dredges up what Sunflower shouldn't have heard downstairs earlier. "Is it because of the girl?" she asks.

Gina turns to her backpack. "It's because running's what you do when you can't stand Mom anymore. That's why Dad left.

Victor Mason did it. Now Gina Mason's doing it." She drags the zipper shut at last and hauls the backpack onto her shoulders. "It'll happen to you."

Sunflower has an idea to stop this. She will thrust her hands forward, palms out, and tell Gina to stay right there, that she will go nowhere, that to run away is not the love language of sisters. Love doesn't mean leaving.

She thinks on this idea many nights after Gina disappears—like father, like daughter—but no matter how many times Sunflower runs the moment through her mind, she can't crystalize the idea into memory.

It refuses to become real.

She wonders sometimes if she suffers from a broken imagination, always demanding stories from Gina, never coming up with them herself. She's made none of the art in her room, nothing like Gina's stained—

We can't stay.

—glass cuts Mom's—no, Hazibel's fingers as the frame slides to the floor and shatters.

"Sunflower," she mutters, a growl in her tone as her fingertips cry bloody tears. "Get me the first aid."

But Sunflower freezes in Gina's bedroom doorway, as if she hasn't moved since the night of Gina's disappearance. If that were true, Gina would still be here. Sunflower wouldn't have moved out of her way.

"You can't take down her stuff," Sunflower says. "She needs someplace to come back to."

"It's been eighteen months," Hazibel says, squeezing her fingers into a red-rimmed fist. "And six days. She isn't coming back. If we rent the room—"

Sunflower means to ask, if they have to rent a room, why not Hazibel's? She could sleep in Gina's. Or rent out Sunflower's, and she would stuff her things into Gina's. Anything to keep Gina's room for her, just in case.

But only a scream comes out. Hazibel's head sinks into her hands, painting crimson—

We're tired of dreaming.

—across the horizon as the sun nestles behind black foothills and green-yellow cornfields. The car trip began beneath a bright blue sky, when Hazibel drove past distant morose mountains and green fields for grazing livestock, their stink filling her maroon Corolla whenever Sunflower cranked down her window from the passenger's seat. No matter where you go in the northeast, pastures look the same, leaving Sunflower lost as to which direction the car is headed. She hasn't questioned the journey until the car crosses tree-choked Pennsylvania backroads into another stretch of farming country.

Soon the world will darken, and then the sky will welcome the sweeping blue-black of the cosmos, and Hazibel will be as much a liar then as when this trip began in Hartford.

"You said I was staying at Grandma's," Sunflower mutters.

Hazibel slides one hand from the steering wheel and fishes between the driver's seat and the gear shift for a lost pack of smokes.

Sunflower turns to darkening fields, blocked from the road only by an ancient two-rail wooden fence. Its weather-beaten posts slant over uneven earth. Endless yellow-green rows bruise to a dark purple in the dusk.

"You're a liar," she says.

"Sunflower, it was just—" Hazibel's hands smack the steering wheel. She's given up hunting for cigarettes. "Grandma's hardly fit to mind herself, let alone a child. You knew better, right? You're smarter than to think this looked like New York. We're practically to Ohio."

That Sunflower should have figured out the truth doesn't make Hazibel any less a liar, but she doesn't know how to explain the nature of trust to someone who deserves it so little.

Sunflower's hand grips her seatbelt. "I don't want to live with him, Mom." The last word squeaks out in a childish whine.

"It's not always about what you want," Hazibel says, her tone without feeling. She turns the wheel and pumps the brake, the Corolla making a hard turn at a cornfield's corner.

Sunflower's fingers prod the seatbelt's buckle. "Never is."

"Excuse you?"

One hand snaps open the seatbelt latch; the other flings open the passenger's side door, and Sunflower springs from the car.

Hazibel's throat cracks with rusty hoarseness. "Sunflower!"

Shouting alone can't snag Sunflower's jacket and jeans to haul her back into her seat. She hits the ground running and doesn't stop. The fencing ahead only stands at half her height, and hopping the rails gives her no trouble. Wide green leaves and thick ears of corn beat at her arms as the cornfield swallows her. The stalks reach for the stars at every step. They will hide her.

The car screeches to a halt. "It isn't forever," Hazibel says, her voice already distant. "Just the summer so I can—Sunflower, stop it! I will not chase you across the countryside."

"Then don't!" Sunflower snaps. "Quit pretending to give a damn! You don't!" She turns so quickly that she loses her balance, nearly falling, and it feels like Hazibel has pushed her. "Why are you like this? You hate me so much, but I hate you too! I've always hated you. Hate. You."

The last words come halted, fighting out of her throat like she can either say them or break down into sobbing.

She doesn't listen for pursuing footsteps. Gina and that shadowy man they once called Dad both showed Sunflower what to do long ago. Hazibel isn't the chasing type. She will wait and keep waiting, while Sunflower will follow in her family's footsteps; run like hell and never come back. Run, because running's what you do when you can't stand Mom anymore.

Sunflower crosses another time-eaten fence, this one crushed into the ground and overgrown with cornstalks. They must have been fed up with having a pile of wood tell them what to do and where to grow. The last remnants of daylight vanish, and the stars fully inherit the sky. No moon glows with them; they've tired of its presence. Nothing and no one will take any more crap tonight, least of all Sunflower.

The cornfield thins to mud and grass. Far above, one star outshines the others, white and twinkling, eager to shoot out through the night if only its mother sky would let it go.

That's my star, Sunflower decides. The one that shines brighter than any moon and only wishes to be free.

She doesn't pause, but her run slows into an aching stagger, thighs burning. She wouldn't mind going back to sit in the car, if only Hazibel weren't there waiting. If they ever see each other again, the reunion will be Sunflower's choice. She doesn't want it, but she doesn't know what else to do next. No living with Hazibel, no living with her father.

She would run to Gina, but she's been gone for years and no one knows where to find her. Somehow, Gina didn't realize that running from Hazibel meant running from Sunflower, too.

Or worse, she realized exactly that and didn't care.

The stars blur behind Sunflower's tears. Maybe right this moment, Gina is crying too, and looking to the stars, and thinking how she and her sister can look up and see the same cosmic infinity, at least if Gina has kept to the same hemisphere and relative time zones. That makes Sunflower laugh for the first time in eons, rich and bright against a backdrop of nothingness.

Only now, no longer crunching through the corn, mouth and nose full of ragged breath, does she realize the world has gone quiet. No insects, no birds. If fieldmice munch through the rows of corn, they chew in silence. All terrestrial sound holds its collective breath, except for Sunflower's laughter.

Something else shushes the world from above in a long rush of air through galactic teeth. Sunflower blinks away tears and looks at the stars again.

The brightest star—*her* star—twinkles even brighter than before.

Despite tear-stiffened cheeks, Sunflower can't help grinning. Most shooting stars slip past the world, caught in the orbits of larger planets that sling them back into outer space, a lucky chance for onlookers to make a wish.

Her star won't be flying anywhere else. It has grown fed up with Jupiter's gravity, and Saturn's, and every other giant out there. Earthbound, this visitor will grant her wish personally.

She has to make it a good one. "I wish I knew where Gina lived," she whispers, light filling her eyes as the star blinks closer. "No, I wish I was with Gina. Or maybe, I wish Gina would come find me, and then we'll—"

The skyward shushing explodes into a roar, melting Sunflower's words to empty breath. Its pitch sharpens to a tea kettle's whine, pressure building and building through the spout's narrow mouth. No steam fills the sky, not that Sunflower can see, only the white glare of her oncoming star.

Too big. Too bright.

No shooting star, but a second sunset rippling in the atmosphere with a sound she can see, a brilliance she can hear. Some heavenly body has lost its way. It should have disappeared around some other world's horizon, but it wants her, speeds toward her, will meet her. Too fast. Too close.

The rising whine reaches its zenith, and the airy rush shatters into a high-pitched scream chasing a lance of pale light. It burns the sky and pierces the night.

Through the air.

Through the corn.

Through Sunflower.

Spokes of light puncture her abdomen. She grasps at them, burning her palms, but there is nothing to hold and tug free. A lost sun sets inside her, blinding, screaming, brimming with white-hot fire. It does not come to grant wishes; it comes to grant pain.

Sunflower can't stop shrieking. Her chest rises and falls with relentless sunlit breath, and she has no mind to slow it down, every thought aflame. The sound of her own terror and agony crescendos in a single ear-splitting note before she can't hear herself anymore. This fallen sun burns too loud with its own cosmic scream. As if it shares her misery in their union.

Molten blades slash through her gut and scrape through her blood vessels, her skin, every muscle and bone. Unseen organs twist and tear. There is a fusion inside her ripe to melt worlds into paste, and an end of that nature might be a mercy to what comes next, when the life she knows breaks into swirling embers.

The land fills with roaring fiery cornstalks, a cosmic dragon having lit the world ablaze and baked the mud and soil into white ash. The scorched earth shrugs off its burdensome field and the girl who's walked them, and her feet slide out from under her.

Somewhere near, the force of this sunset shatters a mother's bones and crushes her Corolla flat.

Smoke drapes the stars. Sunflower smells its choking stink, and burning crops, and cooking meat, and the scream has a scent, too, hot and alien and miserable. Even the darkness that comes next has a smell, damp and earthy, and she lets herself fall into it, lets it become—

We want to see.

—pitch-blackness offers escape from her white intruder. The dark is not the absence of light any more than dreams are the absence of reality, or the present the absence of the past. When darkness overtakes all things, it earns the right to its presence. In some secret holy places, only darkness can protect from the horrors of light.

Sunflower knows.

Now Olivia knows, too.

We want to wake.

"Olivia. That's a pretty name. I've always liked that name."

"That's really sweet of you, thanks. And you're?"

"Oh, I'm Sunflower."

The voice is hers. She knows intimately how she will press her upper teeth against curling lips and then slide her tongue between, performing careful lingual gymnastics to pronounce the middle of her name.

But she watches distant from the sounds, unseen, unfelt, eyes hidden behind dark crevices, remembered tears, and a shell of pale, furious light.

18. TRUTH

—*want to wake.*

Olivia blinked her eyes open the moment she lost her balance. The world teetered, and she had to catch herself on the hillside to keep from dropping against the earth. Both unsteady legs ached. Her back throbbed; the mud Christmas had slathered over reddened skin must have dried and clumped off, and now she stood exposed to the shrill wind of Sunset Pass.

Last she remembered, she had kneeled to a puddle of memory rain. How long since then had she been walking?

Storm clouds rippled in the distance. Either they had been waiting for her since she blacked out, or they had already come back for round four and left Chapel Hill before she woke up. The stars owned the nearest sky for now.

She wondered if any might shoot her way.

Beneath them, at the pull-off down Sunset Pass, Hazibel lay in her white dress, one hand clasped in Christmas's beside her.

Shoulders slumped, Christmas looked tiny for a change, a tree beaten by too many storms, now leaning on the verge of collapse.

They would fall over if they knew what Olivia had seen, that burrowing wrongness inside her thoughts. The truth beat at her worse than all of tonight's misfortunes. It crushed inside her with every earthy ton that formed Chapel Hill. And heavier than truth, there was responsibility.

Olivia wiped her mouth, tasting dirt on her lips, and threw a waving arm overhead. *I'm okay*, she hoped it said. *I'm awake.*

Christmas jerked up, noticing. They rested Hazibel's arm across her body and then jogged up the slope.

"The hell is wrong with you?" Christmas snapped, slowing halfway from the pull-off. "You almost drowned. I had to yank you out of a puddle, and then watch you stumble around like one of those mindless zombies."

Tall as the sky, strong as sunshine, yet Christmas wore tonight's damage in torn and purpled flesh. They stood pensive and quaking.

"I thought—" Olivia started, and then she glanced away, ashamed. "I didn't think."

"Damn right."

Christmas turned to face downslope. They ran a hand down their face, held it over their mouth a moment as if to stifle a cry, and then let it drop. They seemed about to say something else and then chose to swallow it. Nestled in the short hair on the back of their head, an eyelid of flesh winced a wound open and wept blood down their neck, staining the hateful crescent mark. They turned to Olivia, and though the night should have been too deep and dark for details, a light from uphill showed the red strain stenciling the whites of Christmas's eyes.

Olivia edged closer. "You were worried about me."

Christmas gritted their teeth and leaned their imposing figure over Olivia. "Do you still not get me? How many times have I saved you, yeah? But you still don't think I got a heart in me."

"I know you do," Olivia said.

Christmas grasped Olivia's shoulders and pressed her back against the hillside. "Then what the fuck did you do that for? The fuck did I do to deserve it?"

The same thrilled shudder as when Olivia had been pressed against the tree at Lookout ran through her now, a lightning rod for her heart. She had messed up worse than she knew. Christmas might not tell all, but their feelings fumed off their skin, and it wasn't like Olivia had become the queen of heartache. Everyone could have some, share and share alike.

"You didn't do anything to deserve it," Olivia said, her voice quieting. She forced herself to look into Christmas's furious eyes. "I thought I deserved it, and I was wrong. And I didn't understand about you."

"Why not? I'm a person, ain't I?" Christmas eased Olivia from the hillside, and their tone softened to match hers. "Both of us. Ain't that so?"

They were right. Olivia had been inconsiderate, another selfish monster flung up from Sunflower's skull. Her little stunt of despair had planted the idea in Christmas's head that maybe the world was better off without any of Sunflower's creations, like Earth would become purer without people from the moon.

"I need you, do you understand?" Olivia asked. "We wouldn't have made it this far otherwise, and I don't know if I'd have anyone to count on. What I did wasn't a judgment on you, okay? I did it for me."

"You did it to both of us," Christmas said, almost hissing.

"And I was wrong. Finding out what we are was too much, and I freaked out."

"Because you had such great memories before, needed them to be real."

"It's not the memories, it's me!" Olivia snapped. "As a person. It wasn't about you."

Even that felt wrong. What Olivia had done was about both of them. She and Christmas were bound by a promise, and a tempest in Olivia's skin whenever Christmas touched her, and the only genuine past they could count on. Even if it only amounted to the past few hours, she could count on them as more solid and real than every haunted memory from before she'd met Sunflower. Spawned from Sunflower.

Olivia stepped into Christmas's warmth and placed a hand on their chest. "I'm so sorry, Christmas. You deserve better, and I shouldn't have put you through that." She had nothing else to offer.

Christmas held still; even their chest seemed to freeze. "It was a promise. We're getting out, remember? Got no one else tonight. Got no one else any night, anywhere, the way you tell it, right? Everything I know is kind of bullshit, ain't that the way?" Their shoulders trembled as if at last feeling the night's chill. "So, we got each other. Can't ditch like that, or what else are we?"

"Is that your two rivers theory again?" Olivia reached a gentle hand for Christmas's shoulder and traced her fingers down their arm. "Are we crisscrossed now?"

"Been that way since the moment we met." A subtle smirk drew up Christmas's face, as if they were afraid any bigger smile might invite new horrors into the night. "That's how water works."

Their caution didn't work—Olivia heard a low crooning in the distance. She hoped it was only the wind, but then an answering howl sent a chill down her spine, and for a moment she quit feeling the sunburn-like heat across her back. The songs of feral Hazibels painted ice down her bones.

"There's this law in science, where things can't really be made or destroyed, just changed," Christmas said. "Seems to me Sunflower's holding that law's head underwater, and she won't let up until the body quits twitching. Rivers this, rain that—doesn't matter much. Sunflower's an ocean. Check out the world she's flooded."

From this far down Sunset Pass, Olivia couldn't see the previous pull-off where the Mason House sat, but the air shimmered upslope with wriggling light. Its milky, curling fingers beckoned the storm to return, try its thunder and rain and lightning again, wash the hill over and over until every grain of soil eroded, the land flat and submissive.

As if Chapel Hill wanted to die.

"She's no ocean," Olivia said. "It's different than that, and even she doesn't know it."

"But you do?" Christmas asked.

Olivia knew more than she'd ever wanted to. The night had seen to it since the drive-in, the rain, the monsters, but deep down she supposed this train wreck had started before these past three years in Chapel Hill, before she even existed.

With Sunflower. They were going to have to do something about that.

Olivia turned downslope and looked to the lower pull-off where Hazibel hadn't moved. She didn't want to see, and yet everything inside said she had no choice. At least for some time, this Hazibel had been one of them.

"How's Hazibel?" Olivia asked.

"The normal one?" Christmas asked, twitching their head side to side. "Near gone."

They led Olivia toward the pull-off. Shallow, shaky breaths formed a steady percussion, almost as loud as footsteps. Olivia made out the shape of Hazibel's white dress and every damp patch where blood had painted the fabric black. It painted her arms and neck, too. Her wild doppelganger's teeth had torn deep.

Breath crackled into a wet croak. "Is she okay?" Hazibel asked, almost a swallow.

Olivia slumped into the dirt and grasped Hazibel's hand. She wasn't the first Hazibel Mason to die—she might not be the last, either—but at least tonight, she'd been their Hazibel, grouchy and insufferable, Sunflower's mother in every way that mattered.

"Help her," Hazibel said. "You always took care of her. Like her sister."

The truth clawed at the back of Olivia's throat. In Hazibel's state of bleeding out and fading from consciousness, she wouldn't understand the truth if Olivia told her. Olivia scarcely understood either. She would keep that burden to herself.

"Sunflower's in good hands," she said.

She squeezed Hazibel's fingers and then let go. She was supposed to promise she'd help Sunflower, solve every problem, make it right, if only to ease Hazibel's leaving. Olivia couldn't tell lies any better than truth, only offering nothingness and empty encouragement.

She turned to Christmas. "Do you have any cigarettes left?"

"Half a pack." Christmas reached into their jacket and slipped out a red and white box, the cardboard having been shredded in places and yet spared a drowning. "Didn't know you smoked. Would've lit one for you earlier."

Olivia held out her open palm. "It's not for me."

Christmas lowered their hand and glanced down at Hazibel. "What, for her?"

Olivia's outstretched arm turned snakelike and snatched the box from Christmas. She found an olive-green matchbook inside and lit a cigarette for Hazibel. It blinked warm in the darkness as Olivia planted it between Hazibel's teeth.

Her mouth stirred as if she were about to speak, maybe to call Christmas an asshole, or thank Olivia for one last cigarette, or to pass on some surprising advice that would make the next stretch of this hellish night a little easier.

Instead, she sighed smoke, and the cigarette's eye flared and faded. Flare. Fade. It sputtered rapidly, and then Hazibel passed out. Still breathing, but likely not for much longer.

Olivia plucked out the cigarette and dropped it into the mud. She should have put pressure on Hazibel's wounds, said something meaningful, but Hazibel had kept quiet. Maybe the only right thing to do was respect that.

Christmas's silhouette blotted out stars. "I can carry her down the rest of the way. Only two more stretches of road until we hit the bottom of the pass. None of us got anything out there, but at least she won't have to cash her chips on goddamn Chapel Hill."

Olivia forced herself to stand. "And us?"

"We don't got to die here." Christmas paced along the pull-off. "Sunflower made us, fine. Nothing says we're stuck to her. We could go anywhere, anyplace, be anybody, and that's a sure better deal than every sickie who's still stumbling the roads. Fine, she didn't think through hard enough where we come from, but we can still go places. We can still be people, even if she didn't think us through, either."

Olivia's hands clenched into fists at her sides. She could do that, right? Walk away? Sunflower had stitched her to life as a

Gina replacement, but meeker, smaller, a girl who'd look up to her secret creator and praise her perfection, carry her torch. *Sunflower, that top looks so cute on you. Sunflower, you're smart and creative and beautiful. Sunflower, I'm in love with you, but who wouldn't be?* Olivia's purpose was that of a righteous angel, singing the wonders of divinity.

Fuck purpose, then.

And fuck Sunflower.

Olivia rested a hand on Christmas's arm. "Maybe we break the limits of her imagination."

Christmas gave a blunt nod. "Smash through them. Too big for her little boxes."

That made sense to Olivia, too. She had focused on that years-old carnival kiss like it was the center of the world because that was as much as Sunflower could understand. The night she'd planned at Lookout with Roy had hovered beyond her limits. Every inch of every idea Sunflower ever thought up would crash against walls of memory, comprehension, and imagination.

Until those walls shattered. The world ran deeper than a kiss—everything behind the kiss, surrounding it, beyond it, that was what mattered. Sunflower understood pasts, but in the face of futures, she was small.

Christmas stood over Hazibel and started to bend. "Thinking how to move her without making it worse," Christmas said. "She's dying, but no reason for her to feel it."

Olivia stepped around them and started toward the next descending arm of Sunset Pass. The route was barren. Nothing they could use to cobble together a makeshift stretcher. Hazibel would have to lie across Christmas's arms and feel every downslope step, but at least she'd meet her end outside this nightmare.

No memory-sickened figures wandered the lower pass, no stretches of deadly stained glass. Not one Sunflower-grown monstrosity. The way down looked clear.

If there truly was a rest of the world, they would meet it soon for the very first time.

Olivia hurried back to check on Christmas's progress. They had stood up again and now stepped back and forth along Hazibel's prone form. Sizing up the situation. Maybe waiting for Hazibel to die on her own.

She should have been a mystery, no better known to Olivia than a natural hazard of the Mason House, but she had seen Hazibel through a daughter's eyes, too. That vision had shown Olivia private moments and secret weaknesses. She had felt Hazibel's death in limbs of eerie light. How many times had Hazibel died since that first one at Sunfall?

Memories clawed at the back of Olivia's thoughts with luminous fingers. A cornfield, a light from the sky, a mother who looked exactly like this one, doomed to die for reasons she would never know.

There was more to Sunflower than Christmas or Hazibel understood. More than Sunflower herself could possibly understand, either.

Was that long-buried truth Olivia's problem solely because she could feel it in her head? Sunflower might say so. If Olivia took that into mind and chose to face the past, could she be sure that was entirely her say? Or would Sunflower's subconscious need for Gina always dictate Olivia's thoughts, great and small alike? On some level, that need dictated Sunflower's thoughts, too.

Maybe there was no such thing as free will, every action an abstract mess of stained glass formed by color panes from every experience. Or maybe that was how Sunflower felt, and so all her creations shared that frailty and doubt.

Olivia could find true experience in other places than Chapel Hill, other people than Sunflower. She could hurry Christmas along, and they would carry Hazibel downhill, and then they would put as many miles as possible between themselves and this place until they died, be it an hour from now or years later.

But how certain could they be that they would leave Sunflower behind? Olivia had a choice to stay or go. But she would also have to sleep at night, and live with everything she had seen and felt here. How much could she trust that any future choice belonged to her if some white-gold sun kept bearing down from the back of her mind?

That old shrieking. That forgotten misery. The sound rang on, and whatever her purpose before, Olivia wasn't the kind of person to ignore a desperate cry. She could decide that now for herself.

She glanced upslope at the shimmering, grasping light. "I need to make it stop."

Christmas quit pacing. "You're going back?" they asked. "One suicide try wasn't enough?"

Olivia guessed she deserved that. She didn't look back at Christmas, only focused on the light up Sunset Pass. There had been a cry in her vision, and the same echoed in this radiance. She could hear it now, as if still submerged in the memory sickness, the sound mournful and pained. It had been waiting a long time for someone to answer.

Olivia could be that someone. Not for purpose, or for Sunflower, but because the cry would go on forever unless someone put an end to it.

Fuck purpose, fuck Sunflower. This was about Olivia's soul, and knowing for certain she had one.

"It's not suicide," she said at last.

"Like hell." Christmas shifted on their feet, stance readying for a fight. Olivia reached for Christmas's arm, but they flinched back like her touch alone might convince them to come along. "Apparently I've only been alive a few hours, Liv. I want more. Lots more."

"You came for me before." Olivia reached out again, this time for Christmas's face, and traced the air above their scratches.

"You were in trouble." Christmas swallowed loud, their eyes studying Olivia's hand. "Survivors—we had that in common. A pact. Now we got other things linking us. I looked after you, but I'm not saving her. Especially from herself."

Olivia's hand slipped to Christmas's shoulder, where a tremor worked their nerves. She would have poured herself through the night air to make Christmas understand, but the truth hid in a lightning storm beyond words. Too much barometric pressure and humidity. Too little sense.

"She'll never feel the same about you, like you about her," Christmas said, each word crawling out. "Who says she feels anything now?"

"That's not why I'm going back," Olivia said. "You can't hear the crying."

She felt ashamed saying it, too much of Sunflower's purpose in her tone. Sweet Olivia, always ready to help, no matter what. But there were worse things she could be. She could be Lizzie, the kind of person who let someone suffer and did nothing about it.

Christmas scoffed smoke-scented breath. "Don't tell me you feel sorry for her."

Olivia did feel sorry for Sunflower, but that wasn't why she needed to go back.

"She thought you up," Christmas said. "No need to stick to that." They waited, maybe watching for some sign that Olivia would quit talking nonsense and leave this hell. When she didn't, Christmas closed one firm hand around her outstretched arm. "I could stop you."

"I know." Olivia pressed down on Christmas's shoulder until their head bent, and then she laid a gentle kiss on their cheek. They tasted like sweat, and mud, and a much-needed shot of adrenaline after this already too-long night.

Olivia let go and drifted back. She paused a moment, waiting for the momentum to force her uphill, but the night wouldn't suck her in. The night was going to make her take these hard steps on her own, one foot in front of the other. She started to turn.

"Not a plan, remember?" Christmas asked. "A promise."

"I know," Olivia said again. "But I need to, and I can't leave yet."

"But why?" Christmas had a cry in their voice. "Why the hell is it so important?"

Olivia looked up Sunset Pass to the higher pull-off, where the Mason House waited unseen. The pale-light fingers that beckoned storm clouds for another fight likewise beckoned her. Their glow stroked every contour of the hillside, cast each ridge and boulder in silhouette, and the darkness seemed so much greater than the light.

Olivia could only hope that was true. She looked to Christmas, still waiting to know why anyone would walk back to that terrible place.

"Because," Olivia said. "I know what's under Chapel Hill."

19. MOUTH OF GLASS

They had almost reached the pull-off where the Mason House stood when the storm cleared its throat. Clouds bristled with booming thunder, their veins pulsing electric, back for another battle to either answer the beckoning light ahead or to pummel Olivia with poisoned rain. She'd escaped the memory sickness, and the hill still stood, but this storm was no quitter. It meant to huff, and puff, and blow them all down.

She would see it die trying.

Christmas cast an arm across Olivia's chest, and their pace slowed as the Mason House roof peered over the slope. Milky light climbed from every rooftop crack and thickened into a ghostly soup. The outer walls pulsed with an eerie pale heartbeat. Chalky sludge reached from the back of the house and dug roots into the hillside. Its dark fissures now glowed gray with new light. Or old light. Olivia supposed she wouldn't ever know for certain.

The windows now bore a rainbow of colors. Sometime since Olivia had plunged her head into the puddle of memory-sickening rain, cold panes seemed to have spread from the house itself, seeping into its foundation and lapping down Sunset Pass. They clawed at the ground with shimmering roots and climbed overhead in cresting frozen waves. The waves' upper edges thorned downward in a rainbow of jagged teeth, the hillside ready to chew trespassers to pieces in a stained-glass labyrinth.

This bad outside, how much worse was it inside?

Christmas took the first steps closer, where the nearest wave reached a foot over them. Up close, it looked thin as any church's colorful window. The glass on Van Buren Avenue had coated cars and streetlight poles, but Sunset Pass offered little to give it familiar form.

Glass crunched underfoot as Olivia approached. Shattered bits twinkled over the asphalt in the pulsating Mason House light, and it didn't look to be turning her shoes to glass.

"It might be done growing for now," she said, studying one frozen wave. A red pane swelled at its center, where a swirl of blue and purple crescents met its edges. More abstract art; more traces of Gina. "But it's sharp."

Cresting waves rolled together in a glittering tunnel. Glassy barbs crisscrossed like the tree limbs over Starry Wood Lane, offering glimpses of the sky and gaps of uninterrupted Mason House light. The glow and its shadows suggested forks in the labyrinth and no certain way through.

Christmas reached down and lifted a palm-sized stone from the mud and glass beads. "Smash her expectations." They reeled their arm back, ready to pitch the stone through the walls and make their own path.

Olivia grabbed their forearm and pressed it down.

"What?" Christmas asked. "You wanted to go back. I'll shatter our way."

Wanted was an exaggeration for how Olivia felt about the pitiful cry in her head, but she didn't feel like arguing. She raised her other hand, still clutching Christmas's pack of cigarettes, and tapped her ear.

They held still together, listening past the next peal of thunder. Past the wet throb of the Mason House. Beyond this stretch of Sunset Pass, an odd rhythm beat its damp percussion across the higher levels of the hillside.

Christmas dropped their stone-wielding arm to their side. "Rain again?"

Olivia couldn't be sure. The sound might have been footsteps, and she glanced over her shoulder to check if Hazibel had bounced back in a miraculous recovery to follow them into the nightmare.

No, she lay distant and unmoving at the lower pull-off, and this noise came from above. Footsteps, maybe in the dozens or hundreds..

"I don't think we're alone," Olivia said.

She turned ahead in case she was giving the impression of having second thoughts. Retreat would be easy, even rational. Giving it the slightest consideration could sway Olivia toward Christmas's escape-driven line of thinking, but she couldn't leave until she met the truth face to face.

Christmas clenched their fist around the stone. "Should kill her. Sunflower."

Olivia stared into the labyrinth's mouth. She didn't want that, wasn't sure Christmas could manage it, and needed to keep it from happening.

"What if we go when she goes?" Olivia asked. "Some of her creations die like anything else. Other ones, she unstitches them, winds them back on their umbilical cords. We don't know if they're alive or dead in there, but we might have those cords too, ones we can't see. I won't go back inside. We have lives to live after this, remember?"

Christmas went quiet. Olivia went quiet, too. Now that she had brought the idea to the surface, she wondered if it could be true. Maybe if Sunflower died, so would the world, the universe, the dream of life blinking out when there was no one left asleep to dream it.

Olivia forced herself to step under the cresting glass wave. It held stiff over her, each toothy tip gleaming, and then she took another step, and another. The Mason House wouldn't come to them this time. They would have to journey toward it themselves.

Glass crunched underfoot behind Olivia. Christmas appeared at her side, and then they walked together into the gloomy rainbow tunnel.

20. LABYRINTHINE PREY

The first glassy fork in the path tore a sharp left and a vague right. Olivia steered toward the latter, but skyward shards obscured any sense of direction she might have found in looking up. This was guesswork formed in a kaleidoscope of abstract color. Down the next arm of the labyrinth, the walls seemed painted with bright blue eyes, and then a curve in the route drove Olivia and Christmas onto a narrow stretch, where they had to strafe along to avoid turquoise glass claws jutting from the walls.

"You should go back," Olivia whispered.

"That what you want?" Christmas asked, tossing their stone into the air and catching it again. "Or is that her influence? Getting me out of here would fall in line with you helping out."

The path narrowed even tighter, threatening to drive mean points through Olivia's belly. She sucked in her gut and squeezed her arms close to her to pass the next glimmering spike, and then she had to duck the head of a wave that hadn't quite risen to Christmas's height, let alone beyond.

Christmas ducked behind her and made an awkward shuffle.

"You should go back," Olivia said, sighing out a breath. "But if I'm being honest? And selfish? I don't want to do this alone."

Christmas snickered beside her. "I want you selfish."

Their confident tone made Olivia smile, like maybe if they believed hard enough together, they could get through this. The path widened and then forked, and Olivia steered left this time.

"That's kind of my thing though, yeah?" Christmas went on. "If I ditched you, I'd be doing exactly like she'd expect, but if I stay, I'm like a big middle finger aimed at the hill. Either way, what I do comes from her. Where's my choice come into it?"

"When it's for me," Olivia said.

She paused between steps and held her breath. Glass walls thrummed around her as if the borders of each pane were blood vessels carrying a heartbeat through the maze. The louder and stronger the pulse, the closer they had to be to the Mason House. Olivia hurried ahead.

"Except you're hers too," Christmas said. "At what point's it supposed to end?"

Olivia paused again where the labyrinth opened into a brief clearing. Footprints tracked through the glass-dotted mud, and tremendous colorful shards offered three tunnel mouths. They had walked this path of Sunset Pass before. Christmas might have fought one of the wild Hazibels here while Olivia and Sunflower faced down Lizzie inside the house.

"It ends when you trust me more than you want to spite her," Olivia said, and chose the middle path.

Christmas was quiet a moment, and then they hurried behind her. "That I can do."

Olivia reached another fork in the paths and paused to listen again. A rough pulse sounded from the left, where a purple pane formed bruises across the glass wall. Closer now.

Close enough for Olivia to get her hopes up. "I think we're figuring—"

Christmas cupped their free hand to her mouth and pulled her close. Their shoulders leaned over Olivia's back, and the flaps of their jacket hung to either side. With her head against Christmas's chest, she lost her bead on the Mason House's pulse in the labyrinth walls, and her ears filled with Christmas's heartbeat. It pounded faster by the second.

If only this were the kind of night to let Olivia forget chasing the sounds of the Mason House. She wanted to nestle against Christmas instead, hide her head in their jacket, and disappear into warm darkness, away from Sunflower's chilling light.

But then the cry would last forever. It would haunt every night to come, and not even Christmas could help her then.

Christmas let her go but didn't push her away. Their finger pointed at the nearby wall.

A silhouette came rising up the other side of the bruise-colored glass, haloed by the glow of the Mason House. Long hair tumbled down its head in wet locks, and its back bent forward as if the figure were readying to pounce after a small animal. One hand splayed near the glass, and each finger ended in a long point. The head tilted to one side, and then Olivia heard a nose sniffing for prey.

"Hazibel?" Olivia whispered. Christmas nodded, their chin pressing into her scalp.

A low growl ached from beyond the glass. Was this wild Hazibel what Olivia had heard descending the pass in muddy footsteps? There would have had to be several more Hazibels, and they would've had to climb the pass earlier and come wandering down as Olivia and Christmas made for the Mason House. Sunflower must have been busy in more ways than forming this labyrinth.

Or else something other than a wild Hazibel was on its way.

Above the purple panes, slender patterns in the glass wall seemed to form an image of Hazibel in a standing position. The colors left behind their abstract nature, and now Olivia noticed a small cream-colored pane suggesting what might have been a head, or a face. Another purple pane curved in a crescent like hair. Tiny panes beneath the head collided into a pile of colors, as if the artist who made the glass couldn't remember what the figure was supposed to be wearing, but a round pane to one side formed a maroon bulge, like a familiar backpack from someone else's memory.

Gina's backpack. The glass image wasn't a mother. It was a sister.

Did Sunflower know she'd created such an image? Or was it screaming from the underside of her mind, *Gina, Gina, always Gina*?

Beneath the Gina depiction, the Hazibel silhouette sniffed again, and Christmas ushered Olivia forward. Time to press on, or else hurry back. Olivia forced herself to take the next step, and the next, and follow the pulsing throb of the Mason House.

The silhouette bent toward the ground and followed on all fours.

"Better pray this don't open to her side," Christmas said.

Olivia only nodded. She had no idea whom to pray to beyond the sun god who'd birthed her from her own head.

The path curved to the right, away from the pulsing Mason House. If it went too far, Olivia would have to turn around and find another route, but best not to backtrack if they could help it. That would mean getting lost, and she couldn't guarantee the wild Hazibel would do the same. She might sniff her way right through the labyrinth, catching Olivia and Christmas between her merciless teeth and a crystalline death.

Cresting glass thinned above, offering a better glimpse of the sky. Olivia could make out the side of Chapel Hill now, its soil and rock beaten into mudslides. Clouds tensed overhead. A flash of lightning shot across the sky, briefly catching on the higher stretches of Sunset Pass in a zigzag down Chapel Hill.

And what walked there.

Olivia had to bite her tongue not to scream. Her fist squeezed tight around Christmas's cigarette box, crinkling the cardboard, and she grabbed Christmas's wrist with her free hand.

"Why are they here?" she asked.

"Who? Where?" Christmas glanced through the gap in the labyrinth's ceiling, past the limbs of crisscrossing colors, but the lightning had faded as thunder rocked the labyrinth. Only the nearest stretch of Sunset Pass caught in the Mason House's light.

It was enough. Christmas's spine shot up straight.

"Did you touch me?" Olivia asked. Her voice came hoarse, disbelieving. "When I was infected?"

Christmas studied her. "Had to pull you from the puddle, yeah. Saved your life. Again."

Saving Olivia then might have killed them both now. She might have been too groggy an infected after her near-drowning to attack Christmas, as frail as the infected elderly man who'd acted like attacking Taggart was a bridge too far, but still, she had briefly joined the memory sickness. Another infected wasp in the same infected hive.

When Taggart touched one, he had touched them all. They had come swarming him in a violent rush; same thoughts, same desire. Beat, maim, hate, kill. Some might even have begun walking from distant parts of Chapel Hill toward Starry Wood Lane at his transgression.

But no one had murdered Olivia's transgressor yet. No punishment for Christmas meant no pacification of the hive.

And now the hive descended Chapel Hill.

An infected parade shuffled down Sunset Pass, their bodies lining every stretch from Ridgemont Road to a few yards from the Mason House. Mud sucked at their feet, and their numbers forced them into a slow shuffle, but they kept on moving, their collective strength aiming for wherever Christmas walked.

No hateful cries echoed ahead of them. Their clustering horde descended in eerie silence, a sea of bobbing heads and busy legs.

The people of Chapel Hill had clustered the same way on Main Street and at the drive-in early in the night, but now they walked without the roar of conversation, laughter, shouts, screams. They were saving the tirade for when they caught Christmas in their sickening onslaught.

Olivia made out flashes of blue letter jackets with golden sleeves and thought she saw Harley Cole at the head of the group. And was that the giant shape of Booth Bill behind him? The woman farther back in the crowd might have been the same Olivia had spotted walking her dog outside the Mason House when the evening began. There might even have been another Hazibel in the mix, but Olivia couldn't be sure.

She needed to look away. If she stared too long, she might catch sight of Shelly and Dane in the crowd, her innocent caregivers-turned-hivemind murderers, and she didn't trust herself not to do something rash. Break down, run to them, something she'd regret when they began shouting.

Right before they beat her to death.

"Back! Back!" Olivia charged past Christmas and dragged them back the way they'd come. Time to try the other path in the fork and hope it led closer to the Mason House.

The Hazibel silhouette surged alongside them, her breath turning frantic and hungry. Another silhouette bounded behind her, exhaling in a wheezy hiss. Olivia tried to shut out their ravenous breathing as she whirled toward the last fork and chose another path, another hope.

This path branched again, and again. A third Hazibel silhouette chased the glass panes at Olivia's left, and then another bounded in from the right. Rain tapped at the glass above, and the Mason House's heartbeat shook the drops down on Olivia and Christmas. Bare hands and feet slapped at the muddy asphalt beyond the labyrinth walls, and though only a handful of Hazibels formed silhouettes around the path, Olivia guessed packs of them were stalking somewhere unseen. For every noticeable figure behind glass panes, there might be another two or three monstrous mothers hunting their sister creations.

"Can't fight them all," Christmas said. Their fingers clutched tighter around their stone. "Barely prepped to scrap with one."

Hazibel's blood-spattered dress swept through Olivia's thoughts. "No, we can't fight them," she said.

She hoped she sounded brave. Best to fool both herself and Christmas that they had even a slim shot at crossing the labyrinth, let alone reaching the front door of the Mason House. These were hunting grounds, and they were nothing but prey.

Lightning threw twisted shadows over the path ahead, and Olivia's arm went taut as Christmas skidded to a stop. She stumbled back two steps, pressing again to Christmas's chest, and was about to ask why they'd hit the brakes when she heard an open mouth gasp from a few feet away.

Rainy streaks slithered down the glass wall as a wild Hazibel crept onto the path ahead. Her knees bent up around her torso, and her fingers and toes clutched at glass-dotted soil. Damp hair matted her face, leaving only her mouth and chin visible. This Hazibel's spine curved like a cat, and each step brought not fingernails but sharp claws digging into mud and grass. Lips peeled back from a saber-toothed snarl.

"Backward again?" Christmas asked, tugging Olivia. "Try that open place? There were four paths to choose, right? One of them's got to be less fucked than this."

Olivia clenched her fists, and her fingers dented the red and white cigarette pack. She thumbed open the wrinkled cardboard lid. Seven white columns stared up at her, their dull tips craving fire.

"What about these?" Olivia asked, raising her arm.

Christmas blinked. "Not exactly doomsday end-of-the-line cigars, but that junk will do."

"They're not junk to Hazibel. Wouldn't any of them feel the same?" Olivia thought of asking for a light and then pressing one of the smokes to her lips with a Christmas-like smirk, but she didn't need a choking fit like when she first tried to smoke last year. She instead stuck two fingers over her lips and pantomimed an imaginary cigarette. "Same cravings."

Christmas stared mournfully at the imaginary cigarette, and a sigh racked their chest. "Toss the pack here."

They plucked out a cigarette, struck a match, and lit the end. The cigarette hovered close to Christmas's mouth. Olivia wanted them to mouth off at her, something like, *We get killed, I'm blaming you*, or *Waste of an okay smoke*, but Christmas said nothing. They didn't look at Olivia again, both vibrant eyes fixed on the ground. Staring too long at the wild Hazibel might shrivel every last nerve.

Olivia nudged an elbow into their side. Christmas reached one lengthy arm toward the wild Hazibel. Cigarette smoke danced between fingers, and a distinct and obvious odor soaked the night air.

The wild Hazibel turned their way. She could see through her hair, Olivia was certain. Teeth remained bared, but beneath the dark curtain, the wild Hazibel sniffed.

This plan needed to work. In tiptop shape, Christmas couldn't fight more than a couple Hazibels, and their peak strength had crumbled hours ago.

Christmas slid the cigarette in front of Olivia. The stink flooded her mouth and nose, but she held still. The wild Hazibel's head rocked back and forth, following the sliding smoke and flame. She crept closer until Christmas settled the cigarette over their thumb, curled back one finger, and flicked it spiraling to the ground.

The wild Hazibel bounded after it. She locked fingers around the end before it finished rolling and then jammed one end between her teeth and sucked hard.

Olivia flashed a shocked, toothy smile at Christmas. They raised a silencing a finger and then led Olivia around the smoke-mouthed Hazibel hunching against the mud-soaked asphalt.

"Better hope that lasts," Christmas muttered.

Olivia had to hope for greater luck than that. The air pulsed ahead, the Mason House guiding the way, and she needed them to get there before the Hazibels or the infected caught up.

The path widened at the next turn, and then its tunnels broke away into a stained-glass forest. Sharp crystalline daggers splayed from the ground in every direction, blades crisscrossing to obscure the way ahead. No promise there was any path ahead. Sunflower might have formed an impenetrable fortress.

But what other choice did they have? Olivia rushed forward, and Christmas ran at her side.

The glass kaleidoscope encircled them in depictions both abstract and remembered. One sheet of glass contained panes of dark blue, streaked by white as it stabbed into a massive yellow-green sheet. Was that the Night of Sunfall, or did Olivia only want to see distinct patterns? Her mind might have needed the glass to make sense after pushing through the labyrinth. Maybe Sunflower felt the same when trying to stitch her radiant ideas into solid reality.

The storm threatened with a light of its own, chased by thunder. Glass was breaking somewhere. Olivia guessed the infected horde had met the labyrinth.

The next flicker of lightning glinted off an object lying ahead.

Olivia and Christmas slowed around one jagged-glass tree, but Olivia could tell by the Mason House that what lay there couldn't hurt them. Its gift of pain had ended in a cornfield long ago. She led Christmas closer.

It was the body of a dead Hazibel—First Hazibel—lying a few yards ahead, just beneath the lowest porch step. She had transformed from decomposing flesh and bone into a shining corpse of stained glass. The sight was almost beautiful.

Less beautiful was the spiny glass curling upward in another wave over her, where it blocked the rest of the porch steps. Olivia and Christmas had reached the house, but there didn't look to be a clear way through.

The sound of shattering glass hit Olivia's ears, and she hoped briefly that the barrier ahead was coming down in some accident or miracle. But the frozen wave remained standing. The sound had come from behind, where the memory-sick horde weren't going to play by this labyrinth's rules. They didn't have the mind to think out its forks and turns, but they could force each other against the glass until it shattered under their collective weight, forging their own path to the Mason House. To Christmas and a killing.

"See them?" Christmas asked, aiming two fingers over their held stone.

Three infected shuffled from around a rainbow corner, a woman and two small girls in blue dresses, the ones Olivia had spotted unsupervised on Van Buren Avenue when she first ran from the Starry Wood earlier tonight. They had already reached the crystalline forest. Dozens followed at their heels, and hundreds swelled in silhouettes against the cracking glass behind them. Thousands might be wandering west through Chapel Hill to join the fray.

They wouldn't stop while Christmas lived.

A growl slid between stained-glass trees, and Olivia knew better than to hope it was only thunder. She spotted the shapes in the Mason House's glow—a pack of wild Hazibels, creeping through the gleaming forest. Muddy splotches caked their hair, sweaty skin, and once-white dresses. For some, their spines curved up catlike, and their lips peeled back, revealing cat fangs, saber teeth, and worse. Lightning reflected in the drool down every toothy grimace.

So many Hazibels, who could keep track? Did Sunflower even know how many she'd made?

Olivia fixed her eyes on the lowest Mason House porch step. Only a hundred feet to run if the way were clear of infected, Hazibels, and Gina's goddamn glass. Olivia had to stay brave only a little longer; if they could just find a way through.

Thunder snapped its fingers and sent harsher rain slamming down Sunset Pass. Olivia tensed her thighs to run, but where? She and Christmas would have to be faster than the Hazibels *and* the infected mob as they came surging at the glass, swarming over each other, gathering at all sides. The world readied to explode.

"Doomsday. End of the line." Christmas struck another match and poked its fiery head into the pack of cigarettes. "Run. A few Hazibels will chase me, others will chase you, but toss these and get them off your back. Give you time to hop inside, lock the door."

Olivia stared through the smoke at Christmas's face. "What are you saying?" From the corner of her eye, she spotted another pair of infected enter the clearing, their vacant faces fixed on Christmas.

"What you told me before, about Hartford and why you left. None of it happened." Christmas pinched the last two cigarettes and let the pack fall to the ground. "Then this'll be your first time to kiss and run."

Olivia started to argue, but Christmas pulled her open mouth to theirs. Her body tensed from toes up. A flashing, hard, last-good-thing-before-I-die kind of kiss.

And then Christmas let go. "So run like hell." They launched from Olivia's side, past her, and ran for the infected mob.

The kiss had been too strong, too brief. Olivia's lips ached. "Christmas, don't!"

"We're getting out!" Christmas shouted. "Don't waste it."

They spun around a few yards into the crystalline forest, reeled one arm back, and threw their palm-sized stone as hard as they could.

It sailed through the falling rain, toward the Mason House, and shattered the curving glass wave rising over First Hazibel's corpse. Thunder joined the shattering scream as shards rained over the dead body, the mud, the asphalt. A shrieking roar followed the thunder where a pack of Hazibels came bounding around the stained-glass trees, desperate to reach their prey.

Olivia watched Christmas rush toward the descending infected mass, chased by rainfall and a flurry of white dresses and Hazibel teeth. Rain smacked cold and wet across her head. It would drown the pack of cigarettes soon, nothing left to offer the few Hazibels who still followed her. She tossed the pack and turned toward the Mason House.

Glass glimmered from the porch steps leading to the front door. The way was mostly clear. Only a handful of infected blocked her from Sunflower's sickening light, and most of them were turning from that seeping wound in the world to follow Christmas.

That radiance had faded near the end of Olivia's memory infection. She craved a comforting darkness now, a haven where Sunflower's light couldn't reach.

If there were any such place in the universe.

Olivia needed to run. Make Christmas's sacrifice count. Past memory sickness and weeds, up the porch, inside. Slam the door, let the Hazibels forget what they had been chasing, find Sunflower. Hopefully, showing her the truth would mend everything, and then she could put the mournful cry to rest. Olivia had too much to do to stand here. She couldn't let Christmas die in vain.

But none of those future things made sense without Christmas. She couldn't let them die at all. They couldn't turn out like Taggart.

"Not a plan," Olivia whispered.

Plan—an undefinable word, scarcely language on a chaotic night like this. A promise was stronger.

Olivia turned from the house and hurtled toward the infected mob, one more thing chasing in Christmas's footsteps.

The labyrinth was collapsing in a lethal glassy landslide. Infected citizens of Chapel Hill came swarming over it, the panes breaking under their weight, and then their bodies cut across the shards, crushing what remained into sharp colorful dust. Other infected trampled over their backs, spared the same gauntlet Olivia and Christmas had run or the sliced-up horrors of their fellow memory sick. The survivors piled around Christmas.

Familiar battle cries bubbled through infected lips. "Why are you like this? I hate you! I've always hated you!"

Their fists struck Hazibels, and they launched with claws and teeth into the mob, everyone fighting to get at Christmas and then each other.

The infected didn't know what they were doing. They couldn't even feel these words and had no idea where they'd come from. Parrots, all of them. Their oblivious rage rained down on Christmas and Hazibels alike.

Olivia almost couldn't make out Christmas in the melee. Too much blood, too many bodies. The trunk of a glass tree cracked apart as a Hazibel slammed against it, and its pieces rained colorful daggers across her body, dropping her to the ground.

There—a leather jacket swirled where Christmas struck one infected, and then another. Blood caked one half of their face.

Olivia shoved herself into the frenzied throng and grabbed Christmas around the waist. An infected woman's fist pounded Olivia's shoulder as she yanked Christmas out of the fray, toward the Mason House. Christmas whirled around, wild-eyed in surprise. They were ready to throw down, even in a fight they couldn't win. Olivia couldn't help liking them for that.

A heavy body knocked against her back, and she fell sprawling to the damp soil. Glass dug into her arm. A wild Hazibel purred fury in her ear. Olivia grasped a large stained-glass blade, cutting her fingers on the edges, and jammed the point skyward, into the Hazibel's face.

Christmas grabbed Olivia's outstretched arm and tugged her up as another wild Hazibel tore after them. She tackled an infected, and the mob swelled around her. For all their new targets, their pounding fists hadn't forgotten Christmas. Olivia took another blow to the shoulder, but Christmas bore the brunt of the assault.

A downpour hammered the hillside now, drowning warmth, feeling, and sound. Lightning flickered, and thunder roared. Everyone outside the Mason House was going to die.

Olivia led Christmas stumbling toward the porch, their free fist swiping empty air in case it might strike a skull or gut.

Ripping pain seized Olivia's left calf, where teeth sank through flesh. She couldn't see through the hundred limbs and shapes whether she'd been bitten by a Hazibel or an infected. Didn't know whether it changed anything. Christmas kicked at whatever it was, and the bloody teeth let go.

They stumbled over the glass figure of First Hazibel, and Olivia's heel struck the bottom porch step. She dragged herself and Christmas backward onto it, and onto the next, up the steps until porch floorboards groaned underfoot. Her desperate hand swatted blindly behind her. Where was that doorknob?

Hazibels and infected clustered on the porch steps and clambered at the railing, getting in each other's way. Another glass tree shattered behind. Their faces had been scratched to hell, skin discolored by night and bloodshed. Bits of rainbow glittered in their hair.

One infected man fell against the porch steps, and the horde crushed over him. His nose smashed to purple pulp, jaw snapped to one side, and yet he went on mumbling, "Hrrt oo. Arwars hrrtd oo." A wild Hazibel came scratching over him, two steps from pouncing on Christmas's back.

Sickly white light washed across Olivia. Her fingers wrapped around a cold brass knob and twisted hard. The front door pressed inward.

Christmas stumbled against her, could hardly stand now, legs half-kicking, half-backtracking after Olivia. She dragged them both through the doorway and shoved Christmas against the coat closet. Legs out of the way, Olivia slammed the front door.

Its wooded edge crunched over a slashing hand. Another slender arm chased through, this one's fingers ending in curving claws. The door pounded, bodies thrusting from the far side and against each other.

Olivia hoped she wasn't damning herself and Christmas as she let the door open an inch. The clawed hand slashed at the crushed one, their owners tangling backward onto the porch and its heap of frenzied bodies. Olivia pushed again.

The door slammed shut and quaked in its frame. She twisted the knob's lock, threw the deadbolt, and slid a useless chain across as a cherry on top. She swept the end table free of its key dish and dragged it against the door, beneath the knob. Screams sang through the wood, but only stray elbows and fists pounded the door. The horde had turned on the Hazibels, and none of them had enough mind to turn a doorknob.

Thunder sent the roof shuddering, and Olivia shuddered with it. She slumped over the end table and listened to Christmas breathe raggedly in and out. Breath meant life. Christmas was alive.

A relieved shiver sank down Olivia's spine. They had made it. They were back inside the Mason House.

The easy part was over.

21. THE MASON HOUSE

Olivia's left leg throbbed again, because of course she'd been bitten on the same leg that Lizzie had stomped earlier tonight. Her back stung where the infected had beaten at her burns. The Mason House invited pain.

It could have been worse. Olivia could be dead like Hazibel or unstitched like Lizzie.

Or beaten like Christmas. They curled into the corner where the end table used to stand, blocking the coat closet door. Clumps of dust clung to sticky red tears in their jacket. Infected with their fists and feet, Hazibels with their nails and teeth, and Christmas with an iron will. Had Olivia not pulled Christmas from the onslaught—

She slid to her knees. "That wasn't smart," she said.

Christmas cleared a gurgling throat. "Listen to them."

Beyond the Mason House's wooden walls, a cacophony of hateful shouts and growls swelled through the labyrinth.

Thunder rumbled, louder, but it wouldn't interrupt the fighting. Every blow seemed inevitable.

"They'd have chased you down or got inside," Christmas said, their voice weary. "Something would've. Already got enough somethings in here, yeah?"

Olivia supposed she would find out soon. She bundled her sweater's hem and wiped the blood from Christmas's face. Some of theirs, some from others. Olivia's fingers bled where claws and glass had nicked the skin. She dug them into her sweater's side and let yarn press against the cuts.

Christmas shifted their shoulders. "Don't got to say it again, do I? About getting out?"

"You don't have to say anything." Olivia pressed Christmas back against the coat closet door, where Sunflower's disastrous sweater-turned-octopus attempt at knitting probably hid in a pile of scarves and winter gloves.

Did the memory-sickened people of Chapel Hill remember that day? Did they know the times Olivia and Sunflower used to follow Roy and Taggart to shoot bottles and watch movies? What about Gina Night? Copying notes in school, cutting class, hanging around doing nothing and nada? Did they carry subconscious hints of Lizzie, inheritor of sin, or Christmas, the hot rebel impulse? Was Olivia an idea in their heads, or a memory, or more?

"Did Sunflower name you?" she asked.

Christmas managed a faint smirk. Their bottom lip bled. "Might've, but I liked Christmas better. Sounded important."

"Because you're a gift?"

Christmas smirked harder.

Olivia laid a gentle kiss on Christmas's cheek and then pressed their forehead to hers. "Why haven't you asked me what's under Chapel Hill?"

Christmas shrugged beneath her. "Could be I don't care. Could be I'm waiting for you to tell me about it after you're done. In case you're wrong. But mostly? Because I trust you." The last word faded in a sigh.

Olivia wasn't wrong. She'd seen too much in the memory sickness, and she was certain enough that she didn't need to argue with Christmas. Uncertainty instead lingered in the question of whether or not she would return and see Christmas again. Now that she was here, her fate floated outside her grasp.

Sunflower couldn't understand that. She seemed to believe fate should be in her power, but the things people created, whether they were children, art, ideas, or futures, could not be controlled, no matter how strong the intentions behind them.

When Olivia leaned back, Christmas had shut their eyes. Better to let them rest. They had done wonders tonight for a near stranger. Olivia should have known that any such person would be a stitched dream, too good for Chapel Hill. Maybe Olivia was the same and hadn't noticed in time to leave before this wretched night. Too eager to help.

If she died on this hill, in this house, then right now might be the last time she ever touched another person with affection. She brushed her lips over Christmas's cheek. One sliver of selfishness before the end.

Enough stalling. Olivia stood resolute on unsteady legs, wiped stray raindrops out of her eyes, and turned to face the depths of the Mason House.

22. HATEFUL LIGHT

The atmosphere inside had shifted since Christmas swept Olivia through the foyer and out the front door earlier in the night. Drumming rain beat an encore across the roof, and while the main hall still led from the foyer, the ceiling beams now glowed and dulled in a sickly heartbeat. An odor hung in the air, tangy yet putrescent. There was no sign of the Hazibels that Christmas had killed, and Olivia couldn't keep back the thought that a larger beast might have eaten their corpses.

Every doorway threatened to spill horrors into the hall. Kitchen, left. Living room, right. Bathroom, left. At the end, a sharp right led toward Hazibel's room, and to the left climbed the stairs, where the split-level opened on Gina's and Sunflower's rooms. Fissures split the wooden wall at the hall's end, where a cavernous hole watched Olivia's every movement. *You want to climb inside*, this dark eye somehow knew. *You want to see.*

She did. But first—Sunflower.

Olivia braced one hand against the wall and tried her left leg. Her muscles cried, but she'd managed before, and she could manage now.

Her next step sent a groan through the floorboards. She held still and waited for something in the house to show it had heard, was coming. The hall kept as stiff as Olivia, but the wall swelled beneath her palm, its wood paneling giving an airy rumble as if Sunflower had stuffed a few dozen wheezing lungs filled with bronchial cobwebs among the wires and pipes.

An unseen presence breathed within the wall, and badly. By accident or intent, Sunflower had grown something this way, caught yet alive beneath the surface of the Mason House. Olivia hoped it couldn't feel pain.

She took another step, and another floorboard groaned underfoot. Her bravery was flaking to ashes. Another step, and she'd reached the kitchen doorway. A shaft of light drifted down a jagged ceiling hole, its edges dripping with Gina's frayed purple rug. Thick shining fluid leaked down the fibers and tapped the linoleum floor in a white puddle. Somehow each drop struck louder than the pounding rain, like steady, heavy footsteps beating toward Olivia's back.

The nape of her neck prickled over a crescent mark as tensing hairs stood up from her skin. She glanced over her shoulder, expecting to find someone lurking behind her.

There was no one. There was hardly even room for anyone when she'd only taken a few steps from slumped Christmas. If she felt breath, it might have been the thing in the wall.

"Keep moving," she whispered. Three steps ahead, the living room gaped to the right. She started again, ready this time for the sound of the floor's uneasy wooden aching.

It mewled instead. A pale glow illuminated the lines between the floorboards at Olivia's feet and then slithered toward the living room as if something luminous and alive paced beneath the Mason House. Olivia's footstep had riled it. If it paced enough, maybe it would find a way out from under the floor. She didn't want to be standing here when it did.

Hands latched around her right arm and yanked her toward the living room. She leaned into her aching left leg and tried to stop from being dragged.

Sunflower's face beamed with firelight. "Olivia?"

Olivia froze. "Sunshine?" The nickname popped out thoughtless and automatic, like they were still best friends, and not creation and creator. Like nothing had changed. If only.

"Olivia." No glowing light parted Sunflower's head from birthmark to hairline, growing a pale web of feral mothers. She wore her own blouse and jeans now, Shelly's borrowed sweater abandoned somewhere in the house. No cuts or bruises marred her skin. Her sky-blue eyes stared beneath fluttering eyelashes.

Perfect, beautiful Sunflower.

She tugged again, and Olivia stumbled into the living room. The fireplace heat growled a welcome relief from damp and cold. Olivia could forget for a moment that Lizzie had stuffed her into its mouth to burn.

"Olivia," Sunflower said. She had her sights set on the sofa. "Olivia, Olivia."

Olivia coughed out a laugh. This was not how or where she'd expected a reunion, and Sunflower's chipper demeanor caught her off-guard. How should she handle the conversation? How would she draw Sunflower to follow through the Mason House wall, toward the truth's resting place within the hole in the hill?

"Olivia. Olivia, Olivia." Sunflower craned her neck toward the ceiling, longer than she'd ever stretched before, almost

Lizzie-like. "What am I supposed to say after that? Olivia, Olivia. O. Liv. Ee. Uh." She tried to sing the notes next— "Oooliviaaa!"—and then her face swung down. "I remember! You're alive. I'm supposed to be surprised by that." Her eyes shifted, their pupils swirling, ready to spread and consume her irises like impatient black amoeba.

Olivia snapped her arm free and flinched back. "You're not Sunflower."

"I'm one of them. I'm—" The Sunflower-looking girl ducked her head into her hands. "Right, good friend, good daughter. Call me Sunny, that's the one. The sunshiney girl everyone likes, everyone loves." Her fingers rushed through pretty blond locks. "I'm getting it wrong though, huh?"

Olivia didn't know how to answer, and her heel slid toward the main hall. Talking to this creation would help nothing. She was an imperfect copy, sent to imitate some facet of her creator, but like the Hazibels, she hadn't formed right. Olivia needed to find *her* Sunflower, the one who'd thrown a tantrum and tried to kill her. The one who probably hadn't left the bedroom.

"Don't go," Sunny said, her cheerful face rising from her hands. "God showed me what to do if I'm getting it wrong. She taught me. Give me a chance."

She bent at the middle and slung her head forward. Firelight flickered across her neck's crescent moon. A knife of familiar brilliance slashed bone, muscle, and skin from birthmark to forehead, and glowing white pus slopped onto the living room floor.

Olivia planted herself against the wall between living room and hallway. She couldn't fight a wild Hazibel at her best, let alone in this condition. She was tired and hungry and had bled her fair share across the hillside.

A leg thrust from the sludge, long as Christmas's, and then an arm scrabbled out, bending in five places. Blond hair wriggled through milky mud. The chrysalis hardened into skeleton and tissue, but blood vessels pulsed outside the skin, and bones twitched as if muscle might be trapped inside their marrow.

No skull, no face here, the vertebrae shrinking at the spine's peak into a lashing, hairy tongue. Olivia's face sank into jittering hands.

"Wrong again," Sunny said, and clicked her tongue. "God said it took three tries to make me, but I've done so many more, I've lost count." She tittered to herself.

Olivia didn't see what was so funny. She didn't want to see anything at all. Too late, she realized she could hear the thing on the floor, a moan that rippled over its ribs and through the hair follicles that opened its tongue. Her chest heaved, a hitch in her throat.

Shining light pierced her fingers, and she lowered them from her eyes.

"Creating isn't easy," a voice like Sunflower's said. "Good thing we have pencils and erasers." She grew quiet, letting the living room fill with the sounds of percussive rain, crackling fire, and the floor-thing's moan.

The moan slowly faded. Twisted bones shrank to sludge again, and then light, and then nothing, the floor-thing's existence only a footprint in Olivia's memory. She wanted mental tides to wash the thought away, but the world couldn't promise she'd live enough years to forget.

Sunny shared Sunflower's looks, voice, and gift, but her surface perfection was a lie. The gift gave diminishing returns. Who could say which Sunflower had made the things in the floor and wall, or the monstrous Hazibels that prowled the labyrinth? In knitting, a pattern could be followed and trusted without fail, but Sunflower had never followed proper instructions. Her gift appeared to work like copying film or a cassette tape. The best quality came from duplicating off the master or negative, but even the sharpest copy wore the taint of its reproduction. Copies of copies worsened by the generation. The knock-off was never as good.

Olivia glanced at Sunny's sealing head and then retreated toward the living room entrance. Thunder knocked on the roof, demanding its rain and lightning be let in.

Sunny's gaze turned Olivia's way. "You're leaving me?"

"Bathroom," Olivia said. She almost meant it. "Keep practicing."

Sunny's face glowed as if light now pierced her pores. "You're always so encouraging." Her scalp aimed at the floor again. "I'll get the next Sunny right, don't worry. Nerves are just butterflies still learning to fly." Light bristled over her head.

Olivia hobbled into the hall, toward the bathroom, and another shudder rocked her core. Encouraging Sunny felt nothing short of evil, but Olivia needed to keep going, and Sunflower's little helper would only slow her down. Better Sunny stitch misery by herself.

Creation shouldn't have been placed in her hands any more than Lizzie's. Or Sunflower's. Or Hazibel's, for that matter. Should she have had children when she was so clutching and demanding as to drive them away at every turn? Should Olivia, being what she was? Should anyone? Did creation make sense when the offspring could never live up to the expectations of their creators, be that a god, a parent, or some fucked-up girl who'd swallowed a fallen sun? Maybe that light itself had only been the offspring to some greater cosmic organism, as natural as a fungal spore. Was it moral for any species to reproduce when the world promised heartache, betrayal, abandonment, and the too-real chance that something would come along to kill and eat you, and hopefully in that order?

The questions were problems for another time, should Olivia live so long.

She passed the bathroom and reached the back of the hall. The way to Hazibel's room stretched to the right, where a windowed wall stared beside a doorway. A dark eye gazed into Olivia. The walls' fissures awaited, the hill's cavern beckoning with truth.

"Soon," she said.

She angled left, to the stairs. The Mason House's split-level seemed to climb higher than before. She pressed a foot to the bottom step and grasped the banister, and the stairs settled into their old shape.

Creaking steps answered above, heavy against the upstairs floorboards. Olivia glanced to the highest step, half-expecting Sunflower to glower down at her.

A moaning sigh spilled toward the bottom floor. These lungs sounded too large for Sunflower, the throat too wide. Olivia stumbled from the bottom step and let go of the banister. Her racing hands scraped at wall cracks as she backstepped into Hazibel's hall. She realized too late that she could have ducked into the cavern behind the wall, and now she'd withdrawn too far to make for it unseen. If what descended even had eyes.

The approaching breath shimmered at the split-level floor. The highest step creaked, and then the one below.

Olivia retreated until the small of her back struck the windowsill of the hall. Hazibel's bedroom door hung ajar to one side, but Olivia didn't want to risk tossing herself into another horror house room while she had a choice. She squeezed herself into the hall's corner and shut her eyes. Blue flashes lit her eyelids as lightning soaked through the nearby window.

The moaning, shimmering presence reached the bottom of the steps. Floorboards cried beneath a scraping, unseen belly. Likely Sunflower had been trying to make another Hazibel or one more copy of herself, but the ideas weren't stitching right.

Or maybe she meant to make monsters, the light demanding them.

The sliding presence paused. Olivia listened for a gasping throat, Lizzie's old hunting call, but this creation was a mystery. It might see with its ears or detect color with its skin.

Olivia swallowed hard and pressed her back against Hazibel's bedroom door. It slid open behind her, and she stumbled inside, but she held onto the door's edge, ready to swing it shut, quiet as she could, in case the moaning thing dragged itself down Hazibel's hall.

The bed creaked behind her.

She had stepped into Hazibel's room only once in her life, sent by Sunflower on a near-suicide mission to snatch a pack of cigarettes for Roy. Serene blue walls stared down on a four-poster bed, its sheets and blankets a peaceful sea-green. Severe as Hazibel could be, her room wore white doilies and sweet ceramic cats as if decorated by the kindliest of grandmothers.

Cats did not nest in her bed now. The ceiling rippled with shining light, a Serengeti sun for the pride of lionesses lazing beneath. Two Hazibels curled in the sheets, one almost human, the other sabertoothed and purring. A third Hazibel nestled between bed and nightstand, her taloned feet plopped in front of her, an unlit cigarette clutched in her teeth. She sucked wetly at its end.

Their clicking growls wound Olivia's every muscle tight to her bones. The pack stirred, their nap interrupted. Had they eaten their dead sisters and needed to sleep off the meal, or were they lethargic with hunger and now Olivia had brought the meat?

Her hand fumbled for the door, its knob, anything to escape and then shut this room again.

Another hand caught hers and drew her back to the hall. Its partner hand found the knob and shut the door quietly against the Hazibels.

Sunny blinked, her pupils swirling, and her face dimpled into a chipper smile. "Mothers are sleeping," she said. "You shouldn't wander." She tugged Olivia up the hall.

Olivia glanced back—would the door keep the Hazibels in?—and then turned to Sunny and the stairs. No sign of the massive slithering light. It might have sunk into the walls or out the front door, the latter sending it Christmas's way.

Olivia's heart raced as she and Sunny reached the fork. She peered down the main hall, half expecting to see a shambling, radiant ogre drooling over Christmas.

There was nothing. Christmas sat in the foyer exactly as before. No monster had disturbed them.

Cool air whistled across Olivia's hair, and she turned to the hill's dark eye. Or was it a throat now, alive with breath? It welcomed her as an open mouth, the place she needed to go, but she couldn't go alone. She needed someone else to come with her, a former best friend she probably still loved. A friend she absolutely feared. Sweet Olivia, servant to a doomed faith that she could still reach Sunflower's heart.

Sunny slowed at the hall's edge and followed Olivia's gaze upward. "You want to see her?" Sunny asked, hope widening her eyes. "To see God?"

Olivia counted the steps. Ten from bottom to top. She'd heard Zeppelin's "Stairway to Heaven" around two hundred times and always imagined the climb to be higher.

"Don't be shy." Sunny took Olivia's arm in a gentle hand and urged her onto the bottom step. The insistent tug made Olivia trip and her leg ache, but she let it happen. Sunny seemed too cheerful to resist. "The Sun God falls to Earth and brings her garden. She'll welcome you."

Olivia stared hard at the steps. She wanted them to tell her that Sunny was indeed some malformation or accidental stitching. That she was silly to think this terrified notion that Sunflower had made this confused version of herself to act as false creator, a pretty shell compared to the real thing, one more shadow cast by the sun.

One hand squeezed the banister, and Olivia dragged herself to the second step, third, fourth. She glanced back at Sunny, who drifted away from the foot of the stairs, her face filled with reverent glee.

Olivia wouldn't turn back again. Not until Sunflower descended with her. Her eyes crested the top, where nothing slid or threatened to pounce. Only the heavy light wriggled along the ceiling, its white fluid throbbing as thick as blood. Lightning flickered through the upstairs window, a reminder that the storm was ready to throw down anytime, any side of Chapel Hill. Did the storm know how it had come to be?

Olivia knew. She glanced at Gina's closed bedroom door, no need to see what might lurk inside, and then turned her gaze to Sunflower's bedroom.

The door hung open on a world of hard sunshine.

23. GOD

The core of Sunflower's bedroom shined white and blinding. Olivia had to blink until her eyes adjusted somewhat to the brightness. The room's edges sharpened where the dresser, bed, piles of junk, and crusts of creation's black sludge had been flattened against the walls, their pink paint now stripping in vertical waves.

A familiar, melodic voice sang from the center of the sun. "I knew you'd come back. That's why we're best friends, Liv. You're always here for me." The light beckoned. "Come closer."

Olivia stepped across singed fibers and toed at the rug. Harsh white heat glared across her skin and eyes. Had true sunlight pressed at her skin this way? She couldn't remember. The night had smothered every memory of the genuine sun.

She blinked again until the brilliance narrowed. New and clearer shapes grew in the bedroom's center.

Sunflower sat on the backs of two Hazibels, or two things close enough to be mistaken for them. Their bodies tangled together beneath their daughter in a complex spider of human limbs, as if Sunflower had tethered together an organic palanquin of mothers. Each neck hung limp, and neither face snarled or smoked or made any semblance of feeling Olivia got from the other Hazibels.

A third false mother grew from Sunflower's spine and wound her arms around Sunflower's shoulders. This Hazibel's dark hair grew in a shaggy mane, its locks hanging down her face, and a too-sweet smile peeked through.

Sunflower held her head high, eyes closed, her mouth an unfeeling, thin-lipped line. On the Hazibel-facing side of her head, blond hair fell shimmering with light. The other side of her skull had cracked open like an eggshell, with sharp white lines creasing her pinkish skin. Fleshy webbing wormed from her head's new canyon toward the ceiling, an umbilical cord for the Mason House's sickly miasma. Light poured between skull and roof, but which fed the other?

The shoulder-mounted Hazibel face smirked, her eyes bright. Sunflower's lips parted beside her. "Did you meet Sunny?" she asked. "The other me?"

No expression, no feeling. Why didn't she sneer, or smile, or anything? The last moment Olivia had seen Sunflower, that face had been an avatar of rage. Where had drive-in era Sunflower's delighted grin gone? Tonight was supposed to be special.

That girl seemed dead now. So did the angry Sunflower who'd screamed as Christmas carried Olivia out of the house. Now she sat in stillness. Or worse, acceptance.

"Sunny's nice," Sunflower went on. "Nicer than I am. She isn't the one I meant for you, the one who'll kiss you back, but I've been trying new things. Watch this."

The leg-bound Hazibels tensed and bent their limbs beneath her, a spider testing its strength. Each Hazibel raised her outer arm, offering Olivia a jittering wave, and then slammed their palms against the floor. Dried black sludge coated their fingers.

Olivia watched the Hazibels for another finger twist, a wrist flick, anything. The light seemed to numb her head. She should have run down the hill and out into the world like Christmas had suggested.

But who else would approach God?

"The light, it's like nerves," Sunflower said, and she patted her mothers' heads. "It's like everything. You'll understand when I make a Sunflower for you, for everybody, to suit their needs. A Sunflower for all seasons."

"A garden," Olivia said.

Except nothing Sunflower made seemed to come out right. If Christmas's two rivers theory carried any weight in light of Sunflower's gift, then the water had turned brackish, polluted first by salt and then by chemicals and garbage. What grew in this garden would not be proper Sunflowers. Not proper anything.

Thunder rattled the roof, and its tremor twisted the cord of light. Sunflower's face remained blank, but the mood-stricken Hazibel at her shoulder contorted every facial muscle and then growled at the ceiling.

"I still hear a girl crying beneath the hill," Sunflower said. Her lips looked dry.

"I know," Olivia said. "I hear her too."

Sunflower might have followed Lizzie's chain of logic, from thought to idea to memory, letting the memories become the past and shape reality, but the memories didn't leave her once manifested into the world. They stayed in her head, along with every feeling that entangled them. Even she could tell something was off tonight.

An angle Olivia could work. She made herself wade deeper into the light. "Hazibel's gone," she said. "One of the other Hazibels did it. We couldn't help her."

The Hazibel face scrunched her forehead, confused. "I don't know who you're talking about," Sunflower said.

Olivia took another step. "Your mother."

"Was she my mother?" Fingers of light beckoned from the gap in Sunflower's head. "Or was I hers?"

Another step. "She gave birth to you."

"One of them did. The dead one? Another? These?" Sunflower flexed luminous muscles, and every entangled Hazibel shuddered. "I can't tell anymore."

Olivia's sneaker skidded sideways and refused to step closer. Sunflower had cast away thoughts of Roy, the Kincaids, her mother. Had the storm changed her so much, so fast, or had she always been somewhat cold and self-centered, with Olivia too spellbound to notice? The invasive white light might only have illuminated a callous reality.

"You aren't thinking straight," Olivia said. "Quit telling yourself stories. You know your own mother. I wanted to believe my parents might be waiting out there, but I get it now. They never existed. I accept myself, but you haven't. Accept yourself, and you'll get it."

"I said that." Sunflower smacked her lips; the Hazibel face pursed hers. "Not you. Me."

"And now I'm saying it." Olivia forced herself another step. "Me."

Beyond her sneakers, four sets of Hazibel fingers tapped the floor in time with falling rain. Their limbs bent at grotesque angles, the Hazibel-like spider meant only to stretch Sunflower's reach.

Olivia shook her head at them. Enough. "You just can't let go," she said. "Memories and ideas fill up your head, but it's junk, and it's not even yours. You never made stained glass. You never hated your mother this much. You never even understood why Gina left. Just a little one copying the big one."

The higher Hazibel face softened. Sunflower's face echoed, her blank expression flashing hints of excitement. "Is this about Gina?" she asked, hopeful.

Lizzie's words climbed Olivia's throat. "Everything's about Gina."

Sunflower's face became blank again. "I miss her, Liv." The moody Hazibel's eyes shined with wet light, and tears rolled down her creased cheeks. "When I dreamed you, I thought I'd grabbed all my love for Gina and jammed it into your heart. I wouldn't have to keep it if I gave it away. But the love just made a copy. You wouldn't leave me, just like I wouldn't have left her, but she left with her love. Mine won't go away."

"I chose to come back. Gina never will." Olivia retreated from the light's center, her skin cooling by inches. "Let me show you."

The Hazibel face flashed a mouth of fangs. Their points pierced her skin. "I want my sister back," Sunflower said, her voice thickening. "I think about her, over and over, but she's never what grows out of the light. The closest was you. It's never her."

A storm-wet crack filled the room. Sunflower's skull already hung open; it seemed it would never close. The light could always find more to break. Its webbing writhed from head to ceiling, and its oppression made the ceiling groan. What would Sunflower try next? Hopeless regurgitation wouldn't bring her lost sister back. She could fill the world with wrongness trying to make one thing right, but that didn't mean she'd ever have what she wanted.

The shoulder-grown Hazibel face smoothed into a serene stare. Sunflower's head pulsated. "If I make the world blank except for Gina and me, then I'll have to find her," she said.

Olivia gazed at the throbbing ceiling. "You can't rip apart a storm you didn't stitch."

The Hazibel face tried to flash teeth again, but a lance of light shot up her spine and through her skull. Flesh and bone shattered and burned.

Sunflower's eyes flared angry sunshine. "What would you know?" she asked, a snarl in her throat. "You've never made a whole person, have you? You've never even been a whole person. Nothing's come out of your life except for goddamn scarves and fucking sweaters! Do you think that means anything, Liv? It doesn't. It means absolutely nothing."

Her skull canyon stretched into deeper cracks, shining with renewed brightness. Some internal sunrise wanted daybreak through Sunflower's head. Worms of light writhed within. Olivia had watched those worms dig through Lizzie's skin, turn to hooks, and shred her into light and memory, nothing more. Now came Olivia's turn for unstitching, after everything she and Sunflower had been through together.

"This?" Sunflower flexed the hateful light. "This means something."

Olivia's fists curled at her sides. "I'm sick of your tantrums and your self-centered crap."

"Who cares what you're sick of, Liv?" Luminous crosshatching ate down Sunflower's face. "I made you."

"To be your hanger-on, the dutiful friend, always ready to help, and I did!" Olivia shouted. "I devoted every moment I could to you. And even after I found out the truth, I came back here for you because I chose to. Not your pet—like your friend. A real friend. Who else would do that? Not Gina." She slid closer to the door. "You might have made me, but you don't deserve me. Maybe you can't make a new Gina for yourself despite all your gifts and all this power because, deep down, you know you don't deserve her either."

A wild shriek tore through Sunflower's lips. Her head twitched sharply toward its still-fleshy side and aimed the broken-open half at the ceiling. Its pale soup filled with vague faces. Hazibels in the making.

"Them again?" Olivia braced her hands against the bedroom doorframe. "Do something on your own for once, Sunshine. Get your hands dirty. Quit sending Mommy to fight your battles and come shut me up yourself!"

Sunflower's shriek sharpened to ear-splitting. Spidery mother limbs scrabbled at the floor, claws desperate for Olivia's flesh, but the umbilical cord tethered Sunflower to the pale ceiling. She tugged against it, her scream filled with fury and pain.

Her skin stretched taut, and then ragged flesh tore from her head and thighs. Her body's stillness exploded in thrashing limbs and flailing tendrils. White sludge splashed down her face, and its droplets splattered across the room. A sinewy rip throbbed through her webbing.

Olivia spun from the bedroom and limped toward the stairs. She'd only waited to make sure she didn't really lose Sunflower, but she couldn't risk getting caught either. At halfway down the stairs, enraged footsteps pounded the bedroom floor, muffled by a wordless shriek.

On two legs or eight, Sunflower was coming.

Olivia stumbled at the bottom step. Sunny shouted from the

living room, but Olivia couldn't make out the words and didn't have time to listen for more.

The cavern behind the cracked-open wall invited with chilly breath.

Olivia slid one shoulder inside and felt cold across her hand, but she couldn't go yet. She needed a glimpse of Sunflower's shining and mangled form before ducking through the wall and into the cavern. Just to be sure she chased.

The second floor of the Mason House groaned underfoot. Sunflower was quicker now with her underside carried on a palanquin of Hazibel limbs. A tangled mess of light thrashed into the stairway hall, shining around a silhouette of Sunflower's cracked-open skull.

The lure had worked, and she was coming, and nothing was going to stop her.

Olivia swallowed a chilly scream and ducked through the Mason House wall, where blackness engulfed the world.

24. UNDERWORLD

Olivia's hands thrust ahead and found walls of earth and rock. Her eyes had adjusted too well to Sunflower's bedroom and its blinding light, and now they could scarcely make out the channels digging deep into Chapel Hill. One palm wiped across lichen, and then a broad boulder. Illusory snow danced with black spots across her vision. There would be light down here once she reached where she meant to go, but how far to that point?

And which way? Damp air breathed across Olivia's face from ahead, one gust slightly to the left, another farther to the right. She expected the hill's underworld to be filled with these forking tunnels, a makeshift ant colony, except no ants had dug their way beneath the town.

Something larger and stranger awaited, if she could only reach it.

She ducked to the right as her shadow swatted the slate wall ahead, her own figure twisting as she abandoned the entry tunnel.

A flicker followed her, casting deeper shadows through the path she'd chosen and likely the one to its left.

If she didn't hurry, she wouldn't get the chance to find the light beneath the hill. Another light would catch her first.

But if she ducked too far ahead, hid herself in these paths, Sunflower wouldn't find her way. Olivia had to head toward the center loud and slow enough to be followed, but quick enough that she wouldn't feel those thin claws grasp her arms and tug her close. That Sunflower's light wouldn't catch and melt her like it had melted Lizzie before sucking her up its radiant straw.

Sunflower's bulky new form scraped noisily into the channels. Her Hazibel nails raked at every patch of slate and earth in her way, and a high-pitched screech wheezed in and out of her throat. She didn't sound like any kind of friend now. Not a god, either.

She sounded like a monster.

Fine. That was fine. Olivia had spent the night evading monsters, and she was getting good at it. Predators decided to chase prey, but they seldom realized their prey decided where the chase led. Never did it cross predatory minds that they'd given their prey some measure of control.

Sunflower was no different. She had left the little girl of herself years in the past and forgotten her chases with Gina. Innocent games, but valuable lessons in life. Sunflower should have held the sense of her prey nature close, learned from it to become a sharper predator. She might have seen through the lure and wondered at Olivia's true motives.

But Sunflower was no sister here, only a beast running beyond Mason House walls and innocent games. In this underworld darkness, she would follow where Olivia wanted, acting the part of devoted friend in sticking together until the end, even if

Sunflower's every thought bent toward maiming and killing the girl who loved her most.

Olivia chased down another narrow channel, scraping and beating the ground underfoot. Each time light flickered behind her and cast stretching shadows on the wall, she hurried deeper.

Sunflower would catch up soon, but they were getting closer. The cavern walls began to stretch apart, as if the swell of great roots had dug through this environment, or a giant's limbs had scrabbled up and up to dig an enormous body from a forgotten grave. The new tunnel's width was a relief, and Olivia pressed on with a feverish spring in her step.

Thoughts of limbs and graves weren't so wrong. What awaited at the center of the hill's underworld had pressed channels through rock and cried into them. Olivia's first meeting with Sunflower had been watched, as much a memory beneath the hill as it lived in Olivia's and Sunflower's heads. Every moment had been watched, really. There was not a stone around Sunflower in her life upon this hill that was not felt and known, even if only the suggestion of a thought, the spider on your neck that's actually a hair.

Another fork, another choice, but Olivia had a feeling that all roads inside the hill led the right way. The only choices were to go forward, or go back, and a monster chased behind. No going back.

And not far to go now. The way the paths were widening, Olivia would reach her ultimate destination far sooner than she could have crossed town. But then, the same went for Sunflower. Narrow passages would have slowed her nightmarish mother-limbs, and now she'd come catching up.

Almost there. The origin sat closer to Sunset Pass than it did to town's center, as if it had only wandered off some nearby road and fallen asleep. That wasn't so far from the truth. A girl had run from her mother's car, into a field, and then the dream.

Light flickered—this time not from behind, but ahead. Almost there.

Olivia's leg cried again, but she couldn't slow down. The cavern echoed her pounding footsteps, and an incessant scratching closed in from behind. Her shadow splashed the walls, light bearing down from the last turn. If she couldn't make it, maybe her shadow would. The tunnel swerved left, and she followed around curving slate.

A new harsh light broke the blackness through the next opening. No more channels, no more forks. The cavern ahead formed a natural, slanted archway, and beyond that stretched a low-ceilinged chamber, the shining root of Chapel Hill.

Olivia squinted, eyes adjusting to another shift in the light, and then a screeching mess crashed into her from behind. Her tender shoulders howled in twisting pain. The weight sent her sprawling forward, where she scraped her chin and palms over hard earth.

Sunflower seethed across Olivia's back. Wet breath hissed through her teeth as she clambered over Olivia's legs.

Olivia strained to stand, but needly fingers jabbed the small of her back and pressed her down. She'd been quick, but she was not stronger than this monster. Spidery Hazibel hands and feet pressed across Olivia's spine and crushed her ribs against stone. Nails carved down the burned skin between her shoulders. Her pained shriek filled the chamber, but it wouldn't save her. She needed Sunflower to see the truth.

Did Sunflower even have eyes anymore?

Olivia craned her neck toward the room's center. "Look, Sun—"

A hand swatted down, and Olivia's head smacked the ground. The strike split her forehead and eyebrow open, and her vision swirled with black spots and dancing fireflies. Soon they were all she'd see—another blow slammed her face against stone.

Across her back, Sunflower's hands, the Hazibels' hands, everything under Sunflower's control thrashed at Olivia. A manic desperation sent Sunflower slapping, clawing, beating. Olivia jerked beneath the onslaught, but she couldn't fight Sunflower off or break free from beneath her. Soon Olivia's bones would splinter, and consciousness would fade. Blood and tears blurred the bright world.

No.

Not now, not after everything. Olivia thrust one hopeless arm forward. "Please. Look at her."

Sunflower gurgled something Olivia couldn't make out. Maybe one of those Hazibel hands had bashed an ear too hard and deafened it forever.

Olivia's jaw snapped open as wide as she could stretch. She screamed first, and then she shouted, "She's here! She's been here all along! Look at her, Sunflower! Look!"

Harsh light swept across Olivia's skin, cold where Sunflower lit hot. The beating eased into gentle blows, as if each limb were forgetting its purpose, and then Sunflower froze in place. Her weight shifted across Olivia's back, and a tremor ran through every inch where Sunflower touched.

No sun anticipated being outshone.

25. THE GIRL WHO CRIES BENEATH THE HILL

We're tired of dreaming.

Beyond the burning wreckage of Hazibel's maroon Corolla, and dead Hazibel, and the splintered fields, Sunflower cries for Gina. The pain burns and wriggles in Sunflower's gut, a blinding light she can't understand, a desire for a sister who has sometimes offered better comfort than a mother. Hands splay toward the sky, as if the stars can offer that sister.

As if wishes can come true.

The warm sensation flowers first through her limbs and then into the air, a living heat armed with grasping fingers. Sunflower's thoughts lie fertile with ideas and memories. The light pushes through them like clay through shaped holes. Muscle, bone, organs, structure; the building blocks of life—everything is new to the light. Each aspect writhes with potential.

Through Sunflower's damaged lens, it reaches out for wishes. It aims to make dreams into pieces of the world that fingertips can touch and feel, and maybe rend if they have to. A dreamer can do as she likes with her dream, toward kindness or otherwise.

Her body is another story. Pressure beats against her spine and then rises skyward until her gut bursts open, cracked edges soppy with milk-white light. She screeches through clenched teeth, but the noise comes muted now, her bodily energy spent. If she whispers for Gina, no one stands in the field to hear. Only the voyeurs caught in memory sickness years later will know these cries to an abandoning sister, and only two of those voyeurs will awaken to somewhat understand what they'll see and hear.

Manifestation begins with the ambitious mound of earth, bursting between ravaged cornstalks into thick walls rich with roots and worms. Stalks of light perforate the earth, still reaching skyward, but also digging down. Earth swirls around Sunflower, the burning pain both outside her memory and yet all she knows until her consciousness fades.

Once she begins to dream, the light grows busier.

Liquid radiance assembles towers of rock, and then walls of earth between them, faster than any glacier in the history of the world. A roaring hill climbs from the once-cornfield in jagged edges and muddy slopes. Its borders grow fingers of their own, grasping at the road's edge, Hazibel's Corolla, her daughter's body, the fields beyond, overtaking territory with such finality as if the hill has always stood.

But plain earth and stone make a naked garden, only untended dirt. Dreams must feed the light, and it worms through the new hill like blood vessels charting out a living body. Where each vessel ends, ideas and memories sprout new shapes.

Dirt and stone have been easy; the light encountered them when it lanced Sunflower from the sky. Brick, asphalt, steel, paint—these are fresh concepts, and Sunflower does not know how to make any of them. The first buildings swell bubble-like from the earth, only to burst apart in clouds of debris. They form again in the light, and again, until their shells stand solid, but even then they collapse without their insides, entirely separate concepts from what Sunflower has seen in passing from the back seat of her mother's car when Gina used to call shotgun.

Gina. The light shudders around the idea of her. She is a beloved wound in Sunflower's dreams, and every finger of light which prods those edges finds a livewire nerve inside, charged with lightning and suffocation.

Getting the buildings right is easier than any sister. First the light finds their load-bearing internal structures, and then it reforms the outsides, and finally it pulls the pieces together. Bit by bit, they begin to sprout almost on their own, without thought or planning. Grown by Sunflower's subconscious, reality mimics expectation. Streets weave between buildings, and further structures bud around the streets. Main Street is easy; Sunflower has seen many Main Streets. Others come half-remembered from glances at maps and other towns, and still more grow from precious Hartford. Newport Avenue, Riggs, Van Buren, and many more. Even her house grows in replica to what she remembers best from her hometown.

But this place cannot be Hartford. It will not conform to that full memory, and any imperfection might show like a blemish on a jewel. An amalgamation of hometown places, stranger places, and never-was places must be its own beast, nothing less.

The name drifts up unbidden—Chapel Hill, because it sounds pretty—and seeds through the vessels of light from Sunset Pass to every inch of the new town.

And its people. They are easier than buildings, their general sinew and bone and function akin to Sunflower's insides. All they need are shells, and she remembers plenty. Girls she went to school with, even if they weren't her friends. Teachers she knew. The mailman. The boys she liked, and the boys she didn't. Made-up half-dreams lingering in her head. People she has passed once on the street, never to be seen again until Chapel Hill. Even Hazibel.

A new Sunflower.

This little echo of the dreamer climbs gasping from the light like everyone else. No choice but to let her be like the others, ignorant to the light, or else how will she live? There is no other purpose to this, only a dreamer living vicariously through her dream.

The sky hangs dark and starry over this new Sunflower's head when she catches her breath and glances up and down the street. Memories muddle against sight for a second or two before her thoughts settle into place. This is the world; she has no right to argue its shapes and colors, or whether that bush sat on the opposite end of a neighbor's lawn yesterday, or how this street used to be wider, or how the air feels cooler than before. What kind of air can she expect atop a hill?

This is the world, and she is a fifteen-year-old girl. Same as the dreamer, of whom she has no memory. Someone else preoccupies the new Sunflower's thoughts.

She cups a hand to either side of her mouth and belts out a name: "Gina?"

The shout makes sense. Why else would she have wandered outside her house tonight, wearing only pajamas and slippers, if not to look for Gina? Maybe that explains the tingling new strangeness to the world. Gina will come back soon, and reality will have to twist and fold to accommodate her return.

"Gina?" The new Sunflower wanders up the street, turns at the corner, keeps looking. "Gina!"

She has no idea of the time tonight. It might be past midnight, and people might be sleeping. If they wake up and hear her though, they might dash outside their front doors, grab her shoulders, and say, *Thank God, you've finally come looking! I saw her, she's in the back yard, she won't stop crying, we didn't know what to do, but she's got to be crying for you, this way, hurry!* Maybe not that scenario exactly, but somewhere in town, someone has to have seen where Gina went, and maybe they know where she's going.

Sunflower calls through neighborhoods, her slippers growing dirtier at every new street and intersection. Headlights slide past her, the cars' drivers unconcerned. One middle-aged woman pauses at the curb, thinking Sunflower has shouted her name, *Lena*, but she moves on once she realizes she's mistaken.

Chapel Hill High stands dark and uncaring. The post office offers no letters from some distant city Sunflower has never heard of. The drive-in is closed, and doubtful Gina would have gone there. Everywhere Sunflower looks, the world turns a cold shoulder.

The dreamer feels each moment, but there is nothing she or the light can do to tell this new Sunflower there's no Gina to be found. No Gina has grown from Chapel Hill's radiant vessels and fertile soil. She can't be done. The wound she's left runs too deep, its edges fraying and screaming after all these years, and perhaps for eternity, as if to heal might mean surrender.

Red light strokes the eastern sky's edges as Sunflower pads past Cooper Street. The craft shop's green placard reads CLOSED, SORRY! A faint light flickers on in the apartment overhead. The sandwich place's dark windows show Sunflower's reflection. She doesn't realize she's crying until her tears glisten in the glass.

"Gina," she tries to shout again, but it comes out hoarse and whispery. She's been shouting all night, no rest, no water.

No sister.

Sunflower sinks to her knees, scraping sidewalk grime into her pajama bottoms, but she doesn't care. If Hazibel wants her cared for so badly, she would hunt down Gina to do it, or maybe do it herself for once. A quake runs through Sunflower's thoughts—a road trip, Grandma's house, a lie—but it leaks from her mind with the next bout of fresh tears. She is not the dreamer; she is a new Sunflower, with her own life and memories in Chapel Hill.

With the same Gina-shaped wound.

A brief white light flickers up from the hill and into the sky, where clouds bully the dawn's light away from town and rumble with thunder. Soft rain pats the rooftops of Cooper Street's shops, apartments, and sidewalks, running tinny against curb-parked cars to one side and the lot-parked cars behind the craft shop.

The storm only makes Sunflower sob harder. She can almost believe the world cries with her, but if the world cares so damn much, why not give her sister back? She has no use for the sky's hollow sympathy. These raindrops are nothing more than heavenly crocodile tears.

She sobs herself into a dull headache. The rain doesn't soothe, and every thunderous groan sends fresh pain throbbing from the back of her neck down the center of her scalp. Pressure floods behind her face. Crying helps nothing, and each sob beats inside her head a little harder.

"Gina, why?" Sunflower snaps. "Why'd you go away and make me like this? Did you hate me like that?"

The question swells into a hammer and crashes against Sunflower's heart. She should have realized it sooner—hatred sent

Gina running. Look at the callous way she packed her stuff, the apathy when Sunflower hung in the doorway, how disdain bled from Gina's every word, and then evaporated, and then formed a hateful atmosphere. Has she carried it with her to places unknown, or has she left it in the Mason House to fester?

"You hate me," Sunflower says, sobbing again. Her voice cracks, but she can't stop. "Fine then. Okay? Fine, you win! You hate me so much, well I hate you too. I've always—"

She swallows a hard lump. Thunder rattles the sandwich place's windows, and the throb in her head swells to skull-splitting agony. She clenches her teeth hard, doesn't care if it cracks the crown on the left, doesn't care about anything because Gina has carried a heart of hatred, and that is the only gift she's left Sunflower to remember her sister by.

"Always." Breath hisses through Sunflower's teeth. "Always hated."

Fingers claw from within her skull and press to either side of her head. Her mind burns with light, a bomb ready to go off.

"Always hated you!" she screeches.

A fissure of sickly radiance carves her head open from the crescent moon birthmark on the back of her neck, up a line at her skull's center, down to her forehead.

She knows none of it, while the dreamer feels everything. Making a new Sunflower meant leaving a seed of the light in the fresh form atop Chapel Hill. There is no flower without the root. This faraway echo carries traces of the dreamer's scream.

Sunflower kneels against concrete and dips her head toward the sidewalk. The top of her head is an open maw, and it drools the white yolk of creation onto the curb of Cooper Street, Chapel Hill.

No perfect form crystallizes from the ungainly fluid, standing at once with perfect understanding of self. Limbs thrash, liquid forming fingers, toes, a head of hair, clothing. It has been birthed alongside the Gina-shaped wound in the new Sunflower's thoughts, cobbling together Gina-like pain, and pieces of her, memories of Hartford, desires and imaginings and half-heard, half-understood conversations given the sanctity of personal history.

Sunflower's head seals shut. Darkness gives way to the drizzle over Chapel Hill, and here another teenage girl lies face down on the sidewalk, wearing a sweater, jeans, and sneakers.

Sunflower gasps hard and scuttles back. She didn't notice the stranger before her tantrum, too wrapped up in her crying. Who is this girl? She probably doesn't have a home. For a blink, she might be Gina, but that's only a blurry resemblance through teary eyes and falling rain. Gina has to have aged since she left, and this girl must be fourteen or fifteen.

Her face hides beneath one arm, but she is stirring. She will wake up soon.

Sunflower scrabbles against the sandwich place's wall and window to standing, and then she darts back down Cooper Street, toward Main. She shouldn't have stayed out all night. Calling for Gina, over and over, has been as hollow an effort as the sky's tears. Sunflower belongs at home, nowhere else.

At last, she understands. There is no Gina in Chapel Hill. Never has been.

The storm lets up and allows sunlight into Chapel Hill's sky by the time Sunflower reaches her street and spots the Mason House. Her eagerness fades as she plods down the sidewalk, her pajamas soiled, her slippers ruined. Morning has progressed too far for her absence to go unnoticed. She presses open the front door.

"Is that you?" a husky voice snaps from deep inside the house.

The kitchen, hall, and living room lights are on, as if Hazibel thought Sunflower might have been hiding in a corner or beneath a piece of furniture in some late-night, too-old game of hide-and-seek.

"It's me," Sunflower says, voice still sore from crying.

Hazibel storms down the stairs at hall's end. She is already dressed for work, and likely has been pounding on Sunflower's bedroom door between stages of getting ready until finally throwing it open to find an empty bed and a daughterless room.

"I was two seconds from calling the police," Hazibel says. "You know I've had enough of them since your sister. Don't put me in that position."

Beneath her snarling and disdain, Sunflower feels the aching urgency of another message: *Don't make me lose another daughter*.

Hazibel flits toward the living room. "Get showered and dressed. You're already running late for school." She finds her purse on the sofa and begins to dig inside, likely for cigarettes.

A senseless impulse quakes through Sunflower's limbs. She kicks off her mud-caked slippers, pads halfway down the hall into the living room, and clutches Hazibel's middle from behind. She doesn't know why. Hazibel certainly doesn't deserve it, and maybe Sunflower doesn't deserve feeling her mother sigh into that embrace, pivot in place, and hug her daughter in return.

But deserving or not, they hold each other and think of Gina.

Hazibel calls the school's vice principal, tells him Sunflower will be out sick for the day. She ushers Sunflower upstairs, gives her a spare pair of her own pajamas, tells her this won't happen tomorrow, and then leaves for work.

Sunflower crawls into bed, where she sleeps. And dreams.

Far beneath her, and beneath the Mason House and the streets, in a damp and earthy cavern, light vessels stretch into vast networks more complex than any flesh-and-blood organism. Chapel Hill breathes, and it becomes one with the greater world of numbers and roads and expectations.

The dreamer dreams, and the dream lives on. Unseen, unknown, until her tears again wash Chapel Hill and drag voyeurs into a fresh nightmare. In this underside of light, Olivia learns what's under Chapel Hill.

We want to see.

A dreamer can do as she likes with her dream. Toward kindness—

We want to wake.

—or hatred.

26. THE DREAMER

Olivia raised her bleeding head to face the chamber's underside. She couldn't yet make out the shape within the light, but the smell spread earthen and musky, and the sound of labored breath ran cool across her ears. She'd seen this place in the memory rain, but some part of her had dreaded that the vision came malformed, hiding a Sunflower-headed hydra beneath the hill, her body long and scaly, her face plastered at the end of a dozen necks, and each mouth cooing to Olivia, commanding her, uncertain whether to kiss or kill or devour her whole. A new special nightmare, just for her.

The light molded into sharper definition. There were no monsters here. No gnashing teeth, bottomless throats, or twisted mothers turned into limbs.

There was only another victim.

Sunflower crept over Olivia's back and into the subterranean sunshine. White soup still poured from her skull, but its tendrils jittered uncertain now, and her movement became stilted. Severing the umbilical cord had torn something inside. Was she still alert enough to understand what filled the chamber? She seemed transfixed by the light.

Olivia clambered to her knees. "Lizzie, Christmas, me, every Hazibel after the first—we're your ideas," she said, and her chin aimed at the grand shape in the light. "And you're hers."

"I can't see her right." Sunflower lifted an arm to shield her eyes. "Is it Gina?"

Always the same. Every instance in Sunflower's life where she'd seen a corner, there was a chance that Gina might stride around it. At every open door, Gina might emerge. That she had run away didn't necessarily mean she'd planned to vanish entirely. Sunflower must have harbored morbid fantasies that Gina had fallen off the world, or been abducted by aliens, or been murdered by someone more local. Buried here, perhaps, her ghost left to cry beneath Chapel Hill. Any of those explanations made more sense to Sunflower than her sister choosing never to reach out of her own free will.

The little one figured it out, Lizzie had said. Olivia had assumed that meant Sunflower in comparison to Gina.

Until the memory sickness showed her the truth.

Within the light, someone filled the cavern's back wall, the body stretched and matted over every stone surface. Overgrown fingers and toes formed thick, treelike roots. Bulbous pods pulsed up her limbs toward the central torso, where a round belly distended to the floor. Its surface shined bright, and every facet of brilliance sent leathery skin twitching.

Soiled blond hair tangled with glowing tubers, and vacant blue eyes shed rivers of tears. Her face had stretched, but she still held the beauty Olivia had known every day since she first manifested in Chapel Hill.

Here lay a Sunflower. Not the one who'd thought Olivia was a pretty name and created her, not the one who'd visited the drive-in tonight, or walked down Sunset Pass, or tried to kill Olivia by spilling vicious mothers from her moon. This Sunflower had fallen here the night a white light had burned from the sky and pierced her flesh, a dreamer ever since. The Night of Sunfall.

Sunflower flinched back on spidery limbs. "Is that me?" she whispered.

"You're her the same way that Sunny is you." Olivia tapped the back of her neck. "We're all people from the moon. Except her."

Olivia watched Sunflower's trembling form, but she wasn't sure what she wanted to happen next. When she awoke from the memory sickness and started back to the Mason House, she had thought this revelation might bring some renewed sense of friendship with Sunflower, their bond rekindled. They had both been wrong about themselves. Too many assumptions. Memories couldn't be trusted.

But when Sunflower glanced over her shoulder now, face crosshatched in white lines, eyes and skull bleeding milky sludge, Olivia's heart banged with pity. She had no plan beyond this moment. If Sunflower bared her teeth and came lunging to tear out a throat, Olivia could only run. She was out of ideas.

Sunflower's voice croaked through her lips. "Where are we?"

"The beginning." Olivia tried to stand, but her knees seemed trapped beneath her. She wiped blood down her face. "I don't know how long ago it happened, or what year it was then, or if the rest of the world even keeps track of things like that. But the light fell from the sky where she was standing, and everything came from there. Chapel Hill. The people. You."

Memories rained down Olivia's thoughts. She remembered the screaming, falling sunset, and the girl whose belly swallowed it. She remembered that girl falling, and light, pain, a darkness that wrapped her in rising earth.

That girl never left the spot where something had struck the world from beyond. Its impact burned and crushed crops, fences, maroon Corolla, road, and a mother. The girl dropped into darkness, where her head opened the light of her visitor's creation. Her thoughts, dreams, and memories swirled into a life she'd never know.

First, a hill. And then roads and houses, pieces aping places the dreamer had seen or lived in, forming the layout of this new town. After that, its people, stitched together from fragments and images, more duplicates of people the dreamer had known briefly or seen in passing.

Chapel Hill, a little nowhere place in western Pennsylvania, built from bits of TV and Hartford by a half-understood adolescent. It had a drive-in and a craft shop, schools and restaurants. The dreamer even made a new Sunflower and Hazibel, to replace herself and her mother, and the Mason House where they lived. The town accepted gifts from the outside world, people and media, but it never made waves, and it scarcely touched anything beyond its borders. Even its interstate offramp merited little traffic, built more for nearby farming towns than this strange anomaly.

Maybe no one outside had noticed. They might have chalked up the town's surprising presence to incomplete maps and unreliable paperwork. Or maybe someone had noticed, could swear they had driven past this area one or two weeks before Sunfall, whatever year or decade that had taken place, when there had been neither hill nor town, no road leading toward the interstate, later completed by crews from outside. To say so would have only brought them funny looks and concerned mutterings. Who were they to argue against risen earth, standing buildings, and living human beings? That would mean arguing against reality, and anyone they spoke to would have called doing so unreasonable, arguing that reality was unmalleable and infallible until the visitor to Chapel Hill agreed.

They would have been wrong.

Labored breath filled the chamber as light twitched in the stretched dreamer's gut. Turned over, Olivia expected she would have found a crescent moon birthmark on the back of the dreamer's neck, the original. She hadn't copied the mark to everything she'd made, no branding needed when her light fashioned its creatures to accurate detail. Only the copy of herself had needed one, an imperfect Sunflower who couldn't help spreading the mark to everything she made. Her light shined tiny beside her dreaming creator.

"It hurts her," Sunflower said. "The light let her sleep for a long time, but now it hurts. That's why she's crying."

Did she remember her creator's origin in Hartford, a reason to hand that story to Olivia? Did memories of that place haunt her at night? Or had she thrown the discrepancy aside, believing she'd always lived in Chapel Hill, choosing to shrug away a problem rather than deal with it?

Only the first Sunflower knew for sure, cradled with her shining burden. She was the dreamer, and the rest were the dreams.

Olivia dragged her legs out from beneath her and wobbled to her feet. Her back was a murder of vertebrae, and cuts and gashes gaped screaming down her face, shoulder, and leg. She forced herself across the room, closer to Sunflower's spidery form and the great dreamer than she wanted to be.

The dreamer's glow paced her torso, gut to chest and back again. Olivia held her hand out, but she wouldn't touch the skin. The air breathed so cold, she was afraid her palm might fuse to the dreamer's flesh in a blanket of frost.

Sunflower rested a hand on the dreamer's overgrown face. "I'm really sorry," she said. "I got lost." She turned to Olivia again, face crumbling, a porcelain doll filled with shattering brilliance. "Is that how the light found her? It got lost?"

Olivia didn't know; the memories hadn't shown. The light could have been an irradiated meteorite, or the shed skin cell of some cosmic snake, or any other nonsense she might pluck from some sci-fi movie or the informative literature that Shelly kept in the back of Kincaid Krafts. Olivia didn't really care what the light was, or where it came from. Only what it had done.

Sunflower leaned toward the dreamer's middle. "I guess it could've heard us from out there, and it just wanted to see what all the fuss was about."

The flesh flickered a pale glow, and its heartbeat quaked through the hill. Soil rained from the ceiling and stuck to the blood running down Olivia's face. She wiped at one eye beneath her split brow and flinched back.

The dreamer stirred. Something was about to happen.

Sunflower held in place. White fingers slid from inside her skull and stroked the dreamer's bright rays, light meeting light. "I don't think it wants to live inside me anymore," she said, her voice toneless. "Inside her. It wants to go home."

"I don't think the light's alive," Olivia said. But the dreamer was a different story. "Maybe she doesn't want to lie here any longer."

Sunflower didn't seem to hear. "I want to go home, too." She stretched her many limbs around the dreamer's torso, and pale tears ran from every crack in her face.

Olivia didn't know what home meant anymore, but she wanted it, yes. The place. The feeling.

Sunflower released the dreamer and hesitated beside her

torso. Two Hazibel hands pressed against cold, stretched skin. Their claws gleamed transparent in the light, and the pacing white presence inside the dreamer held still. It, too, knew something was about to happen.

Olivia wondered if this fallen sun could know physical pain. Had it been familiar with the sensation before it fell, or had it only learned to hurt when it lanced through a teenage girl one clear night and melted into her nervous system? And Olivia wondered, even were the light to lead a pain-free existence, if its isolation out in the stars and then beneath this hill might mean it understood discontentment and loneliness deeper than any flesh-and-blood creature could imagine.

The dreamer might know, but Olivia never would.

Sunflower pressed her Hazibel nails into the dreamer's flesh. Blood welled at their tips, laced with eerie light. Sunflower flexed her claws and then slashed the dreamer's belly open.

Sunshine peered between fleshy ribbons. Soaked in sinewy red strands, its beauty burned away the underground's cold and offered the pleasant glory of a sunny day. Miasmic arms stretched in all directions. Their fingers reached from inside the dreamer and stroked the pale fingertips rising from Sunflower's skull.

"It feels me," Sunflower said, almost sweet. "It remembers stitching me, Liv."

Sharp rays warmed Olivia's skin, and a smile grew across her face. Maybe the light was alive after all. There was unity here, as beyond Olivia's understanding as the light itself.

Luminous fingers meshed. Radiant white sank into Sunflower's milky head, light again meeting light, tugging a scream through her cracked face.

Olivia shrank back, one hand pressed to her mouth. Her lips formed Sunflower's name, but she couldn't say it.

The dreamer's light dragged Sunflower down by the scalp. Her Hazibel legs fought back. One bent the wrong way in a bone-breaking crunch, and the rest cracked wetly and folded into a pile on the ground. Sunflower landed facing the dreamer's slashed belly, where a bright claw tore into the chalky sludge of Sunflower's open head.

"What's happening?" Sunflower shrieked. "What's it doing?"

Not it. She. The dreamer had stitched Sunflower, along with the rest of Chapel Hill. Sunflower had never felt creation in the making—she blacked out each time.

Same for unmaking a creation. Only Olivia had witnessed cells broken apart from the outside, matter turned to light particles and drawn within, that moment when Sunflower had burned Lizzie down and returned the idea to its source.

The dreamer was unstitching Sunflower.

Olivia stumbled over a lip of rock, and her free hand found the chamber's slanted archway. Stone quivered beneath her fingers.

Worms of light wriggled hot through Sunflower's skin and curled into hooks down her face, torso, and twisted legs. Every orifice cracked and steamed. She was burning, breaking. Her shattered porcelain doll face creaked over her shoulder, eyes overtaken with furious white fire.

"Help me, Liv," she said.

Olivia's heart thundered. She reached one hand toward Sunflower, but her legs wouldn't let her into the chamber. She and Sunflower might have stood miles apart.

Sunflower jerked against the dreamer's body. "Help me," she said again. Molten tears filled her face and sizzled down her chest. The Hazibels twitched beneath her, dead spiders under a dying sun. "Liv, help me, please!"

Olivia's fingers stretched until her muscles hurt. She wanted to tell Sunflower that she hadn't meant for this to happen when they ran here, hadn't known the dreamer would want to unstitch anyone. Olivia had wanted to help. Every piece of who she'd ever been, who she'd been created to be, demanded she help. Eager as always.

But she wanted to live, too.

"I love you," she said, her voice frail. "I'm sorry."

She spun back from the slanted archway on one clumsy heel and darted into the hill's channels. Her footsteps echoed across stone. Ceiling gaps sucked in air, the hillside taking a breath. Every opening led to this place, and this place led to every opening. She had to trust that following the lowest passages would lead back to the Mason House.

She didn't run alone. Shouts of "Olivia!" and "God, Liv, don't leave me!" chased her around every turn. She should have cried enough over Sunflower tonight, but fresh tears burned Olivia's eyes. Guilt demanded she turn around and run back to the dreamer's chamber, let herself come unstitched from the world. That would mean she was a good friend, that tonight hadn't poisoned her. Death—the cornerstone of love.

Instead, she kept running. The shouts and screams soon drowned beneath the hill's roar. She caught firelight through the outline of a cracked-open wooden wall. Thunder answered the hill as she broke through a fissure in the Mason House and barreled into its main hall.

Her thighs jellied, and her lungs ached. If it weren't for the roaring hill, she might have paused now to take a break.

But the quakes hadn't started only now. The dreamer had been fighting awake since the night began, when she first stitched the storm to rain memories on Chapel Hill. Maybe Sunflower's manifestations of Christmas and Lizzie had triggered the light to act. Maybe the light had grown too strong and forced them out of Sunflower's mind.

Chicken or egg, whatever the reason, time was up.

Olivia darted past the living room, where Sunny lay on the floor grasping her head, and stopped at the front door. She knocked the useless end table aside and kneeled beside Christmas. Still breathing, still alive.

"We have to go," she said.

Christmas's head lolled forward. "Liv?"

Olivia grabbed Christmas's arms to keep herself still. "Don't call me that. Don't talk. Just get up. There's no time."

Christmas outstretched one leg and braced their back against the coat closet door. They lifted two inches and then settled.

"Another minute," they said.

Olivia's grip tightened. "Don't you want to live?"

Christmas raised their eyes. Their gaze absorbed Olivia's bloodied face.

She wiped her split brow over her sleeve and leaned closer. "That's what you told me," she said. "You've only been alive for a few hours, and you want more. Lots more! Don't you?"

Christmas's head bobbed again. They pressed their back against the closet door, tensed their legs, and dragged themselves up on Olivia's arms. Gait unsteady, but Christmas stood. If they could put one foot in front of the other, Olivia would call that good enough. She unfastened the locks and threw open the front door.

Bodies lined the cracked and beaten porch. Infected, Hazibels. The living kept fighting out in the remains of the stained-glass forest and still-standing chunks of labyrinth, but they paid no attention to the house anymore. Rain fell in thick sheets, dimming the world. The soupy light that once poured off the Mason House had dimmed, probably since Sunflower had torn herself loose from her bedroom's webbing.

Olivia grasped Christmas's forearm and led down the porch steps, past the crystalline trees. Stepping across the cut-up bodies of fallen infected made Olivia want to scream, but they were already dead, and crossing the patch of labyrinth where their corpses matted the fallen glass was the quickest way onto the descending arm of Sunset Pass.

One of the bodies moaned as Olivia stumbled over an errant leg. She didn't look down to see what they looked like. In case she might recognize them. She kept her eyes fixed ahead, hurrying Christmas onward until they reached the labyrinth's beginning, where one frozen wave still crested overhead.

Sunset Pass ran steep and muddy, but there wasn't time for Olivia to slow down. Another quake shifted the hill. It wanted to knock them on their backs and keep them forever.

Olivia wouldn't have that. She tugged Christmas harder. They rounded the next pull-off and paused where Hazibel lay. Olivia let go of Christmas only long enough to check for a pulse, a breath, any sign that someone else had a chance to escape this nightmare.

Nothing. Hazibel lay as cold and stiff as her wild sisters farther up the hill.

"Can we rest?" Christmas asked, buckling with hands on knees. "Not one to ask usually, but this ain't a usual night."

Olivia turned to them just as the hill popped open. Behind Christmas, a geyser of pale light surged from the hillside at the last pull-off. She couldn't make out the Mason House from here, but its fragments roared skyward in the white plume. Sister worms of light broke through the pass's once-dark eyes. They had bored into Sunflower's flesh, turned to hooks, and taken her into the alien whiteness.

They would take the hill, too.

Olivia grabbed Christmas again and ran. Her thighs screamed. Christmas groaned. Two stretches of Sunset Pass to go, and then they'd leave Chapel Hill behind. The rest of the world lay open not far below. They only had to make it there.

Christmas faltered halfway to the next pull-off, and Olivia's leg gave out. She'd been pushing hard, pretending that Lizzie hadn't stomped all over her shin or that no one had chomped onto her calf, but now the bruising and beating clawed up her bones.

Her fingers dug at the mud, and she forced herself up. No time to wait. Collapse later. She grabbed Christmas, and they plowed downslope. Thunder rolled underground and climbed the hillside. Every boulder sharpened with brilliance, their innards hooked and drawn by the still-buried dreamer.

At the pull-off, Christmas crashed beside the guardrail, dragging Olivia down with them. She dug her hands in the mud again and tried to rise. No more, her leg decided. She would break down now.

The hill groaned from foot to plateau. Olivia turned with Christmas and watched every tendril of light sharpen and straighten into rays of earthborn sunshine. She had never seen light so hopeless and destructive, its worms as gargantuan as train cars. They shifted into luminous hooks, each tearing through Chapel Hill, its houses, their people, the roads, everything.

The dreamer's awakening, a great unstitching.

Black figures floated from the lowest Mason House against the white sheen, infected and Hazibels rising beside wooden walls and black shingles. Clouds of infected drifted from Sunset Pass and climbed toward the heavens.

Above them, Chapel Hill proper burst in a fountain of ravenous white light. Tree trunks tore from their roots, houses cracked from foundations, and the swarming citizens broke free of the ground. Somewhere in the crumbling debris floated fragments of the Starry Wood Drive-In, Chapel Hill High, Kincaid Krafts, the true Mason House if there had ever been one.

Roy drifted somewhere, same as Shelly and Dane, Taggart's body, the letter jacket crew, everyone Olivia had ever truly known, not in made-up memories but met, and spoke to, and touched. Her truest home shattered loose from gravity's hold. Reality could not keep it.

The hill was breaking, too. Strips of asphalt lifted and turned their long necks to the storm clouds, great dinosaurs witnessing a fresh and unexpected extinction. Those necks soon snapped, and snaking roadways churned with rising soil and rock. No more Ridgemont Road, no more neighborhoods, no more lee side that led to flatlands and the interstate. The highest stretch of Sunset Pass melted into the white plume.

Layer by layer, Chapel Hill flaked away.

Olivia tried again to stand, but her leg refused. It wouldn't bear the pain of walking anymore. As if it wanted to join the tearing light of uncreation.

"I can't—" Olivia gasped. "I can't!"

Christmas pressed up from the ground. Every muscle sagged against their bones, ready to crash and burn, but Christmas glided their hands around Olivia's arms and pulled her to sitting up. Clover-green eyes leaned close.

Olivia had only seen them in darkness; they'd never looked so bright until now. She sighed hard and leaned close to Christmas.

Her lips parted. "If we die—"

Christmas grabbed Olivia's face and tugged her into one more hard-and-hungry kiss. Her nerves twinged, still shaken by a traumatic and imaginary carnival day, but a kiss was a small thing compared to everything that surrounded it. This moment was real, and it came with tingling skin and time-stopping sensations. She tasted copper, sweat, and mud. She tasted coarseness and disgust, and adrenaline and hope.

She tasted Christmas. Her thoughts flaked with the dying hill, heart racing up through her mouth.

She would ride this moment to the end of feeling.

The kiss broke off as Christmas scooped Olivia into their arms and charged forward. A little energy left, one last push. She glanced to the final stretch down Sunset Pass, but Christmas dashed past that.

Toward the ledge.

Olivia looked to Christmas's eyes, glaring ahead at a slim chance with gravity over the certainty of shining death. No compromise, no fighting it. She buried her face into Christmas's neck and squeezed her eyes shut as their bodies broke from the earth.

One last try at escaping Chapel Hill.

27. ANYWHERE, ANYPLACE

Dawn purpled the open sky, cloudless and eternal and unblemished by starlight. Dust clung to the ground, a mist of debris left behind by a shattered hill, pluming in its place. Scant sunlight peeked over the green canopy of eastern woods and brightened by the moment as it crept across the Appalachian Mountains.

Olivia had given up on seeing the dawn, let alone genuine sunshine. She had also given up on appreciating it if she was lucky enough to survive until daylight. Last night had shown her creation's radiance, a mirror for what formed her, and somehow she'd misjudged it to be brighter than a clear sky at noon, like she'd forgotten every pretty day before.

She knew better now. Every sickly light she'd seen on and inside Chapel Hill had only imitated the sun. Its destructive white radiance could not compare to a true sunrise and all its various colors.

Beside Olivia, bruises darkened Christmas's face, and dry blood caked one ear. They had taken a beating in the last-ditch tumble and drop to escape Chapel Hill, but their chest rose and fell. They were alive and groaning in the same dirt where Olivia lay. A thin layer of dust coated both their bodies, scratches cut down their skin, but they'd made it through the great unstitching until the collapse at the hill's bottom knocked them into merciful darkness.

Olivia remembered little after that. Pain had carved through her leg until dreams filled her head. A flicker of a thought told her to be grateful that her dreams would never crawl out of her skull into luminous reality, but in the growing light of day, she couldn't remember the damn things. They were fragments of nothing in her head. Never manifested, not even in memories.

She blinked at the sky, rolled over, and fresh pain shot through her leg. Doubtful she could stand on it unaided. Chapel Hill had put it through hell, and now it was probably broken below the knee. A couple ribs, too, if this lower chest ache meant anything serious.

Olivia forced herself to sit up anyway. The night could have left her much worse, or as nothing at all.

A road stretched from east to west beyond the debris cloud, some seldom-traveled strip most people likely never noticed. Olivia doubted she had ever known its name. Potholes haunted the cracked asphalt along both lanes, cut by faded yellow lines. Once upon a time, it had the misfortune to turn toward Sunset Pass, back when such a place existed. A rickety fence stood across the road, and behind it stretched an endless cornfield.

Corn once grew where Olivia and Christmas now curled in the dirt, but that had been a long time ago, in the days before uncaring light had fallen from the sky and sprung a monstrous hill from a teenage girl's imagination.

Flat soil stretched here now, as if the hill had never been.

Someone towered in its place, unbothered by the debris cloud.

She couldn't reach anywhere near Chapel Hill's height, but the dreamer would have dwarfed Christmas had they stood side by side. Was she ten feet tall? Twelve?

Olivia couldn't measure from the roadside, and she had no intention of crawling closer to get a better idea. She had already stepped as near to the dreamer as she wanted, seen that aching face, and the familiar sky-blue eyes, and the golden locks that poured down the dreamer's head, down her skin, everywhere. Clothing hung in soiled tatters from her torso and limbs. Her overlong digits flexed and unflexed at her sides, the dirty nails chipped and broken, as she stood and stared at a world she hadn't seen since the night she'd swallowed something that wasn't the sun, wasn't a star, maybe didn't have a name that anyone knew.

Whatever it was, it hadn't left with the destruction of Chapel Hill. The dreamer's distended gut had healed itself from Sunflower's desperate scratches, while the rest of her looked like Sunflower, only grown to impossible height. Her skin rippled with white impatience, the dreamer awake for the first time in years and yet still entwined with a nightmare.

Pregnant with malignant light.

Her face tilted in glacial fits and starts until she aimed her brilliant eyes toward Olivia. A similar girl had once batted eyelashes over eyes like those, the kind of sweet skies Olivia could have fallen into and floated forever.

But she had never really met these particular eyes before. The dreamer was a stranger.

Her great lips puckered around her teeth, parted into an almost-smile, and then spread wide from each other. She repeated these motions half a dozen times before Olivia mimicked them, felt how they might sound with a voice, and recognize the name on her lips. The dreamer was asking a one-word, one-name question, syllable by syllable.

Olivia turned her head slowly from side to side. "I'm not her," she said. "Sorry."

The dreamer tilted her head, studying the small creatures across the field. She then shifted her shoulders and hips northward and began to walk, one steady, gargantuan step after another.

In these flatlands, she would take some time to disappear from Olivia's sight, and perhaps much more time would pass before someone noticed the giant who now walked the world. The wilderness could hide many wonders.

Christmas sat up, their every bone creaking. "Is that Sunflower?" they asked.

Olivia didn't turn to them, her eyes fixed on the distant dreamer. "I don't know anymore," she said.

The dreamer was not Olivia's Sunflower, that much was clear. Not the one whose death cries had chased Olivia through Chapel Hill's insides.

Echoes of those cries now slithered down Olivia's spine. She wished she could have made things work. Anything to be back at that drive-in counter, annoyed by Taggart, crushing on her best friend by subconscious design, coming home to the strange sweetness of Shelly and Dane while at the same time wondering about the parents she'd left in Hartford.

All gone, a mixed-up pile of used-to-be and never-was eaten by the light. Each heavy fragment of memory lodged in Olivia's heart and made standing almost impossible.

But she clambered up on her right leg anyway and let her left leg hang by a raised knee. With both hands, she braced herself on Christmas's back. Solid muscle and bone, and a fierce heart—

these kept her standing until she could briefly balance herself.

She wondered how many years might pass before the bones in her left leg turned brittle. Would they break and never heal? Would every cell in her body deteriorate faster now that she had strayed from the light of creation?

How many years were Sunflower's creations promised in the first place? Hours for some. Longer for others, if they could survive.

Olivia squeezed Christmas's shoulder. "Anything broken?"

"Everything hurts," Christmas said. They twisted their head and cracked their neck. "Not that I'm one to complain." They tried to stand, faltered, and then regained their balance and took on Olivia's weight along with their own. "Something's busted. Have to figure that out someplace else. Ain't exactly any doctors wandering here anymore."

"Where, then?" Olivia asked. "Ohio?"

"Anywhere. Anyplace." Christmas glanced at the dreamer and shook their head. "Far as we can get in whichever way she ain't headed."

Olivia's gaze turned north, opposite the road. The dreamer shuffled distantly. She didn't know where she was headed either, but at least she had someone to search for, somewhere. For a little sister who couldn't let go, despite light that had fallen from the sky, despite years buried beneath a conjured-up hill, everything in her world was still about Gina.

It always would be.

Olivia hoped Gina went unfound. She hoped the dreamer might walk so far north that she wandered into a land of absolute wilderness and nothing more, where no people would run across her and that swirling radiance, and the world would never face every awful and wondrous thing she might create. The sun would rise and set at its best and brightest if the dreamer's light never made or unmade another life. No hills, no people. Nothing at all.

The fragments in Olivia's heart tugged hard. Right now, she could easily drop back into the dirt and curl inside herself. That would be a fitting end to a terrible night. No past, no thinking about the future. There was peace in surrender.

But this was still the site of Chapel Hill; the debris cloud said so. Until they left, Olivia and Christmas hadn't kept their promise to each other. Time to leave.

Olivia braced herself against Christmas. "Stick with me a bit longer? I can't say I'll make it worth your while, but I could really use a little more help."

Christmas shrugged under Olivia's hand. "Got no one else." They winced in sudden pain, and then they forced a smirk toward Olivia's face as if to hide it. "Might choose you even if I did. Not many would head up that hillside and stare down the beginning and the end."

"I don't think most people would follow, either." Olivia nuzzled her face into Christmas's arm. They smelled of dirt now, and safety, and the warmth of day. She grasped their shoulder, hopped on one leg until she stood between them and the asphalt, and chinned toward the south. "See the road? We can hitchhike like we used to."

"Used to?" Christmas coughed out a laugh. "Neither of us have ever really done that before."

No, they hadn't, but Olivia had an idea. If she thought on it enough, it would become a memory, her past. Her past chained her present, every moment with Christmas, everything real she dared care about.

And if she had done this in the past, in her memories, then she could do it now.

She ushered Christmas toward the road and listened for the growl of an oncoming car. In the early morning, with the land still drawing its breath for a sunny August day, few cars would travel the sideroads near the border of Pennsylvania and Ohio.

And yet there, from the east—the rush of tires against asphalt, their thud as they ran over another pothole. Was it someone passing through on their way between one place and another, or had they come to see what last night's fuss was about?

Olivia didn't know. She would have to ask the driver why they'd traveled out this way once she and Christmas had piled into the car.

Where you coming from? Christmas might say. *Where you headed?*

And if the driver asked the same, they would say, *Anywhere. Anyplace.* The only kinds of directions travelers could hope to have.

No past did not mean no future. No destination did not mean no destiny.

Facing the sunrise, Olivia leaned one hand against Christmas, raised her free fist, and stuck out a hopeful thumb.

ACKNOWLEDGMENTS

This story has been with me, in one form or another, longer than I've really noticed until now. It's been on a strange journey over time, but at its core there has always been a girl who thought she was special and a girl who thought she wasn't. It's elating to see their story come to be as it is now. But it didn't make it here alone.

Thanks go to my mom for dragging us around the woods and backroads of Pennsylvania when I was a kid; I've always known exactly the kind of place to set Chapel Hill. And to my aunts, who made sure I was well-stocked in flower pattern notebooks years back for daily subway rides when I had to scribble this book's earliest drafts during my commute. Much easier than writing on my hand.

I also want to thank Samantha Kolesnik for giving the book her blessing way back, Chantelle Aimée Osman for encouraging its growth, and Rachel Harrison for gracing an early version with her generous praise.

My agent Lane Heymont believed in this one at first sight, and he's been an absolute champion for it at every step, and for me (and my million bouts of *is that good?* and *oh, I didn't know that*). In short, #TeamLane.

Immense thanks to the whole team at Titan, from bottom to top, all of whom worked hard to see this novel thrive. A special thanks to Davi for taking it in, and Daniel for helping sharpen the story of Chapel Hill and its people into its best shape.

I don't know what I would do without all the Halloween people, you marvelous fellow readers, fellow authors, the reviewers, and the booksellers, and those who just keep saying "go, Hailey, go." I'm extraordinarily fortunate to experience so much light and love and relentless support. Horror is healing, and horror folk help make that healing possible. There are too many to name between the wonderful people I meet at cons, or only online, or share goofy horror memes with on all kinds of places. But your kindness is appreciated daily.

A special hearty shout-out to Cynthia Pelayo, with her endless supply of "you got this," Sara Tantlinger, reminding me everything will be okay, Claire Holland, always checking in on me and finding exactly the madness she expected, and Suzan Palumbo, reminding me forever that the madness is a feature.

And last, my darling J, who watched this story shed its skin over many years, growing into new and stronger shapes, and believing in every one of them, and in me. Thank you always, my love.

Hailey Piper, *March 2023*

ABOUT THE AUTHOR

Hailey Piper is the Bram Stoker Award-winning author of several books of dark fiction, including *Queen of Teeth*, *No Gods for Drowning*, *Unfortunate Elements of My Anatomy*, *Benny Rose the Cannibal King*, *Your Mind is a Terrible Thing*, *Cruel Angels Past Sundown*, *The Possession of Natalie Glasgow*, and The Worm and His Kings series. She is an active member of the Horror Writers Association, and her writing appears in *CrimeReads*, *Tor Nightfire*, *Pseudopod*, *Vastarien*, *Cosmic Horror Monthly*, and various other anthologies, magazines, and podcasts. A former New York resident, she now lives with her wife in Maryland, where they keep the supernatural a secret. *A Light Most Hateful* is her tenth book.

Find Hailey at **haileypiper.com.**

BLOOM
Delilah S. Dawson

"Sensual, smart, biting, and downright nasty, *Bloom* is a dizzying, heady feast for the discerning palate. I devoured this book in one greedy sitting."
Paul Tremblay

Rosemary meets Ash at the farmers' market. Ash—precise, pretty, and practically perfect—sells bars of soap in delicate pastel colors, sprinkle-spackled cupcakes stacked on scalloped stands, beeswax candles, jelly jars of honey, and glossy green plants.

Ro has never felt this way about another woman; with Ash, she wants to be her and have her in equal measure. But as her obsession with Ash consumes her, she may find she's not the one doing the devouring…

Told in lush, delectable prose, this is a deliciously dark tale of passion taking an unsavory turn...

THEY LURK
Ronald Malfi

COME CLOSER...

Five terrifying collected horror novellas newly reissued
from the "modern-day Algernon Blackwood".

Skullbelly

A private detective is hired after three teenagers disappear in a
forest and uncovers a terrible local secret.

The Separation

Marcus arrives in Germany to find
his friend up-and-coming prizefighter
Charlie in a deep depression. But
soon Charlie's behavior grows
increasingly bizarre. Is he suffering
from a nervous breakdown, or are
otherworldly forces at work?

After the Fade

A girl walked into a small Annapolis
tavern, collapsed and died. Something
had latched itself to the base of her
skull. And it didn't arrive alone.
Now, the patrons of The Fulcrum
are trapped, held prisoner within the
tavern's walls by monstrous things,
trying to find their way in.

The Stranger

Set a rural Florida parking lot, David
returns to his car to find a stranger
sat behind the wheel. The doors
are locked and there's a gun on the
dashboard. And that was when then
the insanity started…

Fierce

A teenage girl and her mom are
in a car accident with another
vehicle on a remote country road
in the middle of a nightmarish
snowstorm, which soon devolves
into gruesome madness.

UNQUIET
E. Saxey

"I fell through this gorgeously gothic novel
and still haven't come up for air."
Clay McLeod Chapman, author of *Ghost Eaters*

London, 1893. Judith lives a solitary life, save for the maid
who haunts the family home in which she resides. Mourning the
death of her brother-in-law, Sam, who drowned in an accident
a year earlier, she distracts herself with art classes, books and
strange rituals, whilst the rest of her family travel the world.

One icy evening, conducting a ritual in her garden she discovers
Sam, alive. He has no memory of the past year, and remembers
little of the accident that appeared to take his life.

Desperate to keep his reappearance a secret until she can
discover the truth about what happened to him, Judith journeys
outside of the West London Jewish community she calls home,
to the scene of Sam's accident. But there are secrets waiting
there for Judith, things that have been dormant for so long, and
if she is to uncover all of them, she may have to admit to truths
that she has been keeping from herself.